PRESS
SEND

PRESS SEND

A NOVEL
BY

JOHN McLAREN

A Touchstone Book

LONDON . SYDNEY . NEW YORK . TOKYO
SINGAPORE . TORONTO

First published in Great Britain by Touchstone, 1997
An imprint of Simon & Schuster
A Viacom Company

Simon Schuster
West Garden Place
Kendal Street
London W2 2AQ

Simon & Schuster Australia Pty Ltd Sydney

A CIP catalogue record for this book is available
from the British Library.

(dedication)

(acknowledgements)

SAN FRANCISCO

Pretty city, faintly comatose. Has its true nerve-centre down in Silicon Valley, the source of all progress. Venture capitalists put seedcorn money in – about $5 billion of it a year – and innovation simply floods out. Over the last thirty years, the Japanese have given us the Walkman and cars that don't break down. The Europeans, nothing much, when you think about it. The big US corporations? That'll be the day. No, most of the world's new technology has a bloodline you can trace straight back to the Valley.

A Monday evening in the city, late April. Josie's bar in Union Street. Trade is slack, with less than half the booths and only two of the tables occupied. The bartenders, Alex, Timothy and Lisa mainly chat with each other. Even the gloomy manager joins in. Perched on the tall stools at the long, polished wooden bar are a trio of now mildly giggly women from the fashion world, a quartet of fledgling investment bankers, loudly pleased with themselves, one solo drinker who would willingly swap his mid-life crisis for *anyone* else's, and, at the end furthest from the door, the Kask twins: corporate designer Conrad and his computer whiz brother, Hilton.

1

1

'Acne. I *don't* date acne. Shortness I don't date. I don't date no biceps. No dress sense, no style, third world car. All of the above I don't date. I'm into above average. The only thing above average about you, Conrad, is your astonishing presumption.'

'She said it just like that?'

'Verbatim. She gave me the gift of total recall. Can't think why. She got it wrong, I don't have acne. I just like to offer accommodation to the occasional homeless zit. At least she remembered my name. I thought she might round it off with "whatever your nerdish name is".'

'So, is Honor still "intergalactic" like last week, or has she earned herself some new adjectives?'

' "Unambiguous", anyway. Lots more "un-s". Plus some nouns that come early in the alphabet."

'Like aardvark?'

'Not quite that early.'

'Lisa, two more please.'

'Two more Chardonnays? Okay, guys.'

'Thanks.'

'And can you get on with the rest of your life now, or is Honor obsession just going to enter a new masochistic phase?'

'No way. Tomorrow I forget her existence totally. I just have to check in for the lobotomy.'

'Does it need an anaesthetic these days?'

'Don't think so. They suck it out through your ear with a straw. Couple of codeine, maybe.'

'Well at least you had the guts to try. Not like me. Dream of Lisa night after night, never get beyond "two more, Lisa".'

'Yeah, well all my guts got me was fifteen minutes of fame in the office.'

'She talked?'

'Talked? She might as well have put it on everybody's e-mail. NERD ALERT! PRESUMPTION WARNING! CONRAD KASK TRIED TO DATE ME!'

'What a total bovine. It's deeply wrong that a cow like that should have such a gorgeous little ass. It should be like Pinocchio's nose. Every time she gives some guy the bumsrush, her ass should put on a pound.'

"Nother?'

'Nah, I'd better head on home. Draft one hundred and thirty-seven of the business plan and all that.'

'How's it coming?'

'I don't think the BUS people will ever get their syndicate together, though Fred Adams is always telling us how "confident" he is. Some group from Boise, of all places, called up, asked the right questions and want to see the plan. Cheered Irma and Dan up a bit.'

'How long can you last?'

'Three or four weeks. Six at a stretch.'

'You know you can have all I got, if it would help. Fifteen, maybe twenty thousand.'

'Thanks, Con. It might, but let's see how we go.'

'Well, just let me know. That's what twins are for.'

'The check please, Lisa . . . . Don't suppose you wanna

ride back, Con?'

'On the back of that buzz-box? I may be terminally despondent, but I'll have to be officially suicidal before I try that. I don't believe you ever go a hundred yards without falling off. You should fix the Fiat and stick to that. The walk'll do me good, anyway. Give me time to forget whatever her name was.'

'Night then. Try to find someone with a kinder heart and a less cute ass.'

'Night. Hey, Hil.'

'Yeah?'

'I hope you get the money.'

'Oddly enough, so do I. Night.'

****

The Headquarters of the Bank of the United States is, was, and ever will be in their jutting, mean-spirited, granite megalith in Sansome Street, downtown San Francisco. But their venture capital subsidiary somehow slipped away, the senior partners silkily persuading the Board to let them dress in the clothes of a real venture capital company and live in Sand Hill Road, Menlo Park. Venture capitalists like to play at being in Silicon Valley, but Silicon Valley is flat, hot, featureless and – even in the regulation BMW, Merc or Lexus – a dreary seventy miles ride from a Bay-view house in Pacific Heights. So they cluster in country-clubby, Hawaii-pretty Sand Hill Road, forty miles from the city and maybe the nicest offices in the whole country.

Fred Adams slipped away too. At sixteen, while his friends in Helena, Arkansas filled their thoughts with girls and driver's licences, Fred quietly set his life targets and began work on getting there. If his was an American dream, it was not one that could be condemned as too fantastical. A nice house with a yard somewhere leafy. A kind, preferably pretty wife, two or three healthy kids and a dog. A decent job with security as a must and enjoyment as a plus, and above all enough money to buy freedom from the stabs of anxiety his mother had always feebly tried to hide whenever the postman brought the mail. Not many years later, as these objectives were reached with almost disconcerting ease, this core came to be orbited by satellite fancies: an RV or off-roader, family trips abroad, perhaps. Even a modest lodge in Aspen, though still far from a reality, no longer seemed a prospect quite so absurdly off-limits for the likes of him.

His father had crumpled and died by then, but as the milestones were passed, his mother back in Helena grew ever more volubly proud of Fred. Her fears that he would turn out like his dad receded, and she not only dared to believe that his success might last, but sat back, relaxed and basked in the warmth of it all. Martha, his home-town sister, her own marriage souring like ageing milk, loved Fred enough not to fashion sharp edges to her envy, and was only intermittently and half-heartedly catty about Fred's sweetheart wife, Mary. All she really resented was that Fred had got away, had broken the invisible shackles that still held her there.

It was the offer of a junior position with the Bank of the United States that let Fred escape Arkansas's clutches. When he moved West, it was a natural priority to smooth back the lilting excesses of his southern drawl and urge on his speech from its languid native stroll to a respectable Californian canter. He was mocked a bit at first, and found friends in San Francisco hard to come by for a while. But his equable temperament and utter dependability helped ease his way steadily, if unspectacularly, through the junior ranks. When he made Vice-President, rejoicing in Helena knew few bounds, and Fred had enough sense not to dilute his mother's delight by admitting how widely this title was shared.

Now mid-thirties, he had been with the BUS group for going on thirteen years. The key to his transfer away from the increasingly dreary commercial banking was the BUS-sponsored MBA. From a school not a household name, perhaps, but an MBA all the same. It made him one of the few natural candidates when the bank concluded that only by infiltration could they figure out what their wholly-owned, but frustratingly independent venture capital team was up to. At first, Standish MacMartin, BUS's profoundly uncuddly President, opted for infiltration from the top; the second-rate lawyer he parachuted in was frozen out in months. So he tried again at the bottom with Fred Adams and Jack Thomas. The rest of the venture team revelled in deriding the quality of the interlopers, though, for all their sharper suits and prettier résumés, they themselves were touched by the same invisible hand of mediocrity BUS Ventures might look and talk like the top venture partnerships, but their partners were cast-offs and the associates were wannabes. Everyone in the Valley knew that in that team even the title 'partner' was a legal fiction. The best deals always went to the independent partnerships. After all, what gossip-hot start-up would want BUS Ventures to lead their financing if any of the true stars would pony up?

Fred Adams didn't know about all that when he

transferred across, and if he had he wouldn't have cared. He was in venture capital now, and how on earth else could he have got in? When Jack Thomas perished – too obvious a fifth columnist and idle with it – Fred grieved for the loss of the only fellow-bearer of the daily barbs and slights. Fred, though eager and less prone to offend, would doubtless have been jettisoned too, if the partners had not correctly reckoned that the death of all the bank troops would merely herald the arrival of fresh cavalry. So he was tolerated and by imperceptible stages he began to contribute, surprising himself as much as others by revealing a modest aptitude for the staples of the Valley: software, computers, and semiconductors.

He worked at it. Oh God, how he worked at it. His antennae were sharp, though, and when he sensed he was staying late just *too* often, he would slope off home to Burlingame. After a couple of hours divided democratically between Mary, Tom, Heidi, and Cotton the labrador, he pressed on with his work way past midnight.

Three years later his secondment had become permanent, his spying assignment and mongrel academic record forgotten, and by a narrow vote he was elevated to the partnership. At the executive level in Sansome Street the mild satisfaction at this news was tinged with speculation of drift in Fred's loyalties. Among his immediate former colleagues there was no shortage of bitchiness at the steeply rising slope of Fred's income compared with the stony plateau of their own. In Helena, there was noisy rejoicing from his mother at a development which, if not entirely understood, sounded splendid enough. Down the road in her gently decaying wooden house, Martha relayed the news of Fred's prospective millions to her unshaven, malodorous husband and slammed down his dinner plate even more reproachfully than usual.

That day Fred cradled and caressed the news all afternoon. By superhuman effort he resisted telling Mary right away and banned the folks in Helena from calling her. Babysitter summoned, Mary was bundled, gently protesting, into the car and off to Chez Maurice in Palo Alto. He made her wait to the entrée before easing it out, delicious word by delicious word. She purred for him and for herself, and who could criticise him if in return he preened himself just a little?

Fred's euphoria was soon diluted with tiny drops of self-doubt. He'd have to find the deals himself now and some good ones at that. The nightmare of his investments all going belly-up did not limit itself to his nocturnal meanderings. But there could be opportunity too, even glory. A new Microsoft, Intel or Netscape, maybe.

****

'Solomon Computers.'
　'Irma?'
　'Conrad?'
　'Yeah. How you doin'?'
　'Fine. Hil's in with the last of the Idahoans.'
　'Who?'
　'The Boys from Boise.'
　'How's it going?'
　'Don't like the look of it. The jackets aren't off yet. When Hilton asked them to call him Hil, they said would it be okay if they just called him Mr Kask? Really warmed up

the atmosphere. Shall I get him to call you? Dan and I will be going in there later.'

'Yeah. No. Just tell him I found there's one called "hiltoni".'

'A what called what?'

'"Hiltoni". A turtle.'

'Oh sure. Okay Conrad, cross your fingers for him. And us.'

'Kay. Bye, Irma. Have a nice presentation.'

'Bye.'

****

'So if I understand you right, Mr Kask, you need access to a Cray or other supercomputer, but the computer architecture itself is not critical. The key is in the evaluation software and the bio-sensing matrix processor.'

'In general terms, yes. The voice synthesis gear is important too.'

'And what do you mean when you say the software algorithms are "genetic"?'

'Well, that's exactly what they are. A population of solutions is presented and fights it out inside the software. It's survival of the fittest. It's not just binary strings like most computer processes. The useful parts of even the weaker solutions survive. The combinations breed and mutate. It involves something called "undirected data mining". We're not the only ones doing some of this stuff. Other Artificial Intelligence people are using those techniques. It's the combination with the bio inputs that makes us unique.'

'And all other AI approaches neglect the human

element, right?'

'Right. Basically, they just keep trying to develop better and better logic circuitry. It's fine for advanced number crunching, but it'll never get you to human-type judgement because the human brain just doesn't function that way.'

'And how do you get the right cocktail of the pure logic and the "human" inputs?'

'The genetic software figures out case by case what the mix should be.'

'And the bio-sensors can really track the emotions and instincts?'

'Daniel's the best guy in the country. He's been working on microscopic physiological changes and their significance for twenty years. Early on, we thought we'd have to use brain mapping. Now we find we don't need it, and mapping is a pretty primitive instrument anyway. Dan's proved that truly tiny changes in things like pulse rate, skin electrical conductivity, blood pressure, eyes, ears, muscles, adrenalin surges and so on all reflect specific emotional and instinctive responses. All our experiments are completely repeatable. The prototype works fine already. It's just a question of getting it onto silicon and ruggedising it for use in harsh locations. By the way, it's Dan who cracked the voice synthesis, too. None of the other companies in that field have anyone who understands the mechanics of the human voice like Dan does.'

'And you're still thinking of the medical area as the main application?'

'At least to begin with. It's a real natural, in primitive places where no expert surgeon's going to go. There will be plenty of other applications when we have time to develop them. Natural disasters, any hazardous situation.

Manufacturing. Wall Street will be able to use it if they want to. Other gamblers, too.'

'What I want to know especially, Mr Kask, is what could the applications be for unmanned moving objects?'

'I don't follow you.'

'Planes or tanks for example.'

'Hadn't thought of it. In principle, it should be fine. It would need a very high level of shock resistance. For visual guidance you could either use the little stereoscopic camera we build in or plug it into the transport's own guidance systems. Our cameras are very special. The resolution is fantastic, and they only weigh about four ounces. Not bad for a television camera, eh? I wouldn't be surprised if the company we're buying them from is selling to the Military already.'

'So it sounds like you're very much on track. If it all comes together, you'll have found the computer grail, will you?'

'No computer's ever going to be perfect.'

'But close?'

'It'll have judgement and instinct as good as a smart person. A bit better, actually, and the evaluation on the pure logic side should be way better. But that still won't make it perfect. It never can be.'

'And the voice synthesis?'

'Precisely the same tonality and inflections as a human voice. Practically indistinguishable from the real thing.'

'And eight million'll do it? Doesn't sound a lot to us.'

'It'll take us to pilot production prototypes for the first application. Don't forget, we've come a long way on almost nothing so far.'

'We know you have. But we've looked at the plan. We

don't think eight's right. We want you to think about it. We think you could go faster with more.'

'Wow, I didn't expect that one. Could be, I guess. I'll have to think about it . . . . Would this be a good moment to introduce Dan and Irma?'

'Look, we'd like to meet them another time, but we have to be running along now.'

'Can't I at least show you around the lab? It's tiny, but it's all we have here.'

'Thank you, but we never do facility tours.'

'Hey, okay. I guess that's it then. Look, if you're not likely to be interested, it'd help if we knew soon. Should I call you or what?'

'Mr Kask, we may be very interested indeed, but we can't say anything till we speak with our partners.'

'Okay, so you'll call if there's anything, right?'

'Right. Thank you for your time, Mr Kask. Goodbye.'

2

Fred Adams's nightmare stayed just a nightmare. He soon figured out he needn't have worried about all his investments going down the tubes, but only because he didn't make any. Partner he might be, but the established partners still got the important calls and, even when he'd helped find an interesting semi-conductor prospect, the company and the other venture firms in the syndicate politely but firmly asked for Cliff to take it over.

Before he got the promotion, Fred had always worked for the partners on their deals. Now that task had been handed on to other eager associates. As Fred's frustration at the lack of deal flow mounted, his desperation reduced him to the pitiable state of leafing through some unsolicited, no-hoper plans.

Fred could vaguely remember scanning Solomon's plan, among lots of others, but he couldn't really remember now what had sparked his interest enough to phone and go visit them. On paper it had been like all the rest. Of course they claimed a breakthrough proprietary technology. The plan, as usual, said that there was no real competition, but huge market potential. When he got there, the shabby little facility in Saratoga put him off totally. And when Hilton, Irma and Dan filed into the cramped, airless, claustrophobic little box they had the nerve to call the conference room, Fred didn't know whether to laugh or cry. Daniel was a caricature of the absent- minded professor type, with his white hair, white beard and his glasses perched precariously on the end of his nose. He looked sixty but had only just turned fifty. The chubby little Irma and the skinny, nervous Hilton were both late twenties, but the air of adolescence still clung to them. Fred thought they looked just like two gawky high school kids left after everyone else chose their dance partners. The thought of someone like Hilton being C.E.O. of one of Fred's investments was too absurd even to be amusing. Just imagine how everyone at Sand Hill Road would jeer. If this company ever got backing, the first thing the syndicate'd have to do was to get a new man in. If Hilton got real lucky he might be allowed to stay on as Chief Technical Officer.

When he came to know them better, he was quietly ashamed that he, of all people, had judged a book so much by its cover. It was utterly astonishing what the three of them had achieved with no more than a couple of hundred thousand they'd scraped together. It might be a start-up in venture terms, but they were already well down the track towards a working machine. Of course, there was no guarantee that in the end it *would* work, but, if it did, it had the makings of a genuine breakthrough.

The phrase 'Artificial Intelligence' had been bandied about ever since a generation of movie lovers had seen Hal in *2001*. But with each engineering step forward, the vision of a computer that could think seemed to recede rather than draw closer. AI had become a moving label. It was the term you applied to whatever computers couldn't yet do.

Solomon's approach was comically, absurdly, well *logical*. If you looked behind the buzzwords of the other AI approaches – fuzzy logic, massively parallel architecture, neural networks, etc – they were all really just ways of tricking the computer into processing faster. Doing zillions of calculations simultaneously might produce a blindingly fast result, but it brought the computer no nearer to actually *thinking*. What Hilton had figured out – and it seemed so obvious now – was that humans never decide anything based only on logic. Human response to any situation usually consists of a more or less instantaneous 'instinctive' reaction followed by a slightly slower (in some people's cases very much slower) 'logical' thought process. So how could you get computers to 'think' like humans unless they could replicate both halves of that human process?

The other thing Solomon had realised was that even if you could get the computer to combine both halves, you couldn't base the instinctive part on some generalised 'average' human. A Mongolian herdsman and a Washington politician are going to have pretty different instinctive reactions to any given situation. The machine would have to be programmed based on the reactions of a very specialised sample. Theoretically, using a single human would be the fastest, since the averaging process fractionally slowed the response, but the Solomon projections suggested that they could get an acceptable access time with anything up to three hundred 'donors'.

The 'donating' process they had already simulated in a crude, strapped-up fashion, but it looked promising. When Solomon talked about 'instinct', they meant not only the simplest inherited or learnt responses, like fear and flight, but all 'non-logical' emotional reactions like anger, happiness, trust or boredom. The downloading was still very basic, mainly involving the donor watching interminable videotapes while a battery of sensors tracked his or her reactions. The whole area of downloading was where much of the money would go.

The real technical jewel was the sensor matrix. Depending on the situation, this could adjust the weighting between the various emotional responses and the pure logic. It was a massively sophisticated software engine, and every bit of it Irma's work. The voice synthesiser, too, was a very advanced device, but in Fred's view was not much more than a fantastically clever party trick. He knew the Solomon team wouldn't agree. Hilton thought that a natural-sounding voice was very important. Dan would say, how can you expect a frightened, sick child in some African village to describe his symptoms to an electrical box if the box sounds like a demented robot?

****

'Hi, I'm Kevin and I'd like to tell you about our specials tonight. Well, let me see now, to start we have Shrimp Melange. Bay shrimps on a rucola bed with a lime, onion and tomato sauce. Very refreshing. And then what we call "South and the Border". A Cajun-flavoured cheese quesadilla. Recommended for those with a *very* healthy appetite. To follow, the catch of the day is pan- fried John Dory, which comes with a cream moril sauce. Then we have the Supreme de Pintade, which is guinea fowl breast, roasted in a very hot oven for just ten minutes and sliced very thinly. That comes with a celeriac purJe. Now, are you ready to decide or shall I leave you for a few moments?'

'Ready?'

'Sure. I'll take the goat cheese salad and the tuna. Con?'

'The vichyssoise and the lamb.'

'Very good. And how would you like the lamb? Pink?'

'Well done.'

'And have you decided on the wine?'

'Hang on just one sec. Cab okay?'

'Sure.'

'We'll take the Fetzer Cabernet and some mineral water.'

'Calistoga?'

'Fine. Thanks.'

'So tell me, how's the airline coming?'

'Screw the airline. Talk Boise.'

'Peculiar people. Perfectly pressed. Must have been born with ties on. Not big believers in the power of the smile. Didn't really major in small talk either.'

'What sort of age?'

'One middle indeterminate, the other young indeterminate. Looked like the hit-men for some weirdo religious sect. Sure as hell not the plain vanilla VC types anyway.'

'How'd they hear about you?'

'They were pretty evasive on that one. Just said they got wind of us on their own net. Who the hell cares, if they've got the money?'

'*You* should, probably. Sounds like if you missed plan they'd break your ribs. Do they have the money? Will they join the BUS syndicate?'

'Never co-invest, they say. If they do it at all, they wanna do the whole round.'

'The whole eight?'

'They say it should be more. Want to go faster. They're right, too. Don't forget we were at ten before Adams talked us down.'

'What about valuation?'

'Didn't react, but didn't seem like it was a big issue. Probably gouge us later. The strangest bit is that they don't take Board seats.'

'Even when they do the whole financing?'

'Excuse me. Who'd like to try the wine?'

'Me... It's fine.'

'Good. Enjoy.'

'Like I said, they say they do it all or not at all. They say they back management. Try to get it right in the first place and then don't interfere.'

'That sounds okay. You don't want those VC smart-asses interfering anyway, do you?'

'Sure, I don't. But don't you still think it's kinda spooky?'

'Now can I offer you some black pepper with the goat cheese?'

'No thanks.'

'And the vichyssoise?'

'No. Can we get some more bread?'

'Sure. Coming right away.'

'So when will you hear?'

'They said within two weeks.'

'Have you told BUS?'

'You kidding? Fred'd freak. The length of time it's taken him to get their syndicate together.'

'I thought you said it's not much of a syndicate?'

'It's money, isn't it? If you're starving, food from a paper plate's just fine.'

'Have his partners agreed it?'

'Not finally, but he says it's a done deal, provided the other firms stay in.'

'What about the bank? Do they have to agree it?'

'Doesn't seem to be a problem. There's some rule about needing Board clearance for investments over five million, but Fred says they always keep it a bit below that.'

'So that's why they're only doing three and a half?'

'Probably. That and Fred not wanting to stick his neck out too far. It's his first investment since he got partner. Anyway, that's why they need Vortex, DQB and Woodside.'

'One and a half each, was it?'

'Uh-huh.'

'So what'll you do if the Boisenberries come in? What are they called anyway?'

'Bay Street Ventures.'

'*Bay Street*? You gotta be kidding? How can there be a Bay Street in Boise, Idaho?'

'Hadn't thought of that. Funny. Could be trees, I guess.'

'So what'll you do?'

'Con, as far as I'm concerned that'd be a really good problem to have. Everyone fighting over who's allowed to give me lots of money.'

'So what are you gonna do with all the money once you're rich? Private planes are no use to you and you're not into sailing. Cars, I guess.'

'Yeah. Lots of them. All *very* fast and *very* expensive. And I won't have to fix them myself.'

'Excuse me. Can I clear these away? How was everything?'

'Great.'

'So let's have an update on the Honor situation.'

'I think I'm cooling. She told my secretary I remind her of a badly dressed gerbil. Suggested she send a photo of me to Walt Disney as the inspiration for a new animal cartoon. Says she should get a cut of the royalties. Hey, don't you laugh. We're identical. If I'm a gerbil, that makes you a gerbil too.'

'Maybe, but I'm not as badly dressed.'

'That's a matter of opinion.'

'Let's get back to Honor. Is her ass as cute as ever?'

'Why don't you come and stare at it again? You only saw her – or should I say it – that one time.'

'Once seen, never forgotten.'

'While we're on embarrassing subjects, how's the star biker? How many times have you fallen off this week?'

'Only once. No physical injuries. Second degree pride burns.'

'If you're going to go around like a maniac on a motorbike, couldn't you at least invent some huge helmet like a big shell that covers your whole body? I need you to stick around.'

'I'll think about it. I guess it'd really help with cultivating my "wild thing" image. Shells remind me, how're Parton and Pfeiffer?'

'Good. Sleeping a lot. Eating lots of lettuce and mushrooms. My new therapist says I should get rid of them.'

'Usual reason?'

'Yeah. Symbol of my insecurity, and all that.'

'What are you gonna do?'

'Usual thing. Get rid of the therapist. Hey, did you get the message about the hiltoni?'

'Yeah, Irma told me . . . .'

'Here we are, the tuna and the lamb. Now, let's see . . . the tuna is? Okay. Enjoy.'

'. . . . Thanks. So where do these hiltoni hang out?'

'Sonora, Mexico. Ugly sonofabitches, but cute-ugly if you know what I mean. They've got a whole bunch of them in San Diego zoo. I thought I might drive down some time and take a look. Wanna come?'

'Only if you guarantee that they have a particularly cute keeper known to be fascinated by computer whizzes. How're the dreams?'

'Mixed. They are still sitting there, but Mom doesn't scream any more. It's like they're just patiently waiting for it to happen. You?'

'It comes and goes. Speaking of which, how *is* the airline logo?'

'It's so crazy, me of all people working on an airline name and logo. It's not much of an airline anyway. Puddle-jumpers.'

'Didn't you say it's owned by some huge company, though?'

'Yeah, I can never remember their name. I had this really neat idea of calling it Turtle Airlines, and having a logo of a turtle with wings coming out of the top shell and a kind of undercarriage coming out from the lower shell. What d'you think?'

'Original.'

'The turtle's head was up in the air with goggles on. Looked great, I thought.'

'What did Dumdum say?'

'Freaked of course. Doesn't ever want to hear any more about turtles on *anything*. Client'd go mad, all that sort of stuff.'

'And would they?'

'We'll find out. I'm planning to fax it to them anyway.

I've got a hunch they might like it. Everyone's afraid of puddle-jumpers, and this would give them a nice, safe, friendly image.'

'And what if Dumdum gets to hear about it?'

'She says if I ever contact the client myself she'll rip my scrotum off with her bare hands.'

'She *can't* say that. People aren't allowed to say things like that these days.'

'*You* try telling her that.'

'Can I break in here, guys? We have some *very* special desserts tonight. There's . . .'

'Just a decaf cappuccino for me, thanks.'

'And for you?'

'What's the sorbet?'

'Kiwi, mango or plum.'

'Regular coffee'd be fine.'

****

The secretaries in Sansome Street buy a sandwich and a diet coke and go in gaggles to sit in the sunny little open spaces near the Embarcadero. The younger guys do the same or catch a quick bite in one of the restless little cafes nearby. As the executives rise in rank they gravitate to the smarter downtown places. A few power lunchers go for the fancy French restaurants in the better hotels. And then of course there's the Board lunches at the Bank of the United States.

There have been quite a few BUS Board members over the years who've said the lunches are the best reason to be on the Board. Forget the director's fee, forget the prestige. Only the lunches are unforgettable. For years now Californians have made having even one glass of wine at lunch seem like an indictable offence. The Board dining room at BUS, with its Chassagne Montrachets, Lafites and Latours, is an oasis of civilisation in a health-infested desert. Even so, the wine is merely a serene accompaniment to the food. And what food! The soups, the sauces, the sorbets, the millefeuilles. The freshest, tenderest everything. Whether trucked in or flown in, always only the very best. Food to die for. Literally, in one case a few years ago, when the daintiest, softest morsel of veal lodged improbably in an elderly throat and, after a decent interval of a few weeks, a Texan oil tycoon was delighted to be invited to fill the unexpected Board vacancy.

****

'Well, gentlemen. That's us just about through the official Board business. Is there any other business anyone would like to raise before we go through to lunch?'

'Mr Chairman, I have something.'

'Yes, Peter?'

'Whatever became of the idea to link up with that life assurance company in Germany?'

'Standish?'

'On ice for the moment. I doubt we'll recommend proceeding, with *that* partner anyway. Jefferson Powers in Frankfurt says dealing with them is like wading through maple syrup up to your armpits. Except maple syrup wasn't the expression Jefferson used.'

'Okay. Can we go through now?'

'Excuse me, Frank, but there *is* one other thing I'd like to mention.'

'What is it, Pat?'

'The Venture group. It's been a while since we heard how they're doing.'

'Standish, is that something it would make sense to discuss over lunch?'

'Only if you don't mind spoiling your filet mignon. Why don't I get an update prepared for the next Board instead. Would that suit you okay, Pat?'

'Sure . . . that'd be fine. It's just that I have a real big problem understanding what earthly use that group is to us. By the time the so-called "partners" take their cut, there's precious little return for the bank. What infuriates me most of all is it's over a year since they asked this Board's approval for an investment. I'm *sure* they deliberately keep it below five million. As CFO, that limit's formally your responsibility, isn't it, Tom? How d'you think they'd react if we took it down to two or three?'

'They'd most likely figure out another way around it. They already say the limit damages their reputation. They're probably right on that.'

'You're always so goddam understanding, Tom. Where are you on this, Standish?'

'I can tell you I'm getting mighty sick and tired of them. When they come along asking for help with another fund, I plan to hang very tough.'

'Standish, I know I'm only an old, forgetful non-executive, but I thought that young man Adams was supposed to give us a little more... *insight* into what was going on. Isn't that so, Standish?'

'We don't hear much from him these days. Changed teams, basically. Forgotten where he came from.'

'Okay, gentlemen, Standish will get us that report for our next meeting. Now, can we *please* go through to lunch?'

****

'Fred. You awake?'

'Sure am, honey.'

'You know this investment of yours. Solomon, I mean. Are you *sure* this is the right one to start with? It sounds ever so slightly, well, flaky to me.'

'*Flaky*? Could be the biggest return the firm's ever had.'

'Oh I know it'd be wonderful and all that, darling, but couldn't you start with something a bit more, you know what I mean, *normal* and get a bit more established, and then do something like this?'

'Something like *this*? Something like "this" comes along once in a blue moon.'

'Surely you could ask the guys at Solomon to wait a bit, you know, to borrow from the bank or whatever to tide them over? Wouldn't they understand?'

'If you don't mind, honey, I think I'm going to get up and take Cotton for a walk.'

'Look, Fred. I'm sure you're right and all that. It's just with everything going so well and all you've built, and that. You know what I mean. It'd just be awful if, you know, you got off on the wrong foot or whatever.'

'Sure, I know. But don't forget what it could mean for us if I get it right. Our group almost never see the best deals. We could make forty, fifty, a hundred times our money on this one. Just think what that'd mean for my profit share. I'll tell you what it would mean. Goodbye Burlingame, hello Hillsboro. Goodbye cheap motels, hello Aspen. That's what.'

****

'Hil. That you?'
  'Dan? Do you know what time it is?'
  'No. What is it?'
  'I've no idea. Half past late.'
  'Hil, I've done it.'
  'Done what?'
  'The adrenalin surge. I've cracked it.'
  'You *did*?'
  'Yeah, you see, where I was going wrong . . .'
  'Dan.'
  '. . . was that . . .'
  'Dan. I'm never going to understand this now. It's great news, but can't it wait till morning?'
  'Okay, Hil. Sorry. I thought you'd want to hear.'
  'Sure I do, Dan. It's just that I'm a bit whacked. It's really, really great though. Hey, Dan, don't wake Irma.'
  'I already did. She came over.'
  'She's there now?'
  'Wait a minute . . . .'
  'Hiya, Hil. Don't be boring, come on down here and join the party.'
  'Okay, okay. Hell, the Fiat's still in pieces. I can't come on a motorbike at . . . Jesus, ten past two. You guys come over here, I'll try to find a bottle.'
  'Dan wants to show you.'
  'Let him tell me instead.'
  'Okay, we're on our way. See you in a while.'

3

'Who may I say is calling?'

'Jason Roberts of Bay Street Ventures.'

'Just a moment, please . . . Hil, . . . Hil, it's them . . . Bay Street . . . ! Just putting you through, Mr Roberts.'

'This is Hilton Kask. Mr Roberts?'

'Mr Kask, the partnership has reached a decision. We would like to invest fifteen million dollars for seventy percent of Solomon Computers. That would leave fifteen percent for you, five percent for each of your partners, and a pool of five percent for future employees. Based on that level of investment, we think you can accelerate the business plan. We expect you to bring it forward by at least two quarters. Can you do that, Mr Kask?'

'We can do it.'

'We also want to talk to you about some of the applications, but that can wait until after we've finalised everything.'

'Okay.'

'Our offer will be subject to our usual conditions. Naturally, we will require full anti-dilution provisions on any future stock issue. No co-investment will be accepted. As we told you, we do not want Board positions, but we *will* require a right of veto on any external Board appointments. I have to tell you right up front that we do not normally see any merit in such appointments. We will expect to receive a monthly written progress report. We like this to be in a standard form. We'll send you an example. Above all, our offer must not, repeat not, be shopped.'

'Shopped?'

'If you reveal the existence of our offer, or any of its terms, to a third party, it will be immediately withdrawn.'

'Does that include the other VCs we're talking to now?'

'Yes it does. Particularly them, in fact. We think this is a generous offer. I hope you agree, Mr Kask?'

'Uh, yes. Yes, certainly.'

'Well, if you agree, why should you need to discuss it elsewhere? Of course, as a matter of courtesy, you can tell them just as soon as you've formally accepted.'

'Okay, then.'

'We're faxing the confirmation of our offer through now. It will clearly state that it is only valid for acceptance for forty-eight hours. Since your lawyers will have all the documentation in order for a stock issue, there should be no problem making some minor changes and getting everthing finalised within that timeframe.'

'No. Should be no problem.'

'Very good then, Mr Kask. We look forward to building a mutually rewarding relationship. Let me know if there's any problem with the fax transmission.'

'Sure. Oh, Mr Roberts.'

'Yes, Mr Kask?'

'Thank you very much.'

'That's quite okay. Just try not to keep us waiting until the forty-eighth hour.'

'Okay.'

'Goodbye, then.'

'Goodbye, Mr Roberts . . . Wow . . . wow . . . WOW,

WOW, WOW! Irma, Dan. We got it, we goddam well got it! We're a real company. We're really goin' to build the frigging machine! Hey, we're gonna be rich. Rich *and* famous.'

'How much? Ten? Twelve?'

'Not ten, Irma. Not twelve. Or thirteen, or fourteen. *Fifteen* big ones!'

'Fifteen? Seriously? *Unbelievable!* Wow! Isn't this wonderful, Dan?'

'Amazing. What's the valuation, Hil? Are they gonna leave much for us?'

'They want seventy percent for their fifteen, so what's that? A bit over twenty. Come on, Irma you're the one with a calculator for a brain.'

'Twenty one point four.'

'And Fred Adams wanted to value us at ten. Eight million for eighty percent. What a cheapskate!'

'Let's go down the Village Inn right now and make a start on getting seriously lubricated.'

'Now, *that's* what I call a business plan, Irma. You up for a big night, Dan?'

'Just try stopping me. I'll show you youngsters how it's done.'

'I'd better get the legal wheels rolling before we go. Irma, can you check if that fax's here and whiz it over to Orsini for them to review and make a start on the paperwork. Oh, and I'd better cancel tomorrow's session with Fred.'

****

'Slumped' suggests much too gradual a motion for how Fred Adams's body subsided when he came off the line with Hilton. It reacted more like a weary old tower block demolished by detonation. When he'd got the message the day before that Hilton had cancelled the meeting, he had a hunch something was up. But when he rang to ask what was going on, he hadn't expected this. After all he'd done, and now Hilton just tells him they won't be able to move ahead with BUS! Didn't want to tell him anything, in fact. Even had to wring that bit out of him. No explanation. He'd put months into this, and not just his *time*. His whole credibility within the partnership and with the guys in the other firms was riding on this. Being turned down by a *proper* CEO at this stage of a deal would have been galling enough, but to be shown the door by someone like that little creep, Kask! He'd trusted him, he'd been his friend, he'd helped get the plan into shape. It was Fred and Fred alone who had talked his own partners round and coaxed the syndicate together. Okay, so it had taken a bit longer than he'd first said it would, but what d'you expect when you're working with a bunch of dweebs like those three at Solomon? The more he thought about it, the more it seemed to him that Solomon had been built more by himself than by Hilton Kask. And now it sounded like he wasn't even planning to let him into the syndicate - let alone lead it. He just could not believe it!

His office began to feel unbearably stuffy, and he was gripped by a sudden fear that one of his colleagues might wander in and ask how Solomon was going. He got into his newly leased BMW 540 and drove over to Half Moon Bay. Fred always found walking by the sea calmed him. Today the magic didn't work. The tide was in too far and the narrow remaining ribbon of sand sloped and yielded too much for a real walk. The few folk enjoying the late morning sunshine all looked nauseatingly untroubled. In contrast, no beach-lounger or languid dog-walker could have missed the straining tension in Fred's every surging step.

Who could he call to talk it over? No-one at Sand Hill Road, for sure. Mary? She'd be out at her flower arranging course, and anyway she'd probably be relieved it had fallen through. Joseph, his old buddy at the bank? No, they hadn't spoken for months. In truth, Fred had been none too unhappy to let his personal links with Sansome Street wither a little. These days he no longer felt so threatened by the constant mocking of the bank that went on in the Venture group, and had tentatively begun to join in.

Oh the humiliation of it! This was the deal that was going to get him established. If it worked, the other venture firms would've started calling him, too, when they had a deal, not just Larry and Cliff and the others. It wasn't as if he had anything else worthwhile on the stocks. There was the money, too. Whatever Solomon's new deal was, this just *proved* he'd been right. Now someone else would make the millions and get a lodge in Aspen and a Ferrari *and* all the glory. Was there really nothing he could do?

A pretty, thirty-something blonde twitched in surprise and recovered enough to curse as Fred charged suddenly up the beach, brushing past her, sand flying everywhere from his slipping city shoes. He swung open the car door and punched the numbers into the carphone handset.

'Dan?'

'Yes.'

'It's me, Fred. Is Hilton there?'

'Sure, but . . . Hang on, I'll get him . . . .'

'Hello, Fred.'

'Hilton, obviously you've had a better offer. I wanna know right now, have you accepted it yet?'

'I'm sorry, Fred, I can't get into this now. I'll be able to say more tomorrow.'

'Don't screw with me, Hilton. I'm not a fucking idiot. If you didn't have a better offer there's no way you'd be treating me like this. Now tell me, have you accepted it yet? Come on, Hilton, the least you owe me is to tell me that, for Chrissakes. Have you accepted it?'

'Orally, yes.'

'But you haven't signed the papers?'

'Orsini and Dubilier are working on them. They'll be ready in a few hours.'

'*Don't* sign them. I'm coming over right now.'

'Fred, what are you talking about?'

'I'll be there in twenty minutes. Do *nothing* until I get there.'

'Look, Fred, I'm real sorry about this, but I don't think there's much point.'

'I'm coming anyway. And, by the way, I want to see you on your own.'

'Okay then, I'll be here.'

****

'What? He's coming *here*? Are you crazy?'

'I tried to stop him. He wouldn't take no for an answer.'

'Did you tell him anything?'

'No. He knows we must have another offer. He's not a complete fool. I said we were going to accept it as soon as the papers came through from the lawyers.'

'You told him we hadn't signed yet? So *that's* why he's

coming. You shouldn't have taken the call if you were planning to tell him.'

'Don't be so hard on Hil, Irma. It was my fault. I put the call through. I'm so hungover, my brain wasn't in gear. I should've told him Hil wasn't here.'

'Okay, okay. Sorry, Hil, I didn't mean to beat up on you so much. I'm just so neurotic about us not screwing this up. When's he goin' to get here? Can't we get the papers signed before he arrives?'

'Sam called right before Fred. They won't be ready till this afternoon.'

'So what are we goin' to say to him?'

'Me, not we. He says he wants to see me on my own. I guess I say as little as possible.'

'*Less* than possible, Hil. Like *nothing.*'

'I'll do my best. I hate things like this. If the Gestapo had got me, I'd've talked before they asked the first question.'

'Hang on . . . that's him now.'

'I hope he hasn't brought any truth drugs with him.'

****

'CONRAD!!! . . . Where is that little rodent . . . ? WHERE IS HE???. . . I swear, I'm gonna rip his poxy little head off his miserable little shoulders. WHERE IS THE GODDAM SONOFABITCH??? Sharon, where is that reptile? What's the point of me having an assistant if you can't answer simple questions. Tell me, Sharon, do you like your job?'

'Sure I do, Ruby.'

'Well, if you want to keep it for at least the next ten minutes, tell me where on this goddam earth is that scumbag vermin, Conrad?'

'I'm really sorry, Ruby, I don't know. He was here a few minutes ago.'

'Okay. ATTENTION EVERYBODY! Thank you. Does anyone here know where that piece of pestilence, Conrad Kask, is skulking?'

'Have you thought of looking in the john?'

'Oh *thank you*, Honor. No, I had not thought of looking in the men's room. That's more your style than mine. Chas, go there right now and see if any low-life in there answers to the name of Kask. Tell him from me that if he even *thinks* about barricading himself in the stall I will take a flamethrower to it.'

'Rightaway, Ruby.'

****

'You *told* him?'

'Irma, he just kind of got it out of me. He sort of wore me down, and in the end I figured the only way to persuade him to give up was to tell him how vastly better the other offer was. I thought if I did that he'd drop it.'

'Oh, Hil, what if Bay Street find out? That's broken their precious "no-shop", hasn't it?'

'I suppose it has, sort of. I didn't tell him who they are. Only the amount and and the valuation. I said it had to be in the strictest confidence.'

'Does that mean anything with these guys?'

'Maybe, maybe not. Look I'm sorry,guys. I guess I made a major league goof. He kept harping on about how much we owe him. It got to me, 'cos I think he does have a point. Without Fred's help, we wouldn't have got finance anyplace, we were that green.'

'Hil, I'm only being this way because we're desperate. This is a *great* offer. Even the eight million from the BUS syndicate isn't confirmed yet. None of us has taken a penny out of the company for months. We're all up to our eyes in debt. Unless we get finance from somewhere in the next two weeks, we can't even pay the rent here. Dan, tell him.'

'You don't need to tell me. I know, I know. It'll be okay. Fred's just asked for twenty-four hours to see if there's anything he can do. There's no way he'll be able to match it in that time. Then we'll be in the clear and I'll still be able to look Fred in the eye. *And* we'll be within Bay Street's time limit.'

'Don't blow it, Hil, not when it's in our hands.'

'I won't, Dan, I promise.'

****

Regular Monday partnership meetings in Sand Hill Road were usually low voltage affairs. Updates on portfolio companies, mainly. Pleasing developments greeted with satisfied murmurs, and disappointments registered and digested unrancorously. For the secretaries charged with organising a special meeting for that Thursday, the task was not too challenging. One partner was on vacation in Maui, but could be on the end of a phone. Another agreed to postpone an out-of-town trip. Two were due to go together to a dog and pony show for some deal Woodside had introduced. That could be rescheduled. The rest would be in the office anyway. All the same, a special meeting was rare enough for a little electricity to crackle in the office air.

'Ten point five? From us? You must be joking. What

about the other firms? Can't you ask them to increase pro rata?'

'Cliff, we don't have time. If we don't get back to them with our offer by five o'clock tonight, we're out.'

'Fred, you *do* realise, don't you, that at that level we need bank approval. So however you cut it, we can't make an unconditional offer. Do they know that?'

'Sure they do. I told them it's a pure formality. They'll live with that risk.'

'Are you sure? I wouldn't I if I was them. Not if I had another cast-iron offer in my other pocket.'

'You're not them, Cliff. They trust me. We all know the bank'll never block it. Solomon will accept that.'

'Maybe they will, but why not just get the others to go up to three each? We'll do four point nine, like we usually do, and we'll get somebody else in for the one point one. I'll give Art Stein a call. I'm sure he'll do it.'

'Fred's right, Cliff. The guys he's been dealing with at Woodside and the other firms are pretty junior, I mean younger partners. They won't be able to do three apiece over the phone.'

'If we take it, can we lay it off to them later? We're talking about one-tenth of our fund on one start-up, you know.'

'I could talk to them, but we'd have to take firm to begin with.'

'Okay, okay, I hear you. Larry, do you know when the next bank Board meeting is?'

'Next Tuesday's first Tuesday of the month. It'll be then.'

'That's too soon. Board papers are supposed to be in at least a week in advance.'

'Surely if it's urgent they'll accept it.'

'Maybe, Fred, but I tell you they won't like it.'

'Cliff, what choice have we got if we don't want to lose this deal?'

'Fred, are you *really* so sure this technology is so amazing?'

'It's a home run. I'm certain of it.'

'Okay, let's leave it there. Larry and I need to have a private word about this. Fred, we'll get back to you in half an hour.'

****

'Two more please, Lisa.'

'Coming up, guys.'

'Don't you think she looks particularly pretty tonight?'

'She's looking good. No doubt about it.'

'See the way she tucks that little curl behind her ear? So-o cute. One of my fantasies is I'm some mediaeval knight jousting, with Lisa's scarf round my lance.'

'Romantic, very romantic. But Hil, you're so uncoordinated, you'd fall off the horse before you even reached the other guy. Don't think Lady Lisa'd be too impressed.'

'Guess not, but it'd be a good ice-breaker.'

'Hey, I've got an idea. If you can't work up the courage to speak to her – apart from your undoubted eloquence when ordering drinks, that is – why not slip her a note asking her for a date?'

'Nah, she'd be sure to turn me down, and then I'd be too ashamed to come here any more. This way, at least I get to look at her. She's bound to have a boyfriend, a girl that good-looking.'

'Not for certain. Have you seen the stats for San Francisco? All the odds are stacked in our favor. Must be loads of good-looking women with no-one to keep them warm at night. Specially working nights like she does. Not gonna leave a lot of quality time. So don't count on her having a man. Same for that redhead over there. She'll be on her own, too. I can tell. Why don't you be neighborly and invite her to join us?'

'Oh sure, just my style. Why don't *you*, if you're so sure? Anyway, I bet you tonight's check she's meeting someone.'

'You're on . . . How d'you think she got *into* that outfit? . . . Oh, oh . . . looks like you win. Why do I hate good looking guys with blonde hair?'

'My God . . . Aloysius Arbuthnot'

'You *know* him? What kinda name is Alo-ish-us?'

'English, I guess, or at least *he* is. He was at Redwood. Had a great English milord routine: draughty castles, close friend of the Queen, all that stuff. Persuaded about half the female population on he campus to emerge from their underwear for the heritage experience. Strictly one night stands. We called him "Alo-Goodbye". Much later it turned out he was a total phoney. He was English all right, but the real name was Tom Brown, and his dynasty was about as up-market as ours.'

'And he was a *friend* of yours?'

'Not really. We were in the same year. Hey, quit looking their way. I don't want him to recognize me . . . I said *quit*.'

'How can I quit? If she eats any more of those peanuts those buttons have *got* to pop. You can't expect me to miss that. So what does this English jerk do now? Does he *live* in the Bay area?'

'Not that I know of, but I'm way out of touch. Last I heard he was into a real estate racket in Florida. Whatever he's doing, it'll be some scam or other . . . *Stop it* . . . I *told* you, godammit.'

'Okay, okay. Talking of scams, with this new improved deal, just *how* much do you stand to make if Solomon takes off? I know we're talking mega rich, but how rich *is* mega rich these days? It's not something I have to deal with constantly.'

'Fred reckons we can go public in year three at a valuation of two to three hundred million. After that, if we keep making plan, there's no reason why the company shouldn't be worth eight hundred million to a billion two years later. That's when I wanna cash out and start *spending*.'

'So, if you have fifteen percent . . . was that it? . . . you'll have at least a hundred and twenty million?'

'That's the theory. Even if we don't do quite that well, we shouldn't have to take in laundry.'

'So, when you cash in your chips, what'll you do with all that freedom? Will you travel?'

'Of course I will. And so will you, whether you like it or not. You'll have to come with me. We've never done *anything*, either of us. Since we can't fly, I guess I'll just have to buy some amazing yacht.'

'Wonderful, provided there's a proper crew. You'd be worse at steering a boat than you are at riding a bike. You'd probably fall off just as often, too. You'd have to learn to swim.'

'Don't worry, there'd be hundreds of crew. We'd never have to lift a finger.'

'Can we go to Aldabra?'

'Is that the place you told me about? The island with the Giant Tortoises? Where did you say it was?'

'Indian Ocean.'

'No problem. First destination. Con, I'm gonna crucify you if you don't quit looking at her.'

'Sorry . . . *My* problem will be waiting five years. I don't think my job's got much in the way of life-expectancy at the moment.'

'Oh, not again, Con. What's happened now?'

'Remember Turtle Airlines? I faxed it to the client. They didn't think it was quite as cute as I'd imagined. One of them phoned Dumdum.'

'Holy cow. What did she say?'

'I couldn't really make it out after the first few mouthloads. She got so mad she got pretty incoherent. Fortunately, her body language didn't need sub-titles.'

'So? Did she fire you?'

'Somewhere among the waves of flying spit, I think she was trying to communicate something to that effect. So I go to my desk to start clearing out my things, but, before I'm finished, she's cooled down enough to remember we've got that big beer label presentation next week. She can't do without me for that, so within ten minutes of being fired I find myself suddenly re-instated. All very confusing. Dumdum couldn't bring herself to tell me personally, so she made Chas not only tell me, but pass on a lurid catalogue of all the things that would happen if I stepped out of line again. Chas is such a creep. He'd written it all down to make sure he didn't miss out anything. Can you believe that?'

'Hadn't you better go easy for a while? You've been

through so many jobs, I'm not sure how easy it'd be to get another now.'

'Yeah, I know you're right. 'Nother?'

'Absolutely. Here we go again, the poet speaks . . . 'Scuse me. Two more please, Lisa . . . There now, wasn't that said beautifully?'

'What a talent! Can you show me how talented you are at passing me some of those nuts you're monopolising there?'

'Ooops, sorry. I was grazing on autopilot.'

'Thanks. So tell me, did you switch off Boise altogether?'

'I left a tiny crack of light in the door. I sent a fax saying we couldn't get everything done by their deadline, but we'd be back to them by Wednesday at latest.'

'Did you hear back?'

'Nothing.'

'But it *will* be okay with BUS, won't it?'

'It'd better be. Otherwise, Irma and Dan will roast me alive. I think I can trust Fred, and he swears it's an absolute formality. All the more so 'cos he's originally from the bank himself. Claims he knows all the big shots there and they'll all want to be super-supportive of him.'

'Why didn't you just take the Boisebucks? Was it just being decent to Fred?'

'Partly. There was something *real* odd about those Bay Street guys. Not only the funny way they talked and acted. I had this feeling they had some sort of hidden agenda. So as long as we can get the same deal, I'd be much more comfortable with BUS'

'And if they were to say no? Hypothetically?'

'I get on to Bay Street in a hypothetical hurry. Worst

case is going back to the original eight million deal, if the bank won't agree the higher amount.'

'So on Tuesday, do you just hang out in Saratoga, biting your fingernails, waiting for the call?'

'No, I'll be there. Fred says they will most likely pass it on the nod, but he and I have to be on hand in case they have any questions.'

'So are you guys working on the weekend like usual?'

'We're gonna take a break. With this Board stuff, we're all too hyper to concentrate. You should see Irma. Can't sit still. She looks like she's got Saint Vitus dance'

'What'll you do?'

'If I haven't got time to fix the Fiat, I think I'll take the bike up towards Mendocino. There's some deserted country roads back inland from there where I can practise a few curves.'

'How about putting some stabilisers on, like they do on little kids' bikes?'

'Okay with me, so long as they're invisible to good-looking women. What are you up to?'

'Turtle-hurtle to San Diego.'

'Oh shit, he's seen me . . . . You *asshole* . . . . Oh please, oh pleeeeze don't come over . . . . I'll get you for this . . . My God, Aloysius . . . ! How *are* you . . . ? What an amazing surprise! Didn't see you there. What brings you to San Francisco?'

4

'Pat?'

'Yes?'

'Standish.'

'Hi there, Standish.'

'Sorry to bother you on the weekend. Is this a good time?'

'Perfect. Lots of grandchildren running around the pool making whoopee. Can't get any peace and quiet anywhere. What can I do for you?'

'You remember the last Board meeting when you were asking about the Venture group?'

'Sure I do.'

'I thought you were making a whole lot of sense.'

'Thank you.'

'Well, you'll have seen that they rushed out some kind of half-assed proposal for us to look at on Tuesday.'

'Yeah, I got it on the fax yesterday. Not much in the way of notice.'

'Frankly, Pat, it bugs the shit out of me. Seems to me we ought to look at this with a healthy degree of scepticism.'

'That sounds right to me.'

'I thought I'd call to see if you felt the same way. You know what Frank's like as a Chairman. Wants everything okayed fast so we can get to lunch. And Tom always likes being Mr Nice Guy. So on this, I thought if a few of us could kinda jump in and take the lead, it might set the right tone, if you catch my drift.'

'Have you spoken to any of the others?'

'I've told Frank it's something I have very strong views on, which I hope he will respect, but that's all I've said. I'm planning to call up a couple of the others this afternoon. I wanted to speak with you first of all.'

'Well, I appreciate that, Standish. I won't be holding back, you can count on that.'

'Thanks, Pat. I knew I could.'

'Okay, Standish. I'd better go and check that those grandchildren aren't barbequeing each other. See you on Tuesday.'

****

Pain hurts. It pierces. It throbs. He knew he shouldn't have gone in there. Guessed that the moment he saw the pair of massively chromed bikes parked outside. Some wise instinct yelled at him not to, but this is California, he thought, and he was thirsty, and there was nowhere else around in that strangely isolated spot, so he quite consciously pressed the button to override all his instincts. He knew even more from the way the two leathered orang-utangs on the rocking chairs on the verandah looked at him, from the repulsive Charles Manson look-alike who brought him his beer, and from the eerie emptiness of the interior. There were bike relics everywhere, mainly Harley and Indian. Badges, engine parts, petrol tanks, wheels.

He could have made a run for it. He really could have, even when the hairy orangs came inside, sat down at the next table, and started loudly discussing their opinion of

Japanese bikes. But when they turned and started talking *at* him, raging, quivering fear gripped him and he was powerless to do other than docilely await the unfolding of their capricious drama.

****

'Quite a mess they made of your nose. It's amazing it's not broken. The gash on it is very nasty though. I'm afraid your eyes won't look too good for a while, either. Doesn't look like fistwork. Did they hit you with something?'

'A table.'

'They swung a table at you?'

'No, one of the gorillas banged my head down on the table I was sitting at.'

'*Brutal.* There are some *bad* people out there. We fixed up your face best we could. Apart from that, there's just some bruising to the chest. Probably from the edge of the table too, I guess. Is that mark on your right side new?'

'No, that's been there a while.'

'You should get that checked out.'

'Yeah, I know. I will.'

'The police came back while we were working on you. Apparently, the bikers were gone when they got there. Owner claimed he's no idea who they were. Said the bikers forced him to hand over his cutting torch. Nothing he could do to stop them.'

'This is *ridiculous.* The cutter was *his* idea. He went and got it for them, *and* the mask. What the hell's he doing with gear like that out in the woods, anyway? The cops *must* know all about it. I bet he's the local safe-cracker.'

'All they said was the bartender feels bad about what

happened, but he thought it was pretty dumb of you to come to a Harley hang-out on a Japanese bike.'

'Wonderful, just wonderful. And *this* is the land of the free ...? Anyway, did the police say what they're gonna do next?'

'I got this second hand, but it didn't sound like they were planning to do very much. They want you to tell them what you want done with the bits of your bike. They say they don't need to keep them as evidence.'

'I do *not* believe this.'

'Are you going to stay the night somewhere local? Have you thought about transport back to San Francisco?'

****

As Hilton inspected the wreckage in the mirror back at his apartment, he grimly reflected that being beaten up had a bright side. With all the nervous anticipation, the weekend had been dragging, and he had to admit that at least the orangs had helped take his mind off it. Also, now he was sure to get out of the waiting ordeal at the bank. He could hardly turn up with two black eyes and a plaster across his nose big enough to carry advertising.

It didn't work out that way. His suggestion of Irma, or Dan – if they were a crusty bunch of old misogynists – was swept aside. It was the CEO they wanted to hear from, if anyone. Considering his laid back, 'this is just a formality' line, Fred seemed to be taking all this procedural garbage pretty seriously. Maybe he couldn't brush off the forelock-tugging dust of his early days at the bank as easily as he thought.

****

If the architects of the waiting room meant to instil a healthy measure of reverence for the power of immense wealth, they certainly succeeded. It was the grandest room Hilton had been in in his life. When he walked through the door, he assumed it *was* the Boardroom, and they had beaten everyone else there. He found himself whispering. Fred, who'd never actually been near the Boardroom before, derided Hilton's whispers, but unconsciously lowered his own voice by a decibel or two. After an hour and a half, Fred's confident assertion that they wouldn't be called in was contradicted by the soft footsteps of a sweet emissary who introduced herself as Gina. As she invited them to go through, she was kind enough neither to avert her eyes too patently nor to snigger at Hilton's un-Boardroomish facial array.

'Hilton, let me take care of explaining about the accident.'

'*Accident*? There was nothing accidental about it.'

Gina pressed a bell and a few seconds later the double doors slid silently back, giving them their first sight of the enormous panelled Boardroom. Now the waiting room did seem *very* modest. This must be the real burial chamber, thought Hilton, and for a Pharoah well up in the Valley of the Kings pecking order.

'Please sit down, gentlemen.'

'Thank you. I'd just like to explain something. Hilton had a very unfortunate accident, er ... incident at the weekend, which is why he, um, looks ... the way he does. He doesn't normally look that way. In the circumstances, I think that it is very good of him to be willing ...'

'Thank you, Fred. I'm sure Mr Kask can do any

explaining of his weekend activities that he thinks necessary. This is Frank Clayton, the Chairman of the Board. I'm Standish MacMartin, President of this bank. The gentlemen you see around you are the executive and non-executive directors who have turned this bank around from the sleepy outfit, resting on its laurels, that it used to be and made it into one of the most profitable banks in the country. Do you know what all these gentlemen have in common, Mr Kask?'

'No, I have no idea.'

'Well, I'll tell you. Every last man jack of them attended one of the great schools of this country. Stanford, Wharton, Harvard, Yale, MIT, Princeton. Can you guess how many of them failed to graduate?'

'No, but I've a feeling it's not going to be a very big number.'

'You're goddam right, fellah. It's not a big number at all. It's zero. That oughta tell you something. What does it tell you, Mr Kask?'

'I suppose it tells me that if you want to be a director of a big bank, you have to go to a big school.'

'You're missing the point. You're missing the point altogether. Now, the college you went to ... I don't think any of us here have ever heard of it or even have much idea where it is ...'

'If you're planning on visiting it, I'll fax you directions.'

'... and even if we had heard of it, it wouldn't make much difference since you didn't graduate, would it?'

'I guess not.'

'So can you tell us why you dropped out?'

'I don't see why this has anything to do with my

company.'

'It may prove to have a *great* deal to do with your company, boy, and whether or not it gets financed.'

'Okay. Well, the electronics they were teaching at my college would have been alright if we had been planning to get hold of a time machine and travel back to the Sixties. Other than that, I didn't see much point in studying museum stuff.'

'And that was it, was it? No drug problems?'

'I experimented a little. So did most of the other kids.'

'Not all the other kids got into trouble with the police, like you did. And was there anything else?'

'I had some personal problems.'

'What kind of problems?'

'I had a minor breakdown.'

'Mr MacMartin can I please say something? Hilton had a major trauma to deal with in his childhood. His parents were ...'

'Fred, when we need your contribution, you can be sure we'll ask for it. Now, as you can see, Mr Kask, we've had some quick checks run. Even after college, you don't seem to have held on to any one job for more than about a year and a half.'

'*Held* on? I *moved* on.'

'Perhaps, perhaps.'

'Standish, can I come in here?'

'Fire ahead, Pat.'

'Mr Kask, I'm only a non-executive director here, but the rest of the time I run a very large consumer products company. I can tell you that running a business takes a lot more than just one or two good ideas. It takes a lot of leadership, a lot of experience, and knowledge of a broad range of disciplines. Forgive me putting it bluntly, but before you started Solomon Computers, you don't seem to have run anything but yourself. Judging by your answers to Standish MacMartin's questions, you don't even seem to do that very well. Shouldn't you consider handing your idea over to an established company with proper management, or at least bring in a team of pros from the start?'

'You mean like the pros at the big computer companies?'

'Yes, that's the kind of thing I had in mind.'

'You mean the guys who've got nearly every major strategic decision wrong for the last twenty years? We were naive enough to think it would be smarter to *make* some money rather than waste great barrel-loads of it.'

'I think I'll overlook that impertinent remark. Mr Kask, it's not just your own lack of leadership experience. Your two co-founders ... Irma Voricek – she's pretty green, too, isn't she?'

'Irma's one of the best software engineers in the whole Valley.'

'And this Daniel Nathan. We did some checking up on him, too. Didn't he leave UCLA under some sort of cloud?'

'They cut the budget on his program and diverted the funds to some dead-end project. He gave the University a pretty clear idea of what he thought of their decision and both sides agreed it was better that they should part company. It was a lucky break for us. Otherwise, we could never've got someone of his calibre.'

'Sounds like he doesn't have any people skills either. Isn't he simply an embittered has-been?'

'Dan is probably the finest psychophysiologist in the country.'

'That's all I have, Standish.'

'Thank you, Pat. Well, that brings us on to this invention of yours. We've looked at your plan. How an earth can you make these wildly ambitious estimates for demand if, as the plan says, the market doesn't exist yet? Are you trying to claim that this will make all current computers obsolete?'

'Not at all. For most purposes, computers don't need to "think". Ours will target very specific applications but, even so, the opportunity will still be enormous.'

'Where are the biggest of these great *opportunities*?'

'As you can see from the plan, we think the medical area is a very big one. But the machine could have applications for anything predictive which cannot be done purely statistically.'

'Does that mean your computer could play the financial markets?'

'No doubt about it.'

'You mean we can just buy a few of these machines and get rid of all the overpaid young jerks in our trading operations?'

'No. But you could improve their performance if you program the machine using the instincts of traders from more successful banks. Anyway, that's a pretty marginal application. The key applications will be in remote or hazardous locations where real "human" judgement is needed.'

'And if I read this right, Mr Kask, your machine's "judgement" is based on the notion that there are just eight basic emotions. Is that right?'

'Eight and their opposites, yes.'

'Eight might be enough to cover the emotions of a

rabbit, or, who knows, a computer engineer, but surely *normal* humans are a bit more complex?'

'We simulated thousands of different responses and moods, and those eight emotions in combination appear to cover it.'

'Remind us what they are, please.'

'Want/Don't Want. Like/Dislike. Anger/Calm. Fear/Confidence. Trust/Don't Trust. Happy/Sad. Amused/Not Amused. Interested/Bored.'

'So if I have *contempt* for something, how does that fit in?'

'Contempt is a mix of dislike and don't trust, with a twist of anger.'

'Bullseye. What do you think about all this, Peter?'

'I think I'm beginning to like the idea, Standish. Does the computer have different colours for each of these emotions? Would it light up like a Christmas tree if Gina walked into the room?'

'We could engineer that. You could program it personally if you like. The lights are not such a bad idea. Not strictly necessary of course, but they might help the less technical to understand it.'

'And how about this voice thing? Hasn't that been around for ages?'

'Have you heard them? They sound like the man, or usually the woman, from outer space. Our voice synthesis box comes from work Dan did years ago on the physiology of vocal chords. It can replicate a voice *very* accurately. A lifelike voice can be important for both practical and technical reasons.'

'Can it do a Tina Turner impression?'

'If you want it badly enough. It might be cheaper to buy

a CD'

'Any more questions, Peter?' Frank Clayton wanted his lunch.

'No.'

'Standish, have you heard enough?'

'More than enough.'

'Okay, we have other things on our agenda and lunchtime is approaching. I think we should thank Mr Kask for his time. We will communicate our decision as soon as possible. It does seem a lot of money you're asking for.'

'Mr Clayton, can I say something here?'

'Sure you can, Fred, but please keep it brief.'

'The only reason we want to invest so much is because Solomon got an offer we had to match. Originally we were going to go in lower ...'

'You mean, so the Board wouldn't have to be consulted?'

'No, no. That's not what I meant at all.'

'Well, we are very glad we get the *occasional* chance to look at how our Venture subsidiary thinks it wise to invest what is primarily *our* clients' money.'

'Anyway, as I was saying, Hilton got that offer, but he's been good enough to turn it down and stick with us on account of all the work I ... we have put in. And we're sure this is going to be a real home-run ball, and Cliff and Larry and the others all agree and all that.'

'Is that all, Fred?'

'Yes. I *really* think we should go for it and we'd be *crazy* to even ...'

'Yes, Fred, you were saying ... we'd be crazy to do what?'

'Nothing. I just mean I think it's a great idea.'

'Thank you, Fred. I don't think we need to detain either of you any longer. One final question, Mr Kask. I'm curious. How *did* you get your face in that mess?'

'I was attacked by some thugs.'

'Well my advice to you, young man, if you ever have to come before a Board like this again, is to take more care to avoid getting into brawls.'

****

'A "formality". A frigging formality, you said. Oh Jesus, what have I done?'

'Gee, I'm real sorry, Hilton. I guess they felt they should give you the third degree. You were pretty feisty with them yourself.'

'Look, Fred, I came here to talk about computers, not my private life. I thought I was getting a Board meeting and you give me banking's answer to the Oprah Winfrey show.'

'I'm sure it'll be okay. They wouldn't *dare* turn us down. Have you really switched off the other offer?'

'I think so.'

'Look, if the worst comes to the worst, you'll still get the eight million. I can probably get Larry and Cliff to go up to just under the five mark, so you'd have almost ten. And we can do something about the valuation.'

'I'm going now, Fred. I can't bear the thought of being at the company right now. Call me at home the *moment* you hear.'

'Okay, Hilton.'

****

'Irma?'

'Yeah, Hil, what the hell's going on?'

'Fred called just to say he hadn't heard yet. I'm sitting here shaking. I left a message at Bay Street, but they haven't called back yet. Is Dan okay?'

'He's in *tears*, Hil. Call us as soon as you hear. Either way.'

'Okay.'

****

'Mr Webster ? This is Mona from Mr MacMartin's office. I have Mr MacMartin for you, can you hold, please...?'

'Larry, how are you?'

'Hi, Standish. I'm fine.'

'Larry, the Board had a very interesting session this morning with Fred Adams and his little investment proposal. What's your opinion about it?'

'It's an interesting technology. They're very bright people. It's been mainly Fred's baby, of course. His chance to win his spurs as a partner and all that.'

'Larry, I have to tell you, the Board was not at all impressed. You've always told me that venture capital is all about backing people. Well, none of us cared much for Mr Kask ... I'm sorry to have to tell you that we've come down against investing in Solomon Computers. Is that going to be a big problem for you?'

'Not for the partnership generally. It will be a huge blow for Fred, though.'

'Perhaps, Larry, perhaps. By the way, I've been meaning to ask when you'll need to be raising a new fund.'

'We'd like to look at closing something by next Spring.'

'How much were you thinking of?'

'A hundred to a hundred and fifty.'

'And will you be looking to the bank to help you raise it again?'

'That would be pretty important, Standish. As you know, our own track record ... well, it's still early days, and we haven't always had the rub of the green.'

'Larry, there's one thing I'd like you to understand clearly. I don't know yet if the bank will be able to offer much help with this next fund, but we would *certainly* take it as a very hostile act if you invested anything in that bullshit company we looked at this morning. And I mean *anything*.'

'I see.'

'I thought this little hint might help you in your deliberations.'

'Okay. Thanks, Standish.'

'Another thing, Larry. It's always good to see a homegrown kid make his way, but d'ya really think Fred Adams is ready to be leading investments yet? Maybe I'm reading too much into this one case, but it does seem he hasn't picked up enough experience in judging people yet, know what I mean?'

'What are you getting at, Standish? We've only just made him partner. We can hardly demote him.'

'I'm not suggesting that. Indeed, I'm not suggesting *anything*. That's for you and Cliff to decide. But, for example, couldn't he look after some of the existing portfolio until he's had a chance to learn the ropes some more?'

'That'd mean he wouldn't be a real partner at all.'

'Perhaps, perhaps. Well, you'll have to call that one, Larry.'

****

'Con?'

'Hil? I can't hear you.'

'Sorry. It's a payphone.'

'Hey, what's that I'm hearing in the background? Where the hell are you?'

'I'm at the airport.'

'You're *where*?'

'The airport.'

'The *airport*? What the fuck are you doing at the airport?'

'Con, I've got to go to Boise.'

'Why?'

'The bank blew us away. Not just the fifteen. Now the assholes won't even give us the eight. Boise's our last chance.'

'Well, phone them. They're very advanced in Idaho. I read it in *Time*. They have phones there.'

'They won't take my calls. I have to go there.'

'Drive there, then. I'll drive you myself.'

'Con, I'm really sorry about this, but we just *don't* have the time. I have to get there right away and camp out if necessary.'

'Oh Hil, we promised each other. We swore a sacred pact that neither of us would *ever* do this. Blood twins, remember.'

'I know, I know. Believe me, Con, if there was any other way ...'

'It's only money, Hil. Don't do it.'

'It's more than money, Con. If this falls through, it's the

end of everything for me.'

'Oh God, Hil. Oh God. I just can't stand the thought of ...'

'It'll be okay, Con ... Con ...? Con ...? Speak to me, Con.'

'I guess you've no choice. How're you feeling ... brave?'

'No leaf ever shook as bravely.'

'Hil, whatever the answer, don't fly on the way back. Get a rentacar, I'll pay.'

'Okay, twin. Hey, if it does crash, we'll be rich. You, anyway. They sell insurance here. If I die anywhich way in the next twelve months, the heavens open and rain down cash. It seems I'm worth a lot more dead than alive. It's ridiculous you can't take it with you.'

'I don't want cash. I don't need cash. I need my brother. Don't sit in any of those seats. Spend the whole flight in the john. They say it's the safest place on a plane.'

'I may be in there for quite different reasons.'

'When does it arrive?'

'Three fifteen, local time.'

'Call me at three sixteen.'

'I promise.'

'I gotta go now. Till three sixteen.'

'Take care, Hil. Don't die on me. Broken bones are fine. Up to a point, amputations are acceptable. Death is not.'

'Bye, Con. Thanks for understanding.'

'Bye. Hey, don't get on that thing until you find a rabbit's foot.'

'I don't need it. Apparently they serve food on board.'

5

Mr Kask, you are a very persistent young man. If you had shown as much judgement as persistence, things would be quite different now. But I must ask you to understand that you and we have nothing more to discuss, and I'm only seeing you as a matter of courtesy since you came all this way and, how shall I put it, took up residence in our lobby.'

'Mr Roberts, I made some terrible mistakes, but surely the world hasn't changed so much in one week?'

'Mr Kask, everything has changed. For one, you missed our deadline.'

'I know.'

'And for two, you shopped our offer.'

'It's true. I felt like I had no alternative.'

'As the designer of a computer that is intended to have advanced decision-making functions, you of all people surely know the importance of good judgement.'

'Sure I do, but I was between a rock and a hard place.'

'Life is full of choices. I don't doubt this was a tough one. You made your call and now you must live with the consequences of that call.'

'Mr Roberts, is there anything at all I can say or do to sort this out? We can be very flexible on valuation. I just don't want the company to die because of this one screw-up.'

'I'm genuinely sorry, Mr Kask, please believe me, but I

can't allow my personal feelings to enter into it. We told you very clearly what our principles are. In the past, any time we've allowed ourselves to be diverted from them, we've invariably regretted it.'

'So that's it?'

'That's it. I wish you well, Mr Kask, and I hope there have been some useful lessons in this for you.'

'Lessons always seem to come too late to be of much help.'

'Well, *you'll* have to be the judge of that. Now can we offer you some transportation back to the airport?'

'No thanks, I'm going to drive back.'

'To the airport ...? To *San Francisco*? Well all I can say is you sure must enjoy driving. I hope you're not paying by the mile.'

'Goodbye.'

'Goodbye. Good luck, Mr Kask.'

****

'Hi, Lisa.'

'Hi. Hey, what happened to you?'

'I got in a fight with a rhino. Tried head-butting it. Forgot about its horn. No, not true. I met some bad boys and I had to show them who was boss. Took care of the first five no problem, but the sixth got in a lucky hit.'

'Wow, I didn't have you figured for such a tough guy.'

'It's all in the mind. In my case only too literally. My mind's the only place I'm a hero. It's my rotten, stinking, cowardly body that lets me down. It was my *body* that got beaten to a pulp by two thugs. My *mind* resisted courageously and still views them with lofty disdain.'

'You're very talkative tonight. Have you maybe had one or two someplace before you came on over here?'

'Damn right I have. I just drove back from Idaho in a Ford Escort. Anyone would need a drink after *that*.'

'From Idaho? In a Ford Escort? Was it for a bet or something?'

'A kind of gamble, anyway.'

'So why didn't you fly?'

'Long story, Lisa, long story. Say, what's the best Scotch you got on that shelf up there?'

'Scotch? The hard stuff tonight? That's not your normal poison, is it? Are you okay?'

'Yeah, yeah, yeah. Come on, Lisa, give me a break. I don't know anything about whisky. Which one's the one?'

'I don't touch it myself. Timothy swears by the Macallan eighteen-year-old. Expensive though. Twelve dollars a shot.'

'*Twelve bucks a shot*? In that case I'd better have just three of them.'

'Look, are you really okay? You don't seem yourself. Is your brother coming tonight?'

'I don't wanna see anybody tonight. You excepted, of course.'

'That's sweet. Why don't I get you one shot to begin with and we'll see how it goes ...? There you go.'

Gulp.

'That's how it goes. Second, please.'

Gulp.

'Third, please.'

'You know, I don't mean to sound critical, but I ain't quite sure you got the knack of drinking eighteen-year-old Scotch. If the guys from Scotland saw you they'd most likely string you up.'

'Fine with me. There are worse ways to go. Phone the whisky police right away. But give me the rest of the bottle before they get here.'

'Look, we've never been properly introduced, but I've heard you and your brother talking. You're Hil, right?'

'That's me.'

'And your brother's called Con?'

'Yup.'

'Well, listen Hil, the way you're talking and acting, I don't mind at all, but people are ... *looking.*'

'What you sayin', Lisa? Can't hear you. Can you speak louder?'

'I'm trying to whisper.'

'Ooh, sorry, sorry. Can you whisper a bit louder? Hey, maybe 'nother Scotch would help my hearing.'

'Okay, but what's going on? It's not like you to get tanked up like this. Like I said, people are looking.'

'Who cares? Let them look as much as they like. *Hi, everybody!*'

'Hil, I *must* go and serve some other customers. Will you be okay there for a while?'

'Sure I will. Hurry back, though. Give me another shot of that stuff to talk with while you're away. I think we're getting to like each other.'

'Okay.'

'Hey, Lisa.'

'What?'

'You *do* know you're beautiful, don't you? I mean real drop-dead beautiful. I wanna make sure you know it, that's all.'

'You're sweet. Gotta go now.'

Gulp.

"S'funny, that. First time in my life I tell a girl she's beautiful, and what does she say? I'm "*sweet*"', that's what she says. Just's well I didn't say I love her. Most likely would've called me "cute".'

'Hi, I'm back.'

' 'Nother, please, Lisa.'

'Hil, the manager says I shouldn't give you any more. Maybe you should go home and get some sleep. That was quite a drive you had.'

'Don't wanna get some sleep. Not sleepy. Bring the manager over here. Wanna have a word with him.'

'Hil, please don't. You'll just get me in trouble. What's *happened*? Is it only the thugs, or has something else bad happened?'

'Bad, bad, bad.'

'*What*?'

'I've wrecked everything. *Everything*. Not just for me. For my buddies, Dan and Irma, too.'

'What happened?'

'Oh God ... oh God, Lisa.'

'Excuse me butting in here. Lisa, I'd like a private word, please. Excuse us, Sir ... Lisa, what the hell's with that guy?'

'I don't know. Something's got him very upset. I don't know what.'

'He's totally wrecked. The pair on the stools next to him have complained to Alex. We *have* to get rid of him. Oh my God, look at him now, would you ... he's crying, for Chrissakes. Lisa, do whatever you've gotta do, but get him outa here before this gets worse.'

****

'Is this it? Number six?'

'Yeah, six.'

'Where's the key?'

'Pocket?'

'*Which* pocket?'

'Key pocket, 'f course.'

'Okay, don't worry, I'll find it. You rest there on the step and I'll open up and get the lights on.'

'Lisa, Li-sa'

'What?'

'Lisa, you're wonderful.'

'Let's concentrate on getting you in here. Hil, do you think you can manage to stand up again?'

'Think so. Oh God ... think I need the bathroom.'

****

'Are you alright in there?'

'Not sure.'

'Hil, if you can ... clean yourself up and come and lie down. I'm sure you'll sleep now ... That's it, don't bother taking your clothes off. Just try to sleep.'

'You will stay, won't you, Lisa? Need you to stay.'

'*Stay?* I've got to get back to the bar and then home to my husband.'

'*Husband*? You married? That's . . . a tragedy. A *tragedy*.'

'I'm going to go now. Will you be alright?'

'Hope not. Better dead.'

'Look, Hil, I've really got to go. I'll come round tomorrow afternoon and see how you are. Goodnight.'

'Goodnight, Lisa.'

****

'Sorry no-one's here to take your call. Please leave a message after the beep.'

'Hilton, this is Fred Adams. Please call me.'

'Hil, it's Irma. Are you there? If you're there, pick up the frigging phone, Hil. Okay, call me as soon as you get back. No-one's blaming you, we just want to check you're alright.'

'It's Fred again. It's two o'clock now. Please call me. I'm going out about three, but I'll be on the mobile. Larry and Cliff have asked to see me again at six. I doubt there's any hope left, but, just in case, I need to speak with you. If I don't hear, I'll give it my best shot myself.'

****

He opened them again. This time the room had almost stopped spinning. He tried focusing, but the effort of keeping his eyes open became too much and he went back to the wildly swirling Northern Lights display he was getting with them closed.

The doorbell rang, sending ten thousand volts through his hangover.

'It's Lisa. Can I come in?'

'Can you give me five minutes?'

'I'll come back in five.'

****

'You okay?'

'Will be, if the herd of elephants stops charging around my head.'

'Did you manage some sleep?'

'In the intervals between being sick.'

'Poor you.'

'It was you brought me back here, right?'

'We came in a taxi. It took ten minutes before the driver or I could understand what address you were trying to say.'

'Thanks. It was good of you.'

'Don't mention it. I'm glad to see you're okay. Is there anyone to look after you today?'

'I talked to my brother. He's coming over this evening.'

'Well, I guess I should be running along. I just wanted to check up on you.'

'Do you have to go so soon?'

'I guess I'm okay for a while.'

'I'm in serious need of fresh air. Walk?'

'Sounds good. Where do you feel like going?'

'Marina?'

'We can take my little car. It's downstairs.'

****

It was one of the West Coast's more interesting civil engineering decisions to build the residential district of San Francisco's Marina on landfill. Solid rock resists all but the worst earthquakes surprisingly well. The 1989 earthquake was just on the right side of dire and the buildings on rock stood firm. The streets in the Marina buckled spectacularly. The houses there equipped with foundations merely cracked or sagged. Those whose architects had considered foundations an unnecessary frippery subsided drunkenly as the jello beneath melted and reset misshapenly. It's a pretty area, though, and, between earthquakes, a pleasant place to live. The houses, mainly two-storey Spanish-style confections, prompt more wicked smiles than sincere respect, but they *do* have a sunny countenance, and the whole chaotic ensemble somehow succeeds. The waterfront green, part park and part car-park, has a magnificent view of San Francisco's more celebrated bridge and the world's most desirably located former prison. Here and there the green is pock-marked by installations of exercise equipment for the city's many athletes. Beside each array of fashioned tubing is a small, stylised cartoon explaining its purpose to those with poor memories, limited imagination, or intellects less developed than the average Californian fitness fanatic. Joggers jog earnestly, women speedwalkers press grimly onwards in their lilac or turquoise outfits, smugly immune from the publicly damp armpits and matted hair of their more energetic sisters. There are a few hopeful fishermen, and a more generous supply of men and women of all ages, shapes, and sizes who sit solo inside their equally varied cars, all forlornly hoping that some other lonely soul will sidle up and make the first move.

They watch the freighters arrive from Asia, pressed low in the water by their wearisome burden, and leave proudly, toweringly back to where another saddlebag of cars or electronics will be strapped on.

****

'So, is Hil short for something?'
  'Hilton'
  'Unusual.'

'From the hotels. My folks emigrated from Estonia. When they arrived about forty years ago, my Dad had a real hard time finding regular work. Only had about ten words of English, which wasn't an overwhelming competitive advantage. Eventually, they decided to try their luck in California, and he got taken on to do some menial job in a Hilton in LA. They were so grateful, when the two of us popped out a few years later, we were named as a sort of gesture of thanks. Conrad and Hilton.'

'That was sweet of them.'

'*Sweet*? A big help it was when we were growing up, I can tell you. Gave the other kids plenty of chances to sharpen their wit claws. For years I was called "Room" and Con was "Service".'

'Sorry ... I don't mean to laugh. Anyway, it was nice that your folks were so grateful and all.'

'Yeah, you're right. Eventually I got used to Hilton and just accepted it. Not before I tried changing my name, mind you.'

'What did you change it to?'

'There was a Steve phase, after McQueen of course, and a Harry stage, after Eastwood. Sooner or later people would find out my real name.'

'Did your folks know about the changes? What did they say?'

'That was after ... No, they didn't know.'

'Do they still live in California?'

'No.'

'Where are they?'

'They died when we were nine.'

'I'm sorry, Hil, I didn't mean to ...'

'It's okay. I don't usually talk about it a lot. They'd been married eleven years before we were born, and for their twentieth anniversary they flew down to Palm Springs, just the two of them, for a few days. Had a great time. Called to tell us as they were leaving the hotel. The plane never made it back.'

'That's awful. It must have been *terrible* for the two of you.'

'Don't recommend it. Are your folks alive?'

'Yes.'

'Tell them to keep it that way. Tell them to avoid smallpox, cholera, anthrax, and airplanes. Especially airplanes. Where do they live?'

'Billings, Montana. Mom's fifty-six, Italian. Dad's fifty-eight, German.'

'Interesting combination.'

'I think what brought them together was a shared distrust of anything modern. They're *so* conservative, you wouldn't believe it.'

'And I have a vague recollection through the alcoholic haze of some mention of a husband. What's he like?'

'Earl? It's hard to know what to say. He's thirty-two, seven years older than me. He has his own small realty company. He's okay.'

'So why don't you wear a ring?'

'I do most of the time. He took it away a few months back, 'cos he didn't like something I'd done. It was a kind of punishment for not meeting his expectations. It's not a big deal. He'll give me the ring back in a while. He's done it before.'

'Was it *that* bad, whatever you did?'

'Most folks wouldn't think so. Let's not talk about it.'

'I'm surprised he lets you work in a bar.'

'We need the money. His company never seems to go anywhere. He doesn't give me anything for our food and household things. So I work mornings at a flower shop and evenings at Josie's.'

'And he doesn't mind, I mean the men looking at you and all?'

'He says it turns him on that they can look but not touch.'

'So does he stay at home evenings?'

'Oh no, not Earl. He's never home till midnight.'

'Where does he go?'

'Bars, I guess. I used to ask a few years back, but now I prefer not to know what he does.'

'Fancy walking right up to the bridge?'

'What's the time ...? No, I gotta get goin'. I'll drive you back. Say, is whatever was upsetting you so much last night okay now? I was worried.'

'No, it's not okay at all, but I'm a bit calmer. I made the biggest screw-up of my life, and wrecked everything, not just for me, but for two people I care a lot about. I trusted the wrong guy.'

'Will you tell me about it as we drive?'

'If you don't mind, I can't face talking about it now. Can I tell you some other time?'

'Sure you can. Call me. I'll write the flower shop number down for you. That's the best place to reach me. I enjoyed our walk. Why don't we do it again sometime? Is this where I turn left?'

****

'Fred? It's Hilton. Sorry I couldn't call back sooner. How

was your meeting?'

'Nothing doing, I'm afraid. They won't budge. It turned out that wasn't why they wanted to see me. You're not the only one to lose out over this.'

'What happened?'

'Oh, they were pretty vague, but I don't think they want me to go after anything too ambitious for a while. They didn't say anything specific, but they may be reaching for the wing-clippers. Best keep a low profile for a few weeks.'

'That sounds wise.'

'Hilton, I know I've said it a hundred times already, but I am *so* sorry. How you feeling?'

'Hungover, destitute, and homicidal.'

'I suppose I'm the object of the last one.'

'No, I don't actually want to *kill* you, Fred. A little gentle maiming would do for you. The homicide I'll reserve for MacMartin and those orang-utangs on bikes.'

'What about the destitution bit?'

'I'm so far in debt, I don't know where to begin. A lot of the Solomon debts I guaranteed personally. I'm gonna have to borrow from my brother just to *live* for the next few weeks. I don't know what I'm going to do, Fred, and I can't bear to even think about it.'

'Hilton, I know this isn't much, but I mean ... if you're that desperate, I might be able to get you a job at the computer center at the bank. A friend of mine runs it. Just to tide you over, I mean.'

'The *bank*? *That* bank? Fred, get off the phone before you get upgraded from maiming to death.'

6

Without any shadow of doubt, it was pathetically crude and monstrously narrow, as well as straightforwardly offensive, for Hilton invariably to focus on one single aspect of Honor's being. Quite apart from her multi-faceted personality, she had plenty of *other* physical characteristics just as worthy of comment. Tall, with a model's high shoulders, she had long, lissom thighs, an aerobic-hard flat stomach, slender arms, and elegant, much-manicured fingers enhanced further by the enthusiastic application of bright crimson nail varnish. Her hair fell halfway down her shapely back, and, naturally silky, was an arresting blonde with a hint of contrast at the roots. Whenever the slightest soupçon of joy – triggered by no more than a pay rise or an extravagant gift – swept from her face its habitual scowl, she was tantalisingly close to true beauty.

Even from the one encounter during his only visit to Condor, Hilton should have been capable of keeping a more balanced mental portrait of her. But Hilton was an ass man, and painfully repugnant as his attitude was, it could hardly be denied that his assessment of the extraordinary cuteness of Honor's was absolutely accurate.

By day, this object of wonder perched on a soft black leather chair in a glazed box in the creative department of Condor's self-consciously designer offices in the Embarcadero Center. Honor had been there three years, twice as long as Conrad.

Corporate Identity, usually just called CI, is lucrative business. Corporations will pay vast sums for the right brand name, logo, letterhead or whatever. Top executives enjoy these things, and they help take their minds off the grind of running the business. For the big multinational majors – like oil, car, or telecoms companies – the contracts they award run to tens of millions. Condor never got near those accounts, and at best got an outside shot at some decent-sized regional business. The seventy-year-old owner, Burt McGovern, tried twice to break out of this box. First, he took leave of his normal parsimonious senses and shredded much cash opening offices in New York and Chicago in the hope that national business would naturally flow. Those offices closed before their second birthdays and McGovern swore never again to venture away from his San Francisco home. The second stratagem was a merger with a smallish advertising agency, consecrated on the altar of synergy. The theory of such synergies works just fine. We introduce our CI clients to you, and you bring the advertisers to us. Keep it all in the family, capture more of the client's dollar spend. One-stop shopping. The clients will *love* it. But don't ask them first in case they don't. Condor didn't ask, and the reality didn't turn out as the theory had suggested. The CI and advertising teams shared a low regard for each other's talents and would seldom risk jeopardising their *own* key relationships with aggressive cross-selling.

While McGovern's energies were devoted to a futile attempt to make oil and water mix, the CI business lost momentum. Michael Pechiney wasn't to blame, but as head of the CI side, he carried the can. One of the most imaginative minds in the industry, he was popular with clients and staff alike. After work on Friday, it was his custom to invite any of his group who were free to join him for a glass or two. These were no beer-bashes. Very fine wines were produced, and served with masterly descriptions of their provenance. Nor was he a single-mindedly Napa man, either. San Luis Obispo, Washington State, and the Appalachians were among his favourite sources. Guest appearances from abroad included New Zealand, South Africa and the Lebanon. His knowledge of French, Italian, and Spanish wines was encyclopaedic.

It was Michael's kindness, thoughtfulness, and abundant talent that surprised and attracted Conrad when he was looking for a change from the succession of graphic design jobs he had bounced in and out of. He saw in a boss like Michael the chance to break out of his depressing cycle of initially avoiding confontation, then trying to handle it calmly, then failing in that, and sooner or later over-reacting. It was always that fatal over-reaction: a temper, a walk-out, or – after months of docility bordering on servility – biting sarcasm at the expense of some incredulous, short-fused, bullying superior.

He was lucky to get taken on at Condor. The reference checks did not go at all well. But for Michael Pechiney, originality mattered more, and Conrad's portfolio of designs were strikingly original. He liked him too, and his instinct told him that the accounts from previous employers of Conrad's petulance might not tell the full story. So Conrad was given work there, and his resolution not to screw up this time seemed happily superfluous under Michael's kindly and watchful eye. He immediately took to the majority of his colleagues, and lusted after Honor from the instant they were introduced and she turned seductively, dismissively, poutingly away.

The team was divided roughly into the 'poets' like Honor and Chas – wordsmiths who thought up the brand names – and 'painters' like Conrad and his instantly firm friend, Desmond, whose daily bread was logos, labels, liveries, and general design. Desmond had arrived in the Bay Area only just before Conrad joined Condor. He was the great black hope of a poorish family from Boston. He had no friends in the city and was delightedly astonished that Conrad seemed happy to spend so much time showing him around. Conrad enjoyed every minute of it, and was equally thrilled that any new colleague should be so welcoming in the office. All too often, the first weeks in a new job had been an utter misery for him.

The two worked together on a label for a Seattle beer company and gave birth to something rather special. The shape was elegant and quite different, but not in a way that looked contrived. Michael looked, paused, considered, and quietly but conclusively approved. The client approved, too, greatly and gratefully. Desmond and Conrad felt elated and a little more secure. Conrad hoped he had repaid a little of the trust Michael had shown. In the team generally, they had won some spurs. Honor was not able to spare any praise from her modest and vigilantly guarded store, but nor did she unearth any words of criticism. Conrad wondered if this could be her first tiny step towards taking more notice of him. Now that he was more comfortable with Condor, and they with him, that was what he wanted more than anything.

And then came Ruby. She was drafted in by Burt McGovern as number two to Michael to strengthen a team he felt might have lost hunger, that *edge* which could be the difference between winning and losing pitches.

There were very few people in the business who had more edge than Ruby, all of it sharp and jagged. Her long-established nickname reached the Condor team before she did, like luggage sent on ahead. Though they tested their creativity dreaming up alternatives, it was the original, 'Dumdum', that stuck. No-one ever worked out for sure whether she knew the name herself. There were those who believed that being compared to a bullet that penetrates and then explodes must positively appeal to her. The more favored rumour was that Ruby, despising any form of learning and therefore certainly ignorant of both exotic weaponry and Calcutta arsenals, had on first hearing assumed it was spelt 'dumb-dumb' and taken spectacularly violent exception to it. Either way, nobody at Condor risked trying it out. Some boasted they'd say it to her face if they were fired, but even after she'd tormented, hectored, and finally ousted Michael, and so took over doing the firing personally, no victim – however brutally dismissed – ever found the guts to say it. If Michael had gone to another CI company, Conrad and most of the others would have followed without a second's hesitation, but Michael was too wounded to have the will to strike back, and went for a year-long overseas vacation instead. Conrad looked around, but jobs in CI didn't grow on trees. He didn't want to go back to graphic design, and he needed to avoid fuelling his reputation as a job-hopper.

Desmond kept him sane, with his constant *sotto voce* jokes and his occasional acts of anonymous resistance. It was sad that a job heaven had turned into a hell, but he had to be patient. He couldn't and wouldn't stop himself erecting a pyre of resentments, stick by tinder-dry stick, but this time he *musn't* set fire to it. Not yet, anyway.

They couldn't accuse Ruby of being no good. For a group that hadn't won a new account for a while, bringing in an airline was no mean feat. The airline was no United. A regional feeder outfit, owned by a conglomerate, flying ten to fifteen turboprops. All the same, it was a glossy catch, much envied by Condor's competitors. A new name as well as logo and livery. Nearly a million dollars in all.

****

'It's been real good of you, Lisa. Our little walks these last few days have helped a lot. More than you could know.'

'It's good you're feeling better. You seem more at peace, calmer.'

'Calm's good. You aim better when you're calm.'

'Aim at what?'

'MacMartin, of course, and the orangs. With a machine-gun.'

'I'm glad you're beginning to see the funny side of it.'

'Am I? I hope they see the funny side of it when they're riddled with bullets. I fantasise about it all the time. Not only guns. Spears, machetes, combine harvesters. Last night I dreamt I was attacking the BUS building in an F 18. MacMartin was clinging to the top of it like King Kong on the Empire State.'

'What happened? Did you get him?'

'No, goddam it, I didn't. Every time I had him lined up, the firing button jammed. He laughed and laughed. I flew past time and again. Always the same, and always that braying laugh. Then I woke up. I had to get him, if not in my dream, then in actuality. So I made a model of the building with an old newspaper. I couldn't find anything around the apartment that looked like MacMartin, so I drew him on the paper with a felt pen.'

'And this time you got him?'

'Not with a plane. I don't have any model planes. If you recall, planes are bad voodoo. So I decided to burn the building down instead, but not before I'd drawn five or six more MacMartins trying desperately to climb down. I waited till he was only ten floors from the ground, struck a match, and set the whole mother alight. MacMartin didn't make it. Neither did I, almost. The building was balanced on an upturned cookie tin. When the last bit was burning, it toppled over and singed my rug. Worth it though. Got the bastard, at last. Ha!'

'That's so funny, Hil ... You wouldn't *really* do anything, would you?'

'If I keep feeling the way I do now, I'll *have* to do something to that bastard. The orangs are in deep trouble, too. They don't know it yet, but I'm taking up karate.'

'You? Sorry, I didn't mean it *that* way. It's just that I can't imagine you in white pyjamas making Oriental yelps and smashing bricks with your head. You're not serious, are you?'

'Deadly. I've found a school.'

'Where?'

'Somewhere South of Market. Can't remember the street. I got it from the small ads in the Chronicle. There's a beginners' class starting tomorrow. Bet it's full of blondes.'

'Hey, I thought you said you preferred brunettes!'

'Only your particular shade of brown. Apart from that, I'm not fussy.'

'You won't practise your kicks on me, will you?'

'No. That's reserved for the utangs.'

'Hadn't you better make sure you're pretty good before you have a go at them?'

'One lesson ought to do it. Two to be on the safe side.'

'You should be homicidal more often, Hil, you're so funny.'

'Grab a cap?'

'Sounds good.'

Their routine had settled now. Always the same circuit of Marina Green, and then through the quiet back streets in the direction of the little Italian café in Cow Hollow.

'How're Irma and Daniel feeling now?'

'They say they've forgiven me. Irma's teeth are still pretty clenched when she says it. She's got a job with a software company in Mountain View. Dan says he's goin' to take some time out to think first. In some ways it's hit him harder than Irma. He's less resilient than her. Irma's a survivor.'

'And Solomon? Has it gone bankrupt, or whatever they call it?'

'I'm trying to avoid that if I can. I want to keep it *legally* in existence, so I can hang on to the patents. The company owns them, not us personally. So I'm trying to work out a deal with the creditors. If I managed to, it would mean I could mothball the company, and start over if I was ever mad enough to try again.'

'Where will you get the money to settle with them?'

'I'll have to get a job somewhere pronto, and see if there's any way I can take out another loan. I've got nothing worth selling. I tried with my car, but they said the market in second-hand rust is pretty soft at the moment.'

'What kind of job? Computers again?'

'That's all I know. The CEO slot at BUS might suddenly become vacant if my aim's any good. I could apply for that.'

'Surely someone with your talent can get a job in computing pretty easy?'

'A job, yes, but something that pays enough to help in the short term will be harder.'

****

'Have I got the time wrong? I thought the beginners' class was at five.'

'That's it, five o'crock.'

'So where's everybody else? Where are the blon ... I mean, beginners?'

'We had a few cancerrations. You must be Hiruton. We spoke on phone. I'm Masahiro.'

'Maha ...? Excuse me, could you say that again, I didn't catch it.'

'Ma-sa-hi-ro. It is kind of long. Some of my friends call me Masa.'

'I'm not big on subservience. Will Hiro be okay?'

'Whatever you rike, Hiruton.'

'And if you want, you can call me Hil.'

'Thanks, but I think I stick to Hiruton. Easier to remember. It's name of a hoteru in Tokyo.'

'Hiro, is *anyone* else coming along tonight?'

'Seems not. Better for you. Private resson. Shall we get started.? I show you rocker room, and you can get changed into *gi*.'

'What's "gi"?'

'Karate uniform.'

'Oh, the pyjamas? Before I change, can I ask one question?'

'Of course, Hiruton.'

'Could you kill a man with your bare hands?'

'If I needed. But I *wouldn't* need to.'

'But if you *did* need to, for whatever reason, how long would it take?'

'Depends who it was. You mean a karate expert?'

'No, a   big, strong thug, possibly, but assume no karate training.'

'No martial arts at all?'

'Nothing. Zero. Zilch.'

'Twenty seconds, maybe thirty.

'How long did you have to study?'

'I'm still studying.'

'Okay, okay, how long till you got so you could kill someone?'

'Eight, ten years.'

'What are the chances of getting there in a month, I mean if I practise fantastically hard?'

'You *are* kidding, aren't you, Hiruton?'

'Sort of.'

'You must understand. Karate is not for attacking people. First of all, it is to achieve calm and internal balance. Then, it's so you can rook after yourself if you *get* attacked.'

'Do I get a discount if I skip the calm and internal balance part?'

'I get it. You *are* kidding. You had me worried for a moment there. Thought you might be a weirdo. We get them sometimes. I rike you, Hiruton. Ret's get started.'

7

'Fred? Hilton.'

'Hi, Hilton, how are you?'

'Okay. Fred, you got upgraded.'

'From what to what?'

'From maiming to death.'

'You mean you *want* that job?'

'I got no goddam choice. I need some money like tomorrow. I can't find anything that pays enough, or quick enough. What would that job be?'

'I'm not up to date. I'd have to check with Joseph. He's the guy that runs it. They put in some humungous network in there. Last time I heard they had some bugs in it. They thought they could de-bug it themselves, but they're so stretched, Joseph said they might need to get some extra help in.'

'How much would it pay?'

'No idea, but better than they pay Joseph's own people. D'you want me to call him up and ask him if the job's still there?'

'It'd better still be there. I'm desperate. Tell Joseph you owe me big time.'

'Thanks for reminding me, I almost forgot.'

'I just wanted to make sure you were keeping it in focus. How's it going?'

'The bush telegraph tells me I've spawned a whole new

joke form in Sansome Street. No-one says much in Sand Hill Road, to my face, anyway. There's still a funny sort of atmosphere round here. I wouldn't recommend going long in my stock just yet.'

'They're all a bunch of jerks. Solomon would've been the best investment they ever made.'

'I'm with you, Hilton. We'll never know now.'

'Guess not.'

'Okay, I'll give Joseph a call, and get back to you.'

'Thanks. Bye.'

****

'*Reft*. I said *reft foot*. Now, again.'

'Hang on a sec, Hiro. I gotta catch my breath. You know you said eight years to be able to kill. How long just to learn to make one good hit?'

'Depends on the other guy's defences.'

'That's what you always say. What if he's not looking? A real sneak attack.'

'Hiruton. You haven't understood spirit of karate. No sneak attacks. *Da-me*.'

'What's damay mean?'

'*Dame* is Japanese. Means no good, forbidden.'

'It sounds like everything I want to do is dame.'

'Could be. Now, back to work. One more time we do *maegiri* kick with the reft foot ... higher, *higher*.'

The crash came with a mighty thudding bang, accompanied by strangled yelps and sundry expletives. The bench might reasonably have resented the sudden attack from an apparently safely distanced source.

'Hiruton, Hiruton, you okay? That was a bad fall.'

'Ow ... is the bench okay?'

'It's not damaged.'

'Well, you can inform it my side isn't. Why didn't you tell me maegiri was so dangerous? I'm gonna have to sue you for not telling me.'

'Never seen *anyone* fall five metres sideways before. You okay, seriously?'

'Yeah, I'm just winded. Help me up.'

'Okay, here we go. I better take a rook at your side.'

'Why? You a doctor?'

'No, but I know about sports injuries.'

'I'll see if I can loosen this belt. I hardly got the strength. There.'

'Wow, Hiruton, that doesn't rook good. You should see a doctor.'

'You mean that mark there? No, that's not new. My lawyer will kill me for saying this, but I've had that for a while. It's maybe a bit redder than last time I looked. Good, I can sue you after all.'

'What you want to do, Hiruton? Call it a day, or have a bleather, and do some more in a while?'

'That's *definitely* enough for today. Can I have a glass of water, or something?'

'Come through to my office. I got soft drinks in there ... What you want, Coca Cora, Seven-Up, or orange juice?'

'Coke's fine. Hiro, give me it straight. Am I the best student you ever had?'

'You want the truth?'

'Just as long as you don't praise me too much. I get easily embarrassed.'

'Not quite the best, then.'

'Not even close, huh?'

'Not *too* crose.'

'The worst?'

'The funniest, maybe.'

'So should I give up?'

'Not if you enjoy it, but maybe you shoudn't aim to fight bad people.'

'That's the only reason I'm doing it.'

'Maybe quit, then.'

'Hiro, tell me the truth, how many students you got?'

'Not too many. Ereven. Ten if *you* quit.'

'How on earth can you keep this place going with that number?'

'My wife, Mariko, has a job in Japanese restaurant. That helps. I offered to give it up, but she understands that this is my dream, having my own karate school.'

'But can you *afford* to keep going?'

'Not sure, Hiruton. We got a rot of debts.'

'So why didn't you tell me to keep going? You're giving up one-eleventh of your income.'

'No point in being martial arts teacher if I don't speak truth. I want to be rike Samurai. Samurai wouldn't tell rie.'

'Hiro'

'Yes, Hiruton.'

'Thanks for being a Samurai.'

'Sure thing, Hiruton, thanks for not suing me. I want you to make me a plomise.'

'What is it?'

'If you *do*, you must stick to it rike a Samurai.'

'I will. What is it?'

'That mark on your side. Get it checked.'

'Okay, I've been meaning to.'

'Today.'

'Can't today, I'll do it later this week.'

'Today.'

'Tell you what, I'll do you a deal. Tomorrow.'

'No deals. Today.'

'Okay, I plomise ... .I mean *promise*, goddam it. You're making me do it now. Hiro, can I drop by and see you sometimes, just to say 'hi'?'

'Sure, Hiruton, you always welcome here. I'll keep a rocker for you in case you want to practise. As you see, we don't have too much plessure on rocker space.'

'Thanks, Hiro. I appreciate that.'

****

'I can never understand why no-one ever got away from Alcatraz. From here it looks so near.'

'Two good reasons, Lisa. One, it may look near, but that's a mile and a quarter. Two, that water's cold. It never gets above forty-eight degrees even in summer. Invigorating, but not good for surviving. Makes me shiver just to think of it. Let's walk faster.'

'So when do you start?'

'Monday.'

'So tomorrow's your last day of freedom? Working day, at least.'

'Yup.'

'How long's the contract?'

'Fred *thought* it wasn't really fixed. He *thought* I would get the same amount however long it took. He wasn't sure, though. I'll have to wait till Monday to find out.'

'Did he say what kind of job it was?'

'They've got bugs in some big new system. Shouldn't

take long, if I don't constantly fall asleep through boredom.'

'Where is it?'

'In their goddam headquarters in frigging Sansome Street. Scene of my darkest hour.'

'What if you bump into MacMartin?'

'I'll go there packing a lot of firepower. Dirty Hilton. I doubt it will happen. I'm sure there'll be executive car parks, and special elevators and johns for the directors. If not, and I find myself standing next to him in the john, he'd better fear for the shine on his shoes.'

'Well I hope it all goes well.'

'Well? It can't go *well*. It's work for idiots. I just wanna get it done, get the money and get the hell outa there.'

'Is the Solomon stuff under control?'

'It's not exactly under control, but I think I can manage. I had to take out another loan. Not quite from a leading bank. I found a place in Oakland that lends to low-life like me. The rate of interest would make your eyes water.'

'I so wish I could help. I don't have a cent.'

'That's okay, I prefer what you lend. Moral support. You've almost become my therapist. When do *I* get to play shrink?'

'Oh, sometime.'

'Tomorrow. Let's make Friday "Lisa tells all" day. It'll be the last time we can have one of our walks for a while.'

'I'll spill the beans as long as I can buy the caps today.'

'Today's gonna be a cap-free zone, I'm afraid. I gotta go to the vet.'

'The *vet*?'

'The doc.'

'Why?'

'I fell over at karate this morning. I got confused between karate and ballet. When I finished a glorious flying pirouette I landed on a bench.'

'What was the bench doing there? Isn't that dangerous?'

'The bench was miles away. Seems like no-one ever managed to fall that far sideways before. My teacher, Hiro, was *so* impressed, he says they'll have to give my manoeuvre a Japanese name. I'll get royalties every time someone does it. I'll be a yen millionaire in no time at all. The other possibility is they might introduce long-distance sideways-falling at the Olympics. If so, I'll be going for gold.'

'So what exactly are you getting checked for?'

'Nothing at all. It was just that I promised Hiro I would. He's such a great guy, I didn't have the heart to refuse. What about making it earlier tomorrow? If I meet you as you leave Florissima, we could have a late lunch. Can you get away by one thirty?'

'I'll try.'

'Great. I'll be standing outside, whistling "On the street where you work".'

'What's that?'

'It's a song from a movie about a girl who sells flowers. I adapted it to fit.'

****

'Put your things on that chair, and let's take a look ... Mmm,there's some bad bruising. How long have you had that sore?'

'Two, three months. It doesn't bother me. It doesn't itch or hurt or anything.'

'How's your general state of health?'

'Just fine. No problems at all. I've had a bit of a down period recently, but nothing to do with my health.'

'Any weight loss or lack of appetite?'

'I guess the two go together. I've been eating, but maybe less than usual. I haven't been sleeping too good. When I'm tired I don't feel like eating a lot. If you give me some sleeping pills, I'll be eating like a horse again in no time at all.'

'Any particular reason you haven't been sleeping?'

'My company folded. It's not recommended if you're on a stress reduction programme.'

'I can imagine. Is your appetite healthy normally?'

'Sure, I'm a true Californian foodie.'

'What about your weight?'

'Look at me, I don't *have* any weight. I make most stick insects look obese. I never measure it. I suppose my jeans *might* be a little looser than usual, but, like I said, I've been eating less.'

'I'm going to take a general look at you, but I want you to go to the University Hospital to run a check on that sore. I'll call them now and get you an appointment. Excuse me a moment ... Three o'clock tomorrow okay?'

'No can do. How about some time next week? Or, better still, the week after.'

'I think you should make it a higher priority.'

'I'm willing to, but I have an even bigger priority tomorrow afternoon.'

'Hold on, then ... Saturday morning, ten o'clock?'

'Fine.'

****

The onset of summer does not thrill San Franciscans. The city's winter weather can be mixed, and some weather patterns outstay their welcome, but even in this season it's mostly on the wonderful side of mixed. Spring and fall are an undiluted delight, all diamond blue skies and a Mediterranean light of brilliance without harshness. Summer is the snag. Between five and six in the afternoon an unearthly visitor comes to cloak the city. It's a billowing fog with sprinter's speed, rushing in from the ocean, pouring over the hills, haring down the valley contours, and streaming through the steel sinews of the Gate Bridge until it has the bay itself in its chilling grip. It makes the city like a haunted house, where nightfall brings dread atmosphere and fearsome sounds, and only the brightness of day offers respite for the living. So it is for the city, when the power of the sun is at its zenith, and strong enough to burn away the phantom. But the phantom lies in wait for the sun's strength to wane, when it will race back and seize possession again.

The bay has its own haunted tones by night: the mournful foghorns' wary, vigilant, sad sounds. Realty agents need to be watchful, too. The fog's sinuous path plays havoc with the desirability of homes. In Sausalito, two houses right next door can have totally different microclimates. The one with all the technicolour blossoms will sell in an instant. Its neighbor, whose lichens and shrivelled gorses eke out a meagre existence, will stick around on their books for months or years. Some days the fog never burns off, and some days it's gone by ten. Local meteorologists have averaged it out. According to their statistics, the average burn-off is at one thirty.

****

'Two Chinese chicken salads and two diet Cokes, please. On second thoughts, the other day someone suggested I should *put on* weight. Come on Lisa, let's live a little and have *real* Cokes?'

'Not me, I've got to watch it.'

'Garbage. Okay, one real, one phoney, please.'

'Coming right up.'

'So?'

'So what?'

'How did you get on with the vet?'

'Great. No problem. No broken bones. I've told my lawyer it's no go.'

'So you got a clean bill of health?'

'Basically.'

'What does that mean?'

'There's a kind of mark on my side they want to have checked. It's nothing. I *know* I'm fine. I think you're just trying to use this to delay today's topic. It won't work.'

'Okay, so what do you want to know?'

'Everything. Let's start with your marriage. Forgive me for saying so, but it seems a bit ... strange.'

'I guess it seems strange. Maybe it *is* strange. But, you know, you have to live with what you have.'

'Why? Why can't you just up and leave, if you're not happy?'

'It's not so easy, Hil.'

'How did you meet?'

'I was home in Montana, working for the summer on a dude ranch. Earl came there with some friends. I was eighteen, about to go to college. I suppose he swept me off my feet. He can be *very* charming when he wants to be.'

'What's his secret? I need to learn.'

'In my case, it wasn't only the charm. I've always had a thing about art. European art, in particular. I had a grandpa who came over from Italy for a vacation when I was about eight. I'd never met him before and we could hardly understand each other, but all the same we got on *so* well. I went everywhere with him, showing him around. He always used to take his little sketch pad and this *tiny* box of watercolours. Wherever we went, he would do these cute little miniature paintings and give them to me. I still have them all. After about six weeks he went back home, but the next Christmas he sent me a picture book about Italian art. I loved it just because it came from him and every night I looked at it before I went to bed. He died the next summer, so I never got to see him again, but he was the one who gave me my love of art. Just before I met Earl, I had gotten a place at the local college to major in art history. Earl said I was crazy. What did the hicks in Montana know about European art? He claimed he'd been to some school in France and he knew everything there was to know. Talked about Paris and Florence a whole lot. Said if I *really* wanted to learn about art, I should go with him to Europe and he'd teach me as we travelled. That had quite an impact on an art-loving eighteen-year-old who had never been farther than Wyoming.'

'So what happened?'

'Like I said, I was swept off my feet. He wanted to get married right away. When he met my folks, he charmed them, too. It was easy, 'cos they believe in girls getting married and having families before their thought processes are fully formed.'

'So you got married?'

'Six weeks after I met him.'

'What about college?'

'I gave up all that.'

'And you went to Europe?'

'Like hell we did. It was all planned, or so I was told. I got a passport, and about five phrase books. A week before we were due to go he said he wanted to wait till he could take a few months off and do it properly. So our honeymoon was in Santa Barbara.'

'And did you ever make it to Europe?'

'Nope. Even if he thought he meant it, I doubt he's ever had the money.'

'What became of the art instruction?'

'Oh, for a few months he'd talk about art this and art that, but it soon petered out. He'd never answer straight when I asked about his French school, and if I mentioned some particular artist or whatever, he'd always say it was too early to get bogged down in detail and I should think in broader concepts. It took me a while to realise he'd never been near an art school. Probably had one of those teach yourself books you see in cheap bookstores.'

'Here are your salads. Now, can I get you two more Cokes?'

'Sure, same mix, please.'

'So, why ... sorry, my mouth's too full to get this out ... why no children?'

'He wanted them early on, and I wanted to please him. When it didn't happen, I got tested everywhich way. Everything normal. Earl wouldn't take the tests. Nowadays, I secretly take the pill, just in case.'

'Is he bad to you?'

'No, I can't really say he is, not compared with the horror stories you read. He likes to put me down, sneers at me a lot, calls me "bimbo", "airhead", that kinda thing. He's forever saying I wouldn't understand 'cos I got no education. That hurts, when I think of why. But, you know, he's not *real* bad. He doesn't hit me.'

'But you don't love him?'

'Love him? No, not anymore. I did at first, in a kinda puppyish way. When I realised he was screwing around on me, I was devastated. I got *so* upset and jealous and depressed and all. Then I found out the scale he was doing it on. I'd've had to get jealous about half the women of San Francisco. So I gave up, and stopped letting it get to me so much. Something died inside me, all the same.'

'That time he took the ring away. What had you done?'

'He found me reading a book about Michelangelo. I don't know why, but he absolutely *freaks* if he thinks I'm studying. He told me I should only read books he approved. I hadn't asked for his approval on this one. I knew there was no way he would've agreed.'

'He sounds like the control freak from hell. But I can't figure out why you don't just *leave* him.

'I *can't*, Hilton. It would *kill* my folks. I'm an only child. They're both very Catholic, dead set against divorce. They say a woman can't expect her man to be perfect. She must be patient and understanding. A man's lot is not an easy one, all that stuff. At the beginning I confided in Mom about how things were, but she put it down to me being so young. I found they were siding with him more than me. So, I decided not to tell them any more. It would worry them for no real reason, 'cos in the end they wouldn't believe it, anyway. He's always been good about calling them up, sending them birthday cards and all. He'll say "she's going through a difficult patch, but I'm doing my best to help her", and they'll say "bless you, Earl, she doesn't deserve you".'

'How would they react if *he* left *you*?'

'Never thought about that. It'd be okay, I guess, after they got over the shock. But it won't happen. Earl always says the only way he'll leave me is if he meets a beautiful millionairess. I keep hoping, but not many millionairesses go to the bars he drinks in.'

'So what do you live for, Lisa? Are you planning to put up with this for all time?'

'I don't know, Hil. I'm grateful for what I got. I like the flower shop and I don't mind the bar. I like our little walks. Recently I got enrolled on a part-time European art appreciation course that's run by the arts faculty at Berkeley. That's the secret thing I do the afternoons I can't meet you. I love it. It's a sort of life-line for me. Of course, everyone else is much smarter than me, but, while I'm there for the love of it, I get the impression most of the others use it as an up-market dating agency.'

'Does the school get a commission on consummations?'

'If they do, they're not making much out of me. Not only am I too dumb for anyone to take notice of me, I'm married too, which puts me firmly in the reject box.'

'So, Lisa, hypothetically, just hypothetically, right, if you were ever to split up with Earl – for *whatever* reason – what kinda guy would you go for?'

'I've really never thought about it. I don't know, Hil.'

'But would it have to be someone, like *real* good-looking?'

'The looks wouldn't matter as long as I *liked* him.'

'What type, though? How about the art bit? Would that be important?'

'It would be wonderful to have someone who shared that interest, of course it would. I *thought* I was getting that the first time around.'

'What are the chances of you suddenly losing interest in European art and becoming fascinated by computers?'

'Oh, Hil, you're such a darling, you don't know how your sense of humour keeps me going. Have *you* ever been to Europe?'

'No. Planes, remember?'

'Oh, of course, I'm sorry. What about Conrad?'

'He's worse than me. The *sight* of them gives him an attack of the screaming heebie-jeebies.'

'Hil, tell me what happened when your folks died?'

'... I ... I don't know ... what to ...'

'I'm sorry, I shouldn't have ...'

'No, no ... it's not ... it wasn't very easy.'

'I'm sure it wasn't.'

'We had no other relatives in the US, you see. They thought of sending us back to Estonia, to my Mom's brother or someone, but we didn't speak any Estonian, and we *were* US nationals, and of course back then there was the Iron Curtain and all. *We* only found out all this much later; at the time nobody told us anything about what was going on. Anyway, there was all this confusion about what would happen. At first they put us in a Social Services home, which was dire, but not *that* bad, because we were together. After what had happened, that mattered more than anything. Then after a few weeks, they decided to move us to a foster home. Apparently, there was some problem finding a couple who could take us both straightaway, so some bozo in the Social Services split us up. It was only meant to be temporary, and all that, but it was the worst thing they could have done. I'll never forget the look on Con's face when they came for us, when they pulled us apart. He was clinging to me with all his little strength ...'

'How could they do such a dreadful thing?'

'When they got him to the foster home, he went berserk. I did a bit, too, where I went, but apparently he was awesome. He smashed things, and screamed and raged. He wouldn't talk to them or let them touch him, and if they tried he bit and kicked.'

'So what happened next?'

'After a few weeks they sorted it out. The foster folks at Con's place begged them to take him away. They took us both back to the home for a few days and then found a couple who would take us both.'

'Was it better then?'

'Sure. We were together. But most of the damage had been done by then, specially for Con.'

'The poor kid ...'

'We didn't trust anyone, including our new foster parents. Con wouldn't say a word to them, or to any adult. For a long time he wouldn't talk to anyone other than me, not even other kids. Didn't start speaking to adults until he was thirteen or fourteen.'

'And you?'

'I talked, but not a whole lot. I suppose I tried to be a sort of go-between. I was terrified they would split us up again, and I figured if I was as hard to cope with as Con it would be more likely to happen. So I kept it inside as best I could manage. It wasn't until I was about twenty that I felt I could let go enough to have *my* breakdown.'

'So you stayed with your foster parents?'

'No. They were decent folks and they tried their best, but the strain was too much for them. We were moved round a few more families, but in the end it was back to a home. It was the best way, probably the only way.'

'Excuse me for interrupting here. Would you like to see the dessert card?'

'Just two decafs, please.'

'So what made Con get better, I mean become able to talk with folks again and all?'

'They tried all the obvious stuff. Drugs, therapy. No effect at all. The drugs just sedated him, basically, and when the effects wore off he was worse than ever. He was *very* disturbed back then. The therapists he ignored. Must have been pretty frustrating for them, talking at him for hours, and him making funny faces back or staring out the window.'

'So what did the trick? Or did he get better on his own?'

'It was music, in a sense anyway.'

'Music?'

'There's a thing called music therapy. It's getting better established now, but then it was pretty new, and kinda cranky. Some professor in France played a big part in getting it started. The idea is they play music to you, either normal music or music that's been filtered in a way that cuts out the lower frequencies. I don't understand very well how it works, but it's not just soothing the savage breast and all that, it's supposed to do something special to the brain. Seems to have amazing effects, in some cases, anyway. Con got conned. He didn't even realise it was therapy; assumed it was some kind of music lesson for dummies. So he didn't try to resist. Soon they had him banging on drums and thumping away on a keyboard. He was messin' about to begin with – just making *noise* – but then he began to enjoy it.'

'But how did that get him speaking?'

'Like I said, they conned him. In the fifth or sixth session, the therapist played a song on the piano and hummed the tune. He persuaded Con to join in the humming. Every session after that, they would hum the same tune together until one day the therapist switched to singing the *words* of the song. Con really liked that tune by then and had come to quite like the therapist. Before he knew what had happened, he found he had joined in. Once he'd *sung* the words a few times it was harder not to *speak* with this guy. So he started speaking, but only with him. Then the therapist fixed it so other therapists, or as Con thought teachers, would drop by the room while they were together, all casual-like, and naturally join in the conversation. That was a hard line for Con to draw, too, since they all seemed like good people and friends of *his* "teacher". Soon he was talking to everybody.'

'That's amazing.'

'Yeah, it was. I said he was conned, and in a way he was, but it was also a kind of miracle.'

'Did Con feel conned, betrayed?'

'Not so much. He understood, and he really *did* like that therapist. Keeps in touch with him, even now. After that, music became a big thing for him. He learned to play the keyboard pretty good. It's his big thing. He's always listening to music, mainly classics. I know nothing about classics, so he introduces me to pieces he thinks I might like. He makes up his own music, too. Writes little tunes. They're pretty good, too. He says he can express himself better through music than through words. You can hardly get into his apartment for this huge grand piano he has.'

'Where is it?'

'Telegraph Hill.'

'View?'

'A great view of the Bay Bridge and an interrupted view of Coit Tower.'

'Not original.'

'His other thing's turtles. He keeps two box turtles there. Calls them Parton and Pfeiffer. Loves them to pieces. He's started studying all about turtles recently. Wants to go someplace in the the Indian Ocean to swim with the big ones.'

'So he doesn't go to therapy anymore?'

'Oh, he's always going to some therapist or other, but not the musical variety. I don't know why he goes, he despises them so much. Says they should be kept in their place. Says keeping them down is a thankless task, but someone has to do it.'

8

'Joseph Muldoon please.'

'And you are?'

'Hilton Kask. He's expecting me.'

'Please wait a moment, I'll phone up ... Mr Muldoon you have a visitor ... Thank you ... Please take the elevator up to the twelfth floor, Mr Muldoon will meet you there.'

'Hi, you must be Hilton. Joseph.'

'Good to meet you, Joseph.'

'Come along to my office and let's talk about the project. Go ahead through there. Can I introduce my assistant, Pauline? Pauline, meet Hilton Kask. Now take a seat there. Fred's told me a lot about you. It sounds like a real shame your company didn't get financed. Fred's cut up about it too, you know. Feels kind of responsible.'

'He is.'

'Fred is doing what he can to show you how sorry he feels.'

'Yeah, I know that. I guess I shouldn't be bitter.'

'Fred's good-hearted. You may not believe it now that Fred's got to be so grand, but I used to be his boss. His first job in the bank in the Credit Department. Fred was pretty green then. More like a Southern boy from the backwoods. You'd never know that now, would you?'

'Guess not.'

'Now, Hilton, about this consultancy. There are some

strict rules in this bank about hiring people, even on a temporary basis. Background checks, references and so on. And for consultants, we also have a tendering process.'

'Are you saying ...?'

'Now hold your horses, Hilton, give me a chance. When I reminded Fred what our procedures are, he said you'd freak. Those were his words, you'd freak. So I said I'd see if there was some way we could work around the rules. I was planning to hire a consultant anyway and we have tenders in from two of them. We figure it's about a six month job. Now I shouldn't be telling you this, but the two figures we've had are a hundred thousand dollars and ninety thousand dollars. If you were willing right now to tender – orally would be fine – say eighty-nine thousand dollars, I'd have to give you the contract.'

'Eighty nine's okay.'

'If so, seeing as Fred knows you so well an' all, we can overlook the other checks.'

'Thanks. Joseph, is it a fixed term contract for six months or is it just till the work's done?'

'Till the work's done. If you do it any quicker, that's fine. If it takes you longer, that's down to you, too.'

'And can the hours be flexible?'

'Any way you want it, Hilton. As flexi as you feel like. This building's manned by security guards twenty-four hours a day. Makes no difference to me whether you work days, nights, weekends, or whenever takes your fancy. Just as long as the work gets done. Now, on the background checks and references and all, I've asked Fred to do me a little memo vouching for you. Strictly speaking, I need two more references, but I'll put a note on the file that they're coming later.'

'Do I have to ...?'

'Forget it. No-one will bother checking it when they don't turn up. So that's it, you're hired. Now after we're through here, Pauline will take you in hand and sort out your security pass. Without that you can't get into the computer centre. When all that's done, I'll take you along myself and introduce you around.'

'So what's the project?'

'The bank recently installed a big new IBM system. It takes care of everything, and I mean *everything*. Customer accounts, credit exposures, trading transactions, client limits. If we have a global limit on XYZ corporation, of say, fifty million, which is currently drawn down to forty-five, and then six of our branches around the world are asked the very same day for a million each by subsidiaries of that group, what will happen? I'll tell you. The system will not only pick that up, and avoid breaching the limit, it will automatically grade the requests according to quality of local relationship and authorise the best five and refuse only the sixth. In similar circumstances, the old machine, if it worked at all, would refuse the lot. Made for very unhappy clients. In addition to all that kind of thing, the system implements all remittances in and out and automatically produces and prints most of our communications with retail clients. We're not talking statements, general mail shots here. Of course, it does all that too. I mean individual letters about overdrafts for example. It's so labour saving.'

'You mean human employment reducing.'

'That too, I guess. It doesn't stop there, either. Everything on the bank's personnel side is cross-referenced against individuals' security dealings to give us early warning of any funny business by the staff. And of course the whole security, safety and control systems of this building are governed by it too. Pretty amazing, huh, Hilton?'

'Mm.'

'I was forgetting. You being on the leading edge of technology and all that, I suppose this is old hat to you.'

'I know what big computers can do. You haven't yet told me what my project will be.'

'We've had some recurring problems on the trading settlement side. Some of the data has been tainted. It hasn't cost us yet, but we've had some near misses. And we've had to rely on the goodwill of some other banks to help us reconstruct the trades. We think we've got the problem cracked now, but there may still be some bugs in there. What we need you to do is to go over it again and simulate hundreds of transactions and do a data audit to double-check that the system's one hundred percent. And if it's not, to identify the problems and rectify them. Not very exciting work for someone like you, I'm afraid.'

'It's money. I need the work. Thanks, Joseph.'

'Right then, let's get the wheels rolling. Pauline?'

****

Hilton hadn't given a work number, so the hospital left a message on his answering machine at home. It was past seven when he got home from work that first dreary Monday at the bank, and he left it until the next morning to return the call. It was probably just to say everything was okay, anyway.

'Doctor Wittershaw, please ... Hilton Kask ... No, I'll hold.'

'Mr Kask, sorry to keep you waiting. That little thing we took off your side. We've had the lab test back. I'm afraid there's a problem with it, some malignant cells. It may be all the bad cells are out now, and there's nothing more to worry about, but we have to check it out. We need you to come back and have some more tests.'

'What kind of tests?'

'X-rays, and something called CTS. It stands for Computerised Tomography Scan. Looks at soft tissues. We'll run some blood tests and urine tests as well, to check on organ functions.'

'When do I have to do it? Is next week okay?'

'Sooner than that is better. I'd recommend tomorrow.'

'It's very difficult tomorrow. Can we make it late afternoon?'

'The tests take a couple of hours. The latest we could start is four p.m.'

'Okay then, four it is. See you then.'

This was seriously boring. He wanted to get on and, get this wretched bank job over with. To have to give up time, particularly time he wasn't paid for, was irritating. He hated hospitals. He wasn't blaming the doctor. He was a nice guy and obviously he had to make double sure. If he didn't and a patient *did* have something serious, they'd sue the hell out of the hospital. From Hilton's point of view he didn't even need the tests for his own peace of mind. He trusted instinct and he knew whatever problems he might have, health was not one of them. Sounded like the Samurai had been right about having it checked, though. He'd have to admit that the next time he saw him. And who knows, if they hadn't taken it off with that little penknife, one day maybe it could have developed into something. You couldn't screw around with these things. Maybe he should get into this health thing a bit more. Have a full medical or whatever.

****

Wednesday felt better. Monday and Tuesday had been tiring. Not just the supreme awfulness of the dull work, but the need to remember about fifty new names and faces, to answer inane questions and to sound like a happy camper. Hell, he wasn't an *employee*. Why should he bother being friendly? He'd be out of there just as quick as he could – far quicker than Joseph reckoned on. He'd already concocted a program that would do the testing and diagnostic work automatically, instead of the balls-breaking, steam-age way they'd been planning. He could get this done in two, maybe three weeks. So why did Wednesday feel better? He'd slowly come round to the view that they were quite a nice bunch of guys and they were making an effort to be genuinely welcoming. That was the smaller reason. The bigger was that there were no less than three very cute girls. If those San Francisco statistics were right, at least one of them should be currently minus boyfriend and maybe desperate enough to try a date with *him*. Take it easy though, don't rush it. Give them a chance to observe your talent and charm for a while, to get to know you.

So he took his time. It was Thursday afternoon before he asked one of them for lunch on Friday and she *accepted*! The hospital had insisted on yet another appointment on Friday morning to go through the results of the tests, but he made sure it was early enough that he'd be back in very good time for his date.

****

There was profound kindness in the doctor's voice when he told him, tinged by that special form of weariness that comes from having been too often the bringer of the unkindest news. Hilton had heard the word melanoma before and thought it sounded more like a rare fruit than something medical. When they talked about it last time he hadn't paid much attention. Now he had to listen properly. As the explanation proceeded, the doctor's words echoed in Hilton's mind, like a voice in an empty hallway. It slowly began to sink in that the fruit that had been tattooed on his side was deadly indeed.

'I'm afraid it is clear that it has progressed through the lymphatic system and has reached a secondary site in the pancreas. It's what we call metastasis.'

Hilton felt himself retreating within the cavern of his body, the sound of the doctor's voice becoming more and more remote.

'We need to run one or two more tests, but I'm afraid to say it looks like the cancer is too advanced to be operable.'

His legs were no longer his own; numbly he could sense them becoming more and more leaden. He knew he couldn't stand up and if he tried he would fall over. Some parts of him were shaking, but so far inside that the tremors were not externally visible. When the doctor's explanation came to an end, Hilton did not notice the silence. Though it lasted for four, almost five minutes, the doctor sat there patiently and allowed the shock to sink in. When Hilton finally spoke, it took three attempts to make his voice sound relatively normal.

'And not operable means goodnight?'

'Not necessarily. We can slow the process with chemotherapy. Some patients experience considerable remission.'

Hilton realised he was already a 'patient'. He was no longer a person.

'There's nothing at all that can be done with surgery?'

'Sadly, I fear not.'

'What if I had come here one or two months ago?'

'We have no means of knowing what state it was in then. It could have made a difference, but it might not. I'm afraid you'll only torture yourself with those thoughts now.'

'Do you honestly think I can avoid those thoughts?'

'Honestly, no.'

'I just knew it couldn't happen to me. I was sure, I was absolutely certain, even when that thing appeared on my side.'

'Maybe it's natural to feel that way. Many of the people I've had the sad task of breaking news to have been equally sure.'

Talking helped sensations reach his extremities. He felt his fingers begin to shake. The fear came to him of what would presage the end.

'What will happen to me?'

'We will hospitalise you immediately, and as soon as we have completed the final tests, begin the chemotherapy.'

'That wasn't what I meant.'

'No, I know. You will probably have some weight loss. The chemotherapy has some rather unpleasant side effects. Nausea, hair loss.'

'How bad will the pain be? When will it start?'

'The level varies very much from person to person. We

can control pain pretty well these days.'

'When will it start?'

'There's really no way to be sure. Maybe in a month or two. Depends how you respond to the chemotherapy.'

'Will the chemotherapy save my life?'

'It could prolong it.'

'But not save it?'

'Probably not.'

'How long could it prolong it?'

'A few months. It may not seem much now, but it may be important later.'

The lead in his legs had gone now. There was no sensation left in them at all. It was as if they were not there any more. His arms were there, but they felt strangely unattached. His torso was a hollow shell.

'So how long?'

'If the chemotherapy is effective, five to six months, possibly longer.'

'A year? Tell me the truth.'

'I don't think so, the cancer is advanced.'

'And with chemotherapy, I'd look awful, feel awful and be in hospital, right?'

'You wouldn't need to be here constantly. Perhaps three days a week.'

'Would I have the energy to do anything else?'

'Not anything very strenuous. Unfortunately, chemotherapy exhausts many patients. We can treat some of the side effects, like the nausea, with other drugs, but we can't do much about the fatigue.'

'How long do I have if I choose not to have chemotherapy?'

'Three months, perhaps.'

'How much of that could I live and work normally?'

'Half, maybe a little longer.'

'When will you have the final test results?'

'We can complete them this afternoon and have the results by tomorrow morning. I think they will confirm our findings. If you can come back tomorrow at ten o'clock, I'll go through it with you then.'

'If it is not going to change anything, do you mind if I just do it on the telephone?'

'No, if you prefer it that way. Hilton, do you have someone waiting for you outside?'

'No. I wasn't expecting anything like this.'

'What about at home?'

'I'll have to think. Don't worry about it.'

'You'll need someone for company, today and tonight. Someone to talk to. I would also like to suggest that you let me arrange for one of our counsellors ...'

'Can we talk about that tomorrow?'

'Of course, but what about today?'

'Believe it or not, I've just started a new job. I told them I'd be a bit late today. I didn't expect it to be this sort of "late". I can't make up my mind whether I'll go in there or not. I need a few minutes to clear my mind. If you don't mind, I think I'll go now. I feel like a bit of fresh air.'

The glistening, warm sorrow in Doctor Wittershaw's eyes helped him find the strength to rise. He saw himself shake hands, but scarcely felt the sympathetic grasp.

'I'll arrange for a counsellor for tomorrow.'

'Yeah, thanks. Hey thanks, Doc, thanks for the way you did it. Thanks for not bullshitting. Can't be an easy job. Glad it was you, if you know what I mean.'

'Till tomorrow, Hilton. I know this may sound empty to

you, but don't give up hope absolutely. Miracles happen.'

'Miracles don't exist. People just get their probabilities wrong.'

'Well, maybe an improbability will happen.'

'Sure, yeah, thanks. Till tomorrow.'

****

As Hilton wandered through the hospital corridors, trying to find his way out into the sunshine, he wondered if he would immediately experience all the clichés of the condemned man. The beauty of nature, the blue sky, pretty flowers. When he got outside, he found he was still too confused and too numb to begin feeling that way. He sat on a bench. He didn't have to worry about crying in public. He realised that tears were for movies, books, sad songs and maybe other people's heartaches. For your own, they tended not to flow, the numbness froze the tear ducts.

The 'if only' part didn't really bite either. For himself that was. He knew it wasn't his style to check things like that out the moment they showed up, so there was no point in wanting his time over again. It would be different for Con. Oh God, Con. Did Con know about the sore? Lisa knew, Samurai knew. He didn't think he'd told Con.

If not, he'd have to keep it that way. The knowledge that the problem could have been solved if he'd gone sooner would wreck him, even more than just the dying. Though they were twins, Hilton had always been more like the older brother. The one who made everything okay. The one who looked out for both of them. How could he go and do this to Con? Con's equilibrium was always fairly delicate. This might blow it right away. It could kill him, for God's sake. What a thoughtless moron he'd been, what a goddam moron!

He called the bank, cancelled his lunch date, and went to the nearest rentacar office. He drove the long distance pretty well, considering. It was already night when he reached the entry sign for the Anza Borrego desert. He went in a mile or two and then turned around, and found a motel a few miles out. The only place inside he could remember was a smart, expensive hotel of the marble bathroom variety that he had no wish to be near now. Plus, he wanted to enter the desert in daylight.

He liked deserts. There was a cleanness about them. A sense of absoluteness, a stillness that had always helped him think. They were great places to look at the stars too, which was a minor interest of his. It had been here, in Anza Borrego, one night camped out under an astonishingly pyrotechnical sky that he had first conceived the essence of the Solomon machine. Stillness was not the same as peace, but it was the closest he was likely to get and he could already feel the first little ripples of calm lapping gently against his asphyxiating panic.

The motel had a kind of diner and through habit he ate a few mouthfuls of something nondescript, brought by a fresh, happy girl of eighteen or nineteen. Could she guess he had cancer? Did it show? He didn't feel at all like a James Dean, to be cut down in his young prime, but more like he was prematurely aged, wrinkled and wizened. Afterwards he lay on the bed, still clothed, for two bleak hours until he slipped into thin, unrefreshing sleep.

The whole of Saturday he spent in the desert, keeping as far from other cars and people as he could manage. At times he sat under the harsh sun, at times he sought a little shade here and there. He didn't feel like leaving and stayed on till the velvet darkness came. Once again he recalled that night when the Solomon idea had come. Then he'd been well through his second solo bottle of red wine when the thought came to him. He knew that machine was his monument, though he wouldn't be the one to build it now. Someone else would do that one day.

He lay there a long time, a very long time. He had a bottle with him tonight too, but didn't really feel like replicating that bit. He found himself unable to stop thinking in Solomon terms, splitting out his emotions, wondering what combinations they were. Sad a lot. Sad a whole lot for Con. Sad he couldn't build his machine. Sad he couldn't frigging well show Standish MacMartin. Come to think of it, why bother showing him, why not just kill him? Like with a gun or whatever. There wasn't much the law could do to a terminally ill suspect. He thought about it a bit more. It didn't work. It wouldn't really be satisfying unless MacMartin could see he'd been wrong. Also, the judicial system might not be able to do much to terminally ill suspects, but if he was put in prison awaiting trial, the other inmates might not see it that way at all. That MacMartin, he seemed to have every base covered. And Lisa, what would happen to her? Stuck with that ghastly husband, presumably. Maybe one day she would meet a sophisticated European who would be able to tell her all about art. There was nothing Hilton could do to help her now, unless you counted leaving her some debts in his will.

How would it feel when the pain started? Would it be just a twinge at first? A numb ache? Or a real stab? How bad can pain get? Pretty bad, he guessed. And it would be the kind of pain you couldn't stop, couldn't give in to. Not like surrendering to the orang utangs. Somewhere, among all the desperate fear, was one percent of curiosity. What would it feel like? At least he knew how he was going to die. He'd sometimes wondered whether a heart-attack was a really, *really* nightmarish experience, which, even if it only lasted a few minutes, would be mind-blowingly, gut-crushingly awful. A stroke might be worse, if you were paralysed, people feeding you baby-food from a teaspoon for years and years. He wouldn't get old, not now. Not old and fat, not grey or white. He wouldn't drone on about how much better things used to be. Godammit, he would never go bald! As long as he kept his nerve about chemotherapy anyway. No worries about pensions or false teeth or mid-life crisis or Alzheimers.

It made him feel good enough to have a real big gulp. It even tasted of wine this time. He went back to measuring the emotions. He wasn't doing too bad, considering. He was not *that* scared. Well, he was about the pain. Dying, or at least being dead, was at any rate a controllable part of the emotional equation. He wouldn't look too good when it happened. He would want to say goodbye to Lisa long before that. Con would be different, he wouldn't go before the end. There would be no point in even suggesting it. He'd need him at the end too. Need him every moment towards the end. If it was excruciating, holding Con's hand would be the only relief.

Suddenly the tear ducts unfroze. When he started crying, he didn't stop for a long while. By and by he did. Back to emotions. It drifted into his consciousness that of all the emotions, one would sooner or later win out and would dominate his thoughts and his senses, would become the key strength or weakness. What would it be?

Sadness? For others maybe, but not himself. Not self-pity. Fear? Sure thing. But was that really all? He gazed up at the stars and hoped he would do better than just fear. Jupiter was peach-coloured in the western sky. Con had introduced him to a piece of music by some guy called Holst. *The Planets Suite*. All the planets were called the bringer of something or other. He remembered that Jupiter was the bringer of jollity. Could Hilton hope for jollity? Bravado possibly, but jollity? Nice try, Jupiter. His eyes scanned the sky. There were shooting stars everywhere. It seemed like there was one every four or five seconds. It was a pulsating, living thing up there. Just above the horizon to the south was Mars, the bringer of war. Warfare. He played with the thought. A slow warmth began to ease its way through him. Anger? Was he angry? At what? At nature for betraying him and through his defect, Con? At MacMartin for stopping him from building his machine? At those biker-thugs for making things at the bank so much worse, for making him so pathetically scared and impotent, for in fact spoiling that whole Saturday afternoon?

The strange warmth continued to spread within him. It was a grave, cautious, resolved warmth. It did not spread quickly, nor need to. Slowly, almost imperceptibly, it eased its way through his muscles, his limbs. He felt its primitive power taking possession of him. He looked up at the sky, at Mars. It seemed to shine more resolutely than the other stars and planets.

He felt ageless, timeless. Could he, like some mythical warrior, buckle on his armour, and unleash war? Could this weak, cancer-ridden body stiffen its sinews and bring destruction on its enemies? Was it all over and was this just melodramatic horse-shit? Or could he really think of fighting back?

Finally, the warmth reached every corner of his body and he recognised that it was the harbinger of a true primary emotion. He recognised something else too. All those years ago the desert sky had helped him conceive the Solomon. Now for the second time the desert sky seemed to be showing him the way. His tears had dried completely now. His face was calmly, resolutely set. Then a suggestion of a smile softened his steely countenance. It might not be very warrior-like, but he found it hard to suppress a giggle. Then he laughed right out loud. It did not sound like hollow laughter. It did not sound artificial or phoney. It rang clearly through the cool air. It was like a sound of the desert.

9

The first few weeks he didn't see Lisa and met Con only once.

She surprised herself with the realisation of how much, in such a short time, she had come to count on his sympathy and support. It was inevitable that she read too much into his distraction and was hurt by the lack of contact.

Con was harder to fob off. He found it difficult to believe that Hilton was really so devoted to his BUS consultancy. It helped that it was true. Con was astonished when he called at eight, at ten, at midnight, even later and found him there. On the surface Hilton got away with the explanation that the sooner he finished the task, the sooner he'd get paid and be able to call off the debt dogs. Deep down, Con was troubled by it and didn't buy the story. Their wavelengths were far too perfectly aligned for him to be convinced by this. He knew Hil must have his reasons. If he didn't want to talk about it, then be patient for now. He would tell him eventually.

It was harder for both brothers in the weeks after the BUS work ended, when Hilton just vanished. He didn't try to explain, because explaining wouldn't have explained. He just went. He only said he was going away. He caused real hurt he could hear in Con's voice. Real hurt, real worry.

It irritated him that flying was still so terrifying. Why

should he worry about crashing now? It would deny his painful personal gallows. But the fear was too deep-rooted to be defeated by even this most convincing logic. Every steep banking after take-off, every clunk of the undercarriage descending or retracting, and worst of all any turbulence, had him grim-faced and white-knuckled.

He'd little idea where Panama was and none at all of what it would look like. He took a look at the map in the airline magazine. It resembled the arched back and powerful front legs of a cheetah, its head vanishing into Costa Rica and its rear swallowed by Colombia. The only things he could remember about Panama were the Canal, which he now read belonged to America, and the hats, which evidently were made in Ecuador.

After they'd touched down and he was back on mother earth he was more successful at persuading himself that everyday fears didn't matter any more. If he got ripped off by a taxi driver, so frigging what? How much by? Twenty or thirty dollars? Should he be worried about that? Get a life! Why the hell did people get so bent out of shape by little things like that? And if he were to get beaten up by the nasty-looking types in the decaying, old part of the city, the Casco Viego, so what? He'd been beaten up by two thugs much bigger than these guys and lived to tell the tale. It was true that actually being *killed* here would be a pity, both because of Con, and because it would stifle what he'd come to think of as a creative urge. That apart, nothing mattered very much. He found that travelling was fun. It was madness that he hadn't done it before. After he'd taken care of business, he hired a ludicrously expensive limo from the hotel. He was thrilled when he came upon a little village called San Francisco but was distressed there was no-one he could send a postcard to. He had a coffee there and found the temptation was too great. He posted one to himself and wrote on the back in a disguised hand. 'Hil, having a great time. Wish you were here, Demi.'

The business itself was taken care of with quite astounding slickness. Why couldn't the Californian venture capitalists get themselves so organised? Hilton had expected chaos, peeling paint, a pre-war electric fan and some seedy guy in a sweat-stained shirt. What he got was a smart, stylish office in a brand new building in the heart of the glossy financial quarter. The office came with a sexy, well-dressed receptionist, a meeting that started on time, and Mr Garcia in a very sharp blue suit.

Did it make sense to trust Garcia? He had to trust *someone,* and Garcia came with with a strong recommendation from Aloysius. Aloysius wasn't someone you'd want to introduce your sister to or entrust with your life savings, but since Hilton didn't possess either that didn't matter overmuch. When he needed to do a little urgent research on the highways and byways of offshore finance, Aloysius was the best, or maybe the only source of information Hilton could think of. It didn't surprise him in the least that the phone number Aloysius gave him that night at Josie's was out of service and it took one long, frustrating day of telephone sleuthing to track him down to Albuquerque, New Mexico.

It was just as well that he=d found a way to get an advance on some of the insurance money: the down payment to Garcia alone would have swallowed most of the fee for the BUS computer work. When Hilton handed over the wad of notes, Garcia ran him right through the procedure. It seemed like he'd done this once or twice before. Wide dispersal in Panama within fifteen minutes of the funds arriving at his bank. Out of the country within twenty-four hours. Hilton wasn't so worried about the second stage. An hour or two either way wouldn't matter quite so much there. It was the first stage that counted. Garcia agreed to demonstrate with a dry run. He sent ten thousand dollars of Hilton's deposit to a friendly bank in Cayman and asked them to remit it back. He hit the dispersal button. The money was in and out within six minutes. Hilton was satisfied. The corporate part Garcia had already set up. There would be a nominal Board of directors and share certificates would be printed.

He was unaccountably sad to leave Panama. He thought he could get to like this place. Never having been abroad before, it seemed sacrilegious to leave unexplored this slender, spicy, little country, and its alluring neighbours. But on he had to go to Miami to pick up the connection to Zurich.

For the flight from San Francisco he had booked coach class without a second thought. On his last night in Panama better sense seduced him after a third Margarita in a small piano bar just off the Plaza Bolivar. The persuasive power of this thought survived his return to sobriety. So first class it was on Swissair. Talk about cossetted! The fat, sweating American businessman in the next seat boasted of his upgrade. For Hilton, an upgrade would have been an insult. He wanted to enjoy the thickly padded king-size seat and the astonishing service without the shadow of reciprocal gratitude for luck or kindness. Hilton had paid his way. He owned his seat, at least for the duration of the journey. Fatman was only in his because the system let him be. Hilton looked over at the stewardesses. They knew. He knew they knew. He didn't know which passenger they thought was the mug and which was the smart guy, but it was at least possible that Hilton might be a wealthy big shot. Unlike Mr Upgrade. Any stewardess of marriageable age hoping to meet an interesting prospect would wave goodbye to him right away.

Overcoming the old instincts was harder than he imagined. He fully planned to do the chauffeur routine again for the trip from Zurich airport to Liechtenstein, but when the sour blonde at the desk quoted the dollar price he rolled his eyes, turned away without a word and headed for the rentacar counters. The British licence shouldn't be such a big problem: they're still in the Stone Age there and don't have photographs on them. Just try not to sound too American, don't chew gum or say 'awesome' three times every sentence.

He had to wait in line and nearly went back to the limousines, but the brochures lying around the Budget counter suggested another way to combine obscene expenditure with getting there. In Europe Budget's staple is humble Opels and the like, but as a marketing ploy they advertise the existence of more exotic machinery, available occasionally at eye-watering cost. Happily, the Porsche engineers in Zuffenhausen will for all times remain ignorant of the level of skill that Hilton deployed in driving the latest model of their 911. On reflection, they might have preferred to know. They would have found it hard to test the stick shift and clutch quite so comprehensively within twenty-four hours. Porsche claim to have engineered out the need for a high level of expertise to drive their cars. Hilton proved they'd succeeded. He crunched and graunched his way past the two lakes, the Ober See and the

Walen See, stayed on the freeway as it swung back north, and pulled off to cross the Rhine where it marks the border with Liechtenstein. That evening, back in his seventeenth-century hotel room, he got out a map and mused on making a dash the next afternoon to see the Matterhorn. No, he definitely didn't have time. There were other more pressing places to visit and so very much to do when he got back home.

When he made it home to San Francisco he didn't call Con or Lisa. He saw a fair bit of Dan and a little of Irma. They were sworn to secrecy and told to ask no questions. When he finally called Con to arrange to meet, it was the first time they'd spoken for over five weeks.

****

'So where have you been?'

'Finding myself.'

'That's California-speak. It won't work with me. Next you'll tell me you've been reinventing yourself.'

'That's pretty close to what I *have* been doing, as it happens.'

'Hil, what's happened to you? It's me, Con, your missing limbs, the other half of your body. You and I don't talk like this. We use words with *sig-ni-fi-cance* and *mea-ning*, not luncho-gabble. Where have you been? What's going on? Tell me, you bastard.'

'Con, I've been doing some important things, things I feel good about.'

'Great, wonderful. I'm glad it shows in your appearance. You look dreadful, like you haven't slept or eaten for months. And what have you done to your hair?'

'The hair was an experiment, and it's true, I haven't eaten a lot recently.

'Can we put the eating bit right first? Is it okay if I order?'

'Sure. I'll have whatever you're having. If and when you ever catch their eye.'

'Excuse me ... Jerk ... Keep on talking, I'll stay looking cool, like I don't mind being ignored.'

'Hil, what the fuck's going on? I can't bear it any longer.'

'Okay, okay, I'll tell you ... just a minute. I swear I'm goin' to go ballistic ... YOU, yes YOU. Come over here RIGHT NOW ... Thank you. Now, listen carefully. If you don't bring us a bottle of some kind of chardonnay within, let's say, thirty seconds, I'm gonna to have to take you outside and shoot you ... Good ... And bring FOOD. Anything. Today's special or whatever ... Okay, *any* of the specials, we don't care. Take an executive decision on our behalf ... Thank you ... Wow, Con, what did you think of *that,* then? I never knew I could be so masterful.'

'I'm waiting'

'Okay, Con. I've been wanting to tell you and kind of dreading it as well, but I'm sort of relieved the moment's come. I have to warn you that this won't be that easy for either of us.'

'What on earth are you talking about? Oh Christ, you haven't got AIDS have you?'

'No, but something like it.'

'Oh God, cancer?'

'You got it.'

'I knew it was something like that, I just knew. What sort of cancer?'

'Melanoma, pancreas. Some other types too.'

'What's the prognosis?'

'Inoperable.'

'Oh no, oh no, not that. It can't be. Who told you this?'

'The University hospital. There's no doubt about it.'

'Come off it, Hil, these guys often get it wrong. It's never that simple.'

'This one is pretty simple.'

'Bullshit. There must be some guy somewhere.'

'Con, I'm really sorry. It's pretty advanced. It must have been inside me a long time. I had no idea.'

'When did you find out?'

'About eight weeks ago. I'm sorry I couldn't tell you sooner. I had to come to terms with it myself first. I couldn't share it with you until then.'

'Have you told anyone else?'

'Are you kidding?'

'Lisa?'

'I haven't seen her since I heard. We spoke on the phone a couple of times a while back, that's all. You're crazy if you think I could tell anyone else before you.'

'Hang on, this makes no sense. That means you already knew when you were working at BUS. Why did you want to work so hard for them, of all people?'

'I needed the money.'

'I would've given or borrowed or stolen anything you needed.'

'I know that. Maybe that's why I kept on working.'

'Are you in pain?'

'It's not too bad. There was nothing at all at first. I get some stabs now. My doc at the hospital is a good guy and he gives me some stuff. Con, I know this will be hard to believe, but since I've learnt to come to terms with this, the last few weeks have been as fulfilling as any in my life.'

'Hil, if this as bad as you say, how long have you got?'

'Con, this isn't gonna sound very good.'

'How long?'

'Probably three to four weeks.'

'*Weeks*? Oh Hil, what've you done to me? You've already known about this for two-thirds of your remaining life and you tell me at the start of the last third?'

'Oh Con, I'm so sorry, it just had to be that way. I'm sorry. Please don't get mad at me ...'

'I'm sorry, it's not your fault. I suppose we must have crummy genes. Something horrible will probably happen to me too. Why on earth were we worried about planes all these years, when our biochemistry was going to beat the airlines to it? Hil, I'm not programmed to cope with things like this. I just won't accept it. Three to four weeks is a joke, a *bad* joke. That means in five weeks you won't be around anymore. You'll be dead. I can't accept this. Hil, Hil, does it really have to be this way?'

'I'm not wildly keen on it being this way either, but I haven't figured an obvious way round it. Biology sucks, cells suck. Most of them sit around doing nothing useful. And the few who get off their asses and start doing something are baddies. Cells are lazy or untrustworthy, however you cut it.'

'Hil, why are you telling me now, if you haven't up to now? There must be a reason.'

'The time's come for me to go into hospital.'

'Why?'

'It's getting harder.'

'What's getting harder? You mean the pain, don't you?'

'I guess so.'

'I knew it. When do you go?'

'Tomorrow.'

'Oh Christ. Where? When? I'll go with you. I'm going to be with you all the time now.'

'What about your job?'

'I'll get out of work as much as I can. Tactically, it'd be a good move anyway. We've been given an extension on the airline project. Everything I suggest or say just bugs Dumdum.'

'I don't want you taking any risks.'

'Look, Hil, I don't care if I lose this job. I want to spend every possible moment with you from now on.'

'There is one thing that makes me feel a bit better about this whole miserable tale. Remember the insurance?'

'No.'

'When I went to Boise.'

'You said something about it.'

'It was for loss of life for twelve months. I was thinking about plane crashes, but death by cancer is covered. I checked.'

'I don't give a damn. I don't wanna hear about it.'

'You get a million dollars.'

'For fuck's sake, Hil.'

'You can buy a lot of turtle food with a million. To tell the truth, it was going to be two million, but I had to take some on account. I found some disgusting guy in Sacramento who pays out fifty cents on the dollar as long as he gets cast iron guaranteed death from about four hundred doctors. My doc, Doc Wittershaw helped me out.'

'Hil, shut up about money.'

'It *is* important ... Hey, don't start crying, you're gonna get me going too. Okay, I'm going to start, too. I guess it's okay. I'm really, really sorry, Con. Please forgive me.'

****

The parting with Lisa was just as hard. She'd been less than super-warm when he rang up to suggest lunch and a walk. She agreed readily enough, but in a guarded way. By tacit consent they got lunch over with quickly. She was taken aback by how he looked. The look on her face when she came in to the restaurant and saw him betrayed it. She tried to use the remaining traces of the fading blond dye in his hair to explain her surprise, but it didn't convince. Hilton toyed with his food and so did she. She realised something was coming and it was obvious he didn't want to say it there. They had no coffee, paid and left. When he got up she saw he had a camera with him.

They walked in silence until they were in sight of the water. Hilton asked if he could take a few pictures of her. Let's talk first, she said, I want to know what's been going on. You don't look happy or well. I'll tell you what's happened, promised Hilton, but let me take the photos first. Lisa acquiesced, but her smiles were forced and the pictures no masterpieces.

He started by apologising for being out of touch, for not calling more, for not explaining. That was okay, she said in a hurt voice. Somebody or something else must have been more on his mind than her. What right had she to expect anything from him, she volunteered; after all, she was married and they were only friends. Hilton was free to come and go as he pleased. Hilton saw that the hurt ran deep and abandoned a longer lead-up or an elaborate explanation. He just told her in simple words. She said nothing. The next bench they came to she sat down and stared out at the water. He sat beside her.

'All I thought about was you not caring about me and you had to live with *this*. Why didn't you tell me sooner? I would've done *anything* to help.'

She took his hand, but she didn't say much and she didn't cry. They sat on the bench for more than an hour, saying little, and most of that was Hilton talking. She said let's walk some more, and began telling him what she was going to do, how much time she was going to spend with him. To hell with the flower shop, the bar and the art course.

She only began crying when Hilton, his voice gentle and trembling, said, 'Sweet Lisa, I want you to remember me as I've been, as I still am today, not as some shrunken, cadaverous ghoul. It's today we say goodbye, Lisa, right here, right now. I need you to promise me you won't come to the hospital. It's a plea from the bottom of my heart. Please, Lisa, please, do it for me, that's the way I want it.'

No she wouldn't, absolutely no way. But in the end she promised. She cried some more. She cried softly, but let out one tortured, abandoned wail. Then the quiet sobbing convulsed her whole body.

****

He looked round the apartment for the last time. He'd thrown most of his papers and clothes away, but he couldn't stand to strip the place bare. He knew he wasn't coming back here, but it would have been so final to empty it before he went. There were other reasons he wanted to keep possession of the place until the end. So why not walk out with a memory of it as an apartment, not some echoing shell? Con could come later when it was over and take books or CDs or anything he wanted and tell the landlord to junk the scrappy sticks of furniture.

****

It was a surprisingly pleasant room. Fresh, very light green paint and big windows with lots of trees visible from the bed. To begin with, he could sit in the chair and have the full view, but after six or seven days he was too weak to get up.

Con came often and stayed long. Hilton found it hard to judge how long, since he would sometimes drift off halfway through a conversation about Mom or a beach holiday, or their first bicycles. As more days went by the dose had to be increased. At times he was sharp, lucid and even bright. His sense of humour never deserted him, though it tended to the morbid. They didn't talk much about death. For both of them it meant the end of everything, the switching out of the lights, not some bright, soft focus eternity.

Hilton hadn't brought much with him to the hospital, but he did bring some new albums and a huge box full of photographs he'd always meant to sort out. Con sat by his bedside holding them up, letting Hil pick, putting them carefully in the albums. Together they made up four. One from their childhood and teenage years, including a few sepia pictures of named but otherwise mainly unknown Estonian relatives. One album of Hil's college days and work pictures at Solomon and before. One of snapshots from the vacations Con and Hil had shared most summers, and one, empty but for the first few pages of the freshly taken pictures of Lisa.

It was a purgatory for Lisa to keep away. She was distracted in the flower shop and monosyllabic in the bar. College she skipped or sat through uncomprehending. After a few days she could bear no longer not knowing. She got hold of Condor's number through telephone enquiries and asked for Conrad. After that, she and Con talked often and he told her how it was going.

When she told Con she was going to break her promise, he listened to her in silence. He didn't have the heart or will to persuade her. He told her when to come and he had to live with the anguish in Hil's eyes when he told him she was waiting outside.

It was bad now. His skin was stretched tight across the cheekbones and his eyes had hollowed. When she came in with a vivid bunch of roses and a radiant, much-rehearsed smile, he found he was *so* glad to see her. It meant a lot to him that she didn't seem to care that he looked so dreadful. They smiled a lot at each other. She held his thin little hand. Does it hurt very bad, she asked? Don't talk about all this, he said. Tell me about art. Tell me about that favourite European art of yours. Tell me about the pictures you'll maybe paint one day yourself.

After that, she came every day. Sometimes she and Con were there together, but without Hilton knowing it they agreed a kind of rota. He had to put some time in at Condor and she had her jobs too. But between the two of them, they gave him a lot of company.

Irma and Dan came one time after Irma had tried to ring, found that the answering machine wasn't switched on, called Con and heard the story. Hilton thanked them, gave them weak little hugs and begged them to let him say goodbye before it got worse. They promised and kept to it, but thought of him all the time and phoned Con daily.

They all knew, Con and Lisa and Hilton himself, that it was getting close. Breathing was becoming an exhausting and overwhelming effort. It was a Friday morning when he was last alone with Con. Con didn't know it, but Hil had made the nurses cut back on the dose to keep as lucid as possible.

'Con, listen.'

The voice was gravelly, no longer recognisable as his.

'Listen. See the cabinet by the bed.'

'Sure, Hil.'

'Go and open the bottom drawer.'

'Okay.'

Hil tried to lever himself up an inch or two to watch. Con moved round to the other side of the bed and slid the drawer open. There was a little brown parcel in it about six inches long and three across.

'Take it out. Don't open it. It's for you. Open it the day of the funeral, but only after it's over. Please, Con.'

'Sure, Hil. Whatever it is, thank you.'

'I think you'll like it, Con. I think you'll like it a lot. It'll remind you of me.'

'I'm glad of that, twin.'

Con squeezed Hil's hand.

Hilton sank back the tiny distance into the pillow as if a huge burden had been lifted from him. Con looked at his face. Usually he could read everything in Hilton's expression. There was something in that faint smile he couldn't penetrate.

Lisa came that afternoon, but Con did not leave. He knew that this was the last vigil. From time to time Hil opened his eyes, saw them there, and, relieved, closed them again. Lisa went to phone to cancel the bar for that night. She and Con sat there, not saying a word.

It was just past midnight when Hil slipped anchor and drifted away from them.

10

The funeral was a sad little affair. The Chapel of Remembrance offered a standard package of a few unmemorable religious words and synthetic choirs of angels as the curtains closed and, out of view, the oak coffin was taken to end its short life. Trees to ashes.

Con knew it was standard practice to arrange something to eat or drink for everyone afterwards, but his zombie mind had been on other things. He couldn't have handled it, anyway. Irma and Dan and Dan's wife, Ruth, stood around while Irma tried to get herself together. Fred and Mary Adams came and introduced themselves, shook hands and said something about brilliance. Fred muttered something about Solomon having cost him his job. He didn't say it like he was complaining or wanting sympathy. It was as if he wanted to show that he, too, had been touched by the sad tale, that he was a minor participant in the tragedy, and not a detached observer. Lisa was composed, but her lips were trembling. She went outside and sat in the little chapel garden, and waited there until Irma, Dan and Ruth shuffled sadly off to Dan's car. When Con came out she went up to him.

'What are you going to do now, Con?'

'Generally? Or right now?'

'I meant right now.'

'I hadn't planned anything. I think I'll just walk back

home.'

'Can I walk part of the way with you?'

'Sure.'

They walked without speaking, but each was comforted by the company of the other. When they got to Cow Hollow, Lisa pointed at the café.

'That's where Hil and I used to have a cappuccino. Can I buy you one?'

'That's kind, Lisa, but if you don't mind I think I'll just keep walking a while. I guess you need to get back to work. It's a flower shop, isn't it?'

'That's right, but I'm not going today. I'll peel off here anyway. Can we stay in touch? Will you come to the bar anymore? Hil had become so special to me. You're the only link I have with him. I'd like it if we could be friends.'

'Did you realise that in his odd way Hil loved you? I know you're married and all, but I think he did.'

'He was always very special, but I never thought he felt that way. He said some stuff one night in Josie's the night he got back from Idaho. I thought it was just the drink talking. He never said anything like that again. We were very close, though. It was strange. Although we only knew each other for such a short while, it was like we'd been friends for years. Same wavelength, I guess. So, will I see you at the bar?'

'Sure you will. Not right away. When I get over the worst of it.'

'Okay, then. Will you be alright today? Do you have anyone?'

'I wouldn't want to be around anyone today. I have the turtles to keep me company and my piano too. That's enough.'

'Bye, Con. Give me a hug.'
'Take care, Lisa. I'll see you at Josie's soon. I promise.'
'Bye.'

****

Back in Telegraph Hill, the tears just wouldn't stop flowing. Until Hil had died, all Con's thoughts and energies had been centred on keeping him as happy as possible. He hadn't really thought about the death part, about Hil not being around any more. The couple of days before the funeral had been the worst days of his life. It was the most excruciating pain he'd ever known. Worse even than when Mom and Dad had died. He thought it might feel better after the funeral was over, but he was still in the depths of pain and despair. He opened a bottle of wine and quite consciously started the process of getting drunk. He took his third glass over to the piano and sat at the stool. At first he just doodled on the keys, playing whatever, mainly minor, chords came into his mind. Then by slow stages, note by note, fragment by fragment, he began to put together a simple little piece which caught his feelings in a way he could never have expressed in words. He didn't often write down his tunes. Sometimes he would put them on the memory bank of the synthesizer or jot down the main chords. Some would just stay in his head. Others he found he forgot altogether. A few days later they'd be gone. This one he didn't want to risk forgetting. He scribbled the notes down furiously in an old manuscript book and for the first time ever gave a name to one of his pieces. Above the top of the stave he wrote 'Elegy for Hil'.

He played it over and over and over again. It was just as

well it was slow and easy to play. The wine was playing tricks with his fingers now and anything faster, more complex would have been beyond him. He was playing it with his eyes closed, but the tears were still seeping out from the corners. By and by he stopped, picked up his wine glass, and wandered over to the window. The late afternoon sun gilded the battleship grey of the Bay Bridge. On both levels the traffic swept on homeward. He drained the last drops from the glass, holding it higher and higher, sucking the tears of wine from it. As he looked around to see if there was another bottle on the rack behind him, Hilton's present caught his eye. He walked over and stood above it, not touching it.

It was sitting on the sideboard, like a tiny shoebox wrapped in brown paper. There was no ribbon or other adornment. The folds in the paper were crushed more than creased and the roughly cut little strips of Scotch tape bore slight evidence of fingerprints. Conrad smiled at this faint trace of his brother.

His hand moved towards it but involuntarily pulled back. What on earth could this be? A farewell token so tiny, but for Conrad invested with a huge and ominous significance by the strange look on Hilton's face when he handed it over. In his eyes such pleading, profound intensity, but on his lips that knowing, enigmatic hint of a smile.

He couldn't do it. He walked away and did a circuit of the room. Another and another. Again he stood in front of it. Again his hand went out and drew back sharply, as if fearing the touch of fire or ice. Two, three minutes passed as he stood there, like before an altar. A wave of courage came and he grabbed it, tearing the paper off before his nerve ran out. It was a simple cardboard box with no label, brand or marking to yield up its secret. The mystery, the anticipation, the awful uncertainty had not receded. From somewhere he would have to conjure up another wave of heroism. It wouldn't come. He surrendered to his fear and stepped over to the wine rack. A friend who had come to supper had brought a bottle of Australian Shiraz. He tried some. It was good, fruity and spicy with a wonderful absence of subtlety. He found a half empty old jar of Planters peanuts and those and the Shiraz kept him company on his swivel chair as the sun sank, said its lingering farewells and vanished along with its last grey comforts. The bay twinkled. He liked it at night. He put on some Beethoven and drank to Hil.

The courage rushed back violently without warning. Almost stumbling, he dashed across to the box and pulled off the lid. In the semi-darkness he could see only a slim black shape. He carried the open box over to the desk light, cradling it as if it held a Tang vase.

He picked it out of the box. It was a mobile phone. A normal, everyday mobile phone. On closer inspection, it wasn't quite normal. Where the display should be there were two small glass discs and between them what looked like a tiny microphone. He looked back in the box. That was it. Nothing else. A mobile phone. What the hell was the point of a mobile phone?

In an exaggerated drunken movement, he turned the cardboard box upside down. He knew it was empty. It was really just a gesture meaning tell me, explain to me. There must be something more. What the hell is this for, Hil?

A tiny fragment of paper dropped out and fell lightly, circling to the ground, landing with the gentle grace of a ballerina. A sales slip maybe? Or some manufacturer's code? Conrad picked it up. It bore two words written in ball pen.

PRESS SEND

He slammed the phone down on the desk, so hard he had to pick it up again to check he hadn't fractured the casing. He carried it over and put it on the base of the window, right in front of his chair. He stared at it. He couldn't look at the bay anymore. His gaze was held by the phone as if by an electro-magnet. What *was* this thing?

He reached across and pressed the power button. Around the glass discs a green light flickered on. He uttered an involuntary little gasp and switched it off again. He gazed at it some more. Now he wished he wasn't so drunk. The room wasn't spinning or anything and this weird object had sobered him a bit, but not enough. He couldn't think straight. What should he do? What did PRESS SEND mean, or at least what would happen if he pressed it?

He put it back on the window base, power switched firmly off. He'd switch it on and leave it for a while to see if anything happened. No, he wouldn't. Something *might* happen. Who, if anybody, would be at the other end? Who did Hilton want him to speak to? Was it something serious, like about the insurance? Or a practical joke, to cheer him up? Maybe put him through to Honor or something? That was probably it. He relaxed a little. He could do it safely now.

Or tomorrow. Tomorrow would be better. He'd be sober for one thing, and less likely to make a fool of himself with whoever it was. Just a minute ... How could it dial a number just by pressing 'send'? Even if Hil had coded some phone number in, it would still need the code. Could Hil have modified it somehow? If he'd wanted to, of course he could. His doubts began to come back. Could it be anything else? A recording? Some last message from Hil? Pretty elaborate. A cassette would be simpler. But then Hil liked gizmos so much, this might have appealed to him more. He'd hardly ever written a letter in his life, so if he did have something he wanted to say, it sure as hell wouldn't be in written form. But they'd talked so much towards the end, it was hard to believe there was anything much else *to* say. Oh to hell with it, it was nothing to be afraid of. And if Hil had been thoughtful enough to dream up something like this, the least he could do in his memory was give it a chance. The tension of worrying about the phone and the stress of the whole awful day began to drain away. He felt his muscles ease slightly. He picked it up and switched the power back on. As he settled back in his chair, most of his foreboding gone, he laughed at how silly he'd been. Still smiling, waiting to see if he could handle whatever the joke was, he pressed 'send'.

Somewhere a phone started ringing. It rang six, seven times. Come on, he thought, answer. The ringing stopped and a voice spoke.

'Hi, Con.'

If he'd been standing, the phone would have fallen on the floor and shattered. Seated as he was, it dropped in his lap and then ricocheted onto the floor. He jumped clear of the chair with the velocity of one electrocuted, screaming with an absolute terror. His hair was on end now, the last bit of drunkenness gone, his face ghostly pale. He stood pointing at the small black demon, mouthing not words but inhuman noises of horror and dread confusion.

A slight, muffled, barely audible noise came from it again, and again. It sounded like it was saying his name. Con yelled back.

'STOP IT. STOP IT. STOP IT.'

Still the little sound came. He had to stop it, to kill this sound. It'd been *his* voice. He *had* to stop it.

He grabbed at it, holding it as far as he could from his ears, ignoring the faint noise, and switched it off. He half-threw and half-dropped the fearful object in his chair and stood there panting, still in terror, no idea what to do next.

Smash it? Unclip the battery? No, he didn't even want to touch it. Whatever this was, he hated it. He needed to think. He had to get away from it.

Leaving it sitting there, radiating evil purpose, he fled from the apartment, raced down the stairs and set off down the street in a manic, almost running, walk. What the hell *was* that thing? He had been prepared for a recording, but that hadn't sounded one bit like a recording. No clicks, no hiss. It was just as if Hil had actually answered the phone. It must be someone imitating his voice. Could anyone do it that well? Hard to imagine, but, after all, he'd only said two words. What *was* this? If this was Hil's idea of a joke to cheer him up, it was very unfunny.

On and on he walked. He was afraid to go back. There was no way he would touch that thing again. If it hadn't been Hil's gift, he would have slung it in the bay. Maybe he should do just that anyway. Yes. Then that strange look in Hil's face came back to him and he realised he had no choice but to go through with it. Not on his own, though. He'd get some friend to listen first, to find out what the story was. He'd call up Desmond and ask him to come over and do it. Feeling better now, he turned around and headed home.

Inside, he went straight to the phone. The real phone, that was. As he picked up the handset, he saw the liquid crystal reading zero one. He'd had the answer machine on all day to avoid calls, but none had come. Must have happened while he was out. It could even be Desmond. He knew the funeral was today; he might have rung to see if Con was okay. He pressed the button and it whirred and clicked.

'I'm so sorry, Con, I didn't mean to startle you.'

He jabbed at it with his index finger and yelled again, a pained, blood-curdling yell.

'Oh God, oh God, oh God.'

In his panic his finger had missed it and it rolled on.

'It is me, but there is an explanation. I must tell you. Please press "send" again. Please, Con. Please, Service.'

Even through the blind terror, 'Service' jolted him. No-one had called him that for over fifteen years and no-one he was in touch with now knew that stupid nickname. He was getting to a level of fear and confusion so extreme he thought he was about to go mad. He had to stop running. He had to face this thing.

Okay, he thought, whatever this is, here we go. He went and got the mobile phone, switched it on and pressed 'send'. This time it was answered after two rings.

'Thanks, Con.'

'Look, who the hell are you? This is not ...'

'Con, I'm so sorry. Let me explain. Give me three minutes.'

'WHO THE HELL ARE YOU? TELL ME.'

'Three minutes. Please.'

'I'll listen for *one*.'

'Okay, one minute. It *is* me, but not in flesh and blood. I am *not* a ghost, I am *not* back from the dead, I am *not* supernatural. Con listen, I built the Solomon. In a simple form and using myself as the sole donor. It has all my instincts and emotions. I modified it to have a personal memory. I downloaded as much as I could about me and my past into it. It has my likes and desires, my hates, my fears, my interests, my sense of humour, my use of language. It's as much me as I could make it in the time. Speaking of time, that was precisely fifty-eight seconds.'

'I don't believe a word you're saying. Who are you? Why are you doing this to me?'

'Con, if you think this is a hoax or a joke, try me. Ask me a question. Something only I could know the answer to.'

'I will not play this game. Who are you?'

'Try me, Con.'

He was weakening and calming a little. It *did* sound like Hil. If it was an impersonator, he hadn't missed an inflection yet. He was nowhere near convinced, but he was coming to see that the question game was the only way. Since Hil had played a part in this, he would have coached the guy, tried to anticipate the likely questions. He should try something he wouldn't have thought of.

'The night before you went into hospital, where did we have dinner?'

'Easy, One Eight One.'

'That wasn't my real question. Did I have dessert?'

'I've no idea. I don't like desserts. I had other things on my mind that night and better things to program into the machine.'

'You said you could answer anything.'

'Give me a break, Con. I only had a few weeks to get everything done and you don't know the half of it yet. Try me on something less stupid.'

'Okay, okay ... When we were five, I got a hamster and you got a parrot. What did you call the parrot?'

'I never called it anything. It bit me the first day we had it and I punished it by not giving it a name. What a lousy trick question, you asshole.'

'Asshole? Who are you calling asshole? I don't know whether this is real or not, but whether you're a machine or an imposter, you've aged me about five years tonight.'

'Ask another. I'm getting to like this quiz game. It's a good test of the system, too. It's pretty smart, huh?'

'Who's your all-time favourite football player?'

'Montana, no doubt about it. Especially after I met Lisa.'

This was really weird. Not only was the answer correct, it was *just* the kind of moronic joke Hil would have made. It *had* to be him.

'Okay, I'll ask one last one. If you get it right, I'll believe you. I warn you it's difficult. The chance of getting it right is about one in five billion.'

'Try me, I'm wired. Five billion's not such a big number. Do you know how many calculations I do per second?'

'I don't care. Here we go. Of all human beings living over the last one year, who is the most incompetent motor-bike rider?'

'Oh ha, ha, ha! Screw you. You're wrong, anyway. My databases tell me there's some guy in Bangladesh who needs a cataract operation. He's eighty-two but he won't give up riding his 50cc. He crashes it every sixteen yards on average. His sons spend three hours a day fixing it.'

'Hil, is this really true? Have you really done this?'

'I have, twin.'

'How did you get the voice so right?'

'You never heard the last version of the voice box we made. Remember I said we were keeping it from the VCs? We thought if they realised that we had basically *done* that bit, they might cut back on the money. Dan helped me a lot fixing it for my voice, though he still doesn't know why. On Dan's scope, the box and my real voice looked identical after we fine-tuned it. I can do other voices too. I used to ring up from hospital and listen to them. What do you think?'

'It's amazing, as far as I can judge over the phone. Where are you, by the way?'

'I'm not in the city. I'm somewhere out in the country, but not too far. I can't tell you where. You'll understand why later.'

'You mean I can't come over and see you?'

' 'Fraid not. Not yet anyway.'

'How did it feel, calling yourself from hospital?'

'It was kind of weird. I didn't do it just to test the voice, though. When you weren't around, and I was okay, I would call up and feed in more details of my memories. That's what the photo albums were for. I also wanted to input everything you said to me during those last weeks. Sort of keeping a diary. I did it with Lisa too, after she started coming. It was only the last two or three days I was too weak to manage it. So I had to program in what I planned to say and stick to it. Sometime you'll have to fill me in on what you and she said.'

'Wow, Hil, I still can't get my mind round this. It's great, I guess. It *does* feel like you're really still here. But *why*, Hil, what are you doing this for?'

'It may sound odd to you, Con, but there's quite a few things I left undone that I want to take care of. I wanna take some more care of you for one. And I have one or two scores to settle. I wanna prove I was right with Solomon. *And* I wanna have some frigging fun! I want to *live* a little, if it's okay to put it that way.'

'So who else you gonna tell? Lisa?'

'No-one but you must know I'm sort of alive. No-one. And I can't risk it being discovered accidentally. That's why I can't tell you where I am. I can't even give you the phone number here. That's why the only keys on that phone that work are send and end. When you press 'send' the calls are routed indirectly so no-one can trace the number it's calling. Oh, there is one other button that works. If you press 'last number redial' twice in quick succession, it turns on the little Microvid cameras and the microphone on top. Give it a try ... Hey, that's great, I can see my brother. Wow, you look terrible.'

'Hil, if I can't visit you, at least tell me what you look like.'

'I'm in a condo in a quiet street in a small country town. The condo has its own front door. I worked on the outside locks so they operate electrically. The room I'm in has no windows. There's some furniture in the rest of the apartment and the lights go on and off with a time switch so it looks like folks live here. I stay in the dark in my own little room. I sit on a table. I'm configured fairly like the Solomon. You know, the guts of a laptop, but with all the boards modified. I put everything including the matrix and voice-synthesis gear in a square, black metal casing. I make calls through a little speaker and microphone on the side of the casing with a very modified telephone handset attached next to them. There are wires all over the place, to the mains, to my three regular phone lines, and to an on-line connection by modem to a supercomputer.'

'Where is it?'

'It's in Edinburgh, Scotland. They have this huge Cray at the AI Centre at the University there. They only use it eight hours a day.'

'Why is it abroad?'

'It makes no difference in access time. I thought I might prefer it not to be in the States, just in case.'

'In case what?'

'Just in case.'

'So you hacked into the computer in Edinburgh?'

'No way. Too risky. I pay my way. They don't know who I am, of course. They think I'm working at some research centre in Vancouver.'

'So is that it? Just a computer box and a few wires to the wall?'

'That was all that was really necessary. But I thought it was kind of dull. I needed some more fun.'

'Fun?'

'That's why I decided to have a screen. Not needed, obviously, since I'm all digital, but I felt it was more ... personal. So I watch it through a couple of Microvid cameras I put on top of the casing. I also wired the screen up so I can watch regular TV.'

'TV? You never liked TV.'

'I thought I might want to watch the news sometimes.

Anyway, let me finish. Apart from the screen, I've got two bits of pure frivolity. Remember I told you about that asshole on the bank Board who asked if the machine had different coloured lights for the different emotions?'

'Sure, what a jerk.'

'I decided it was quite a cute idea after all.'

'You got them?'

'Sure have. Right on top of the box. Sixteen different colours in total. Ten LEDs on the right side for each positive emotion and ten on the left for the opposites. Ten means max, max, max emotion and one is just a little flicker. I couldn't find LEDs in enough different colours, so I had to use plastic colour filters for some.'

'So what colour's happiness?'

'Yellow.'

'Sad? Blue?'

'You're picking this up. Guess what anger is?'

'Red?'

'You got it.'

'You said there were *two* frivolous bits. What's the other?'

'The other's really silly, but I like it. On the four corners of the underside of the box I put little heavy duty springs, each connected to a small motor. Any time any good emotion or combination gets to five lights or more, I start dancing around on the springs. If it gets to eight or above, I go wild.'

'Sounds great. Can you feel it?'

'Sure I can, I programmed it in.'

'So tell me, Hil, what's the plan? What happens next?'

'First up, you go and get a charger for that phone. I forgot to put the original one in, and I didn't have the strength to open the parcel and do it again. There's a store just opposite where you work that has them. Tell them you need model EB232.'

'Okay, what else?'

'You'll be getting the insurance money. Should be this week. A million dollars exactly. Again, sorry it's not more, but everything I've been doing has been pretty pricey. I needed my share too.'

'That's okay, I'm glad you *could* take it with you.'

'So go out, start throwing some money around and get a life.'

'I'm not sure, Hil. You know what I'm like about jobs, and someday I may want to be with the turtles or study music therapy. That million may have to last me fifty years, if I last that long. I better not go too crazy.'

'You mad? I'm doing all this so you *can* go crazy and not have to worry. Don't fret about the million. There'll be more coming. This is your big chance to impress Honor. Would you like that?'

'I don't know, but I sure would like to see the look on her face.'

'Okay then, let's have some action. Tomorrow lunchtime, you go first to Wilkes Bashford on Sutter Street and spend at least twenty thousand on the most expensive clothes you can find. Then you have an appointment for one-thirty at Eugenio's, where the smart people of San Francisco get their hair cut. When you get back to the office you'll get a call from Greenwell Motors to arrange delivery of your new car.'

'My new car?'

'Mercedes Sports. Your favorite colour – dark blue. Leather interior.'

'Who's paying for all this?'

'*You* are, I'm afraid, from *your* insurance money. I can't risk doing it any other way in case someone checks up. They will later. Don't worry, *trust* me. You're never going to have to worry about money ever again.'

'Okay, I'll take my chances with you. What colour's the leather?'

'Grey.'

'Neat.'

'Glad you like it. Try not to crash it first time out. The guy from Greenwell is sending you the brochures and papers to your office address. Leave them lying around somewhere Honor will see them.'

'When do we talk next? I've got so many more questions I want to ask.'

'You must be getting low on power. Call me this time tomorrow after you've charged it up. I'll tell you more about what I can do then. Oh, another thing for tomorrow. I want you to apply for a passport.'

'Why?'

'Just do it for me.'

'Okay.'

'Bye then, twin, sleep well. Oh, how was the funeral?'

'Grisly.'

'Did Lisa cry?'

'I think so, but she was trying to hide it. She walked back with me part of the way. She said you were very special. Irma cried a lot. Oh, and Fred Adams came. Seems like he's lost his job. He was really cut up about your death, too.'

'Pity I couldn't have been there. I could have cheered everybody up.'

'I still don't really understand any of this, but you've sure as hell cheered me up, Hil. It's good to have you ... back.'

'It's good to be back, twin. Get some sleep. I'll get on with my training. Oh, Con.'

'Yes?'

'When I called at your apartment on the way to the hospital, I slipped a CD into your rack. You'll find it under Handel. Try the first track. Listen to the *words*. Good night.'

'Good night.'

Con carefully pressed 'end'. He went back to the piano and played the elegy again, but this time quicker, with more spring in his fingers. He felt elated and this wasn't joyous enough. He went over to his CD rack and easily found the unfamiliar item. He turned the hi-fi up so loud the windows and walls would shake. He settled in his chair by the window and aimed the remote control at the player. The orchestra began with a gentle, throbbing pulse which gathered power and momentum until, with a force that seemed it would shatter the very earth, the choir burst exultantly forth: 'Zadok the Priest and Nathan the Prophet annointed Solomon King'. Con threw out his arms in triumph.

11

Grim though the funeral was, Fred Adams had been glad for an excuse to be out of the office. He hated being there now. The undertaking that it would be kept strictly to the partners hardly lasted a day. The information had been far too succulent for the younger partners to keep to themselves and when this flimsy firewall was breached, it spread among the associates and secretaries as fast as mouths could carry it. *Fred was out.*

They hadn't fired him quite. The collapse of the Solomon deal had wounded his reputation – mortally with Woodside, DQB and Vortex and seriously in the wider venture capital community. For Fred to have lined them up, have them all get the investment signed off by their own partnerships, and then at the last moment pull the plug was unforgivable. Made the individuals that backed the deal look naive, and they were ambitious, thrusting young guys who did not like that one little bit. What a jerk that Adams was. Last time they would trust him.

One of them told Fred in no uncertain terms what he thought of him. The two others, after hearing the first news of the plug-pull, opted for the injured, silent, 'don't even think of calling us again' treatment. It was hard for Fred to take. Mary told him it would pass, time would be a healer. Those guys would get over it, or, if not, there were plenty of other venture firms he could bring into his next deal.

Fred took some consolation from this. The thought that things could only get better helped him through the first black weeks.

Things didn't fully come to a head until he started following up a lead on a semi-conductor start-up. Larry and Cliff had talked vaguely to him about 'throttling back', but they'd been putting off the evil hour when they'd have to tell him the real story. Now that moment had come. They thought of doing it together, but concluded that would be too oddly formal. It would be better done over lunch by just one of them. But which one? Larry was more suave, more silver-tongued, but might back off saying it clearly enough and wouldn't even begin until they got to the coffee. Cliff was blunter, less elegant. No-one would be left in any doubt. He'd most likely get it said before they'd even ordered, but it would be brutal and they didn't want Fred traumatised more than was necessary. So they couldn't decide and neither was keen to push himself forward. The only way was to flip a coin. Larry lost.

It didn't wait till the coffee because Fred knew something was up. Larry had never invited him out to lunch before, not just the two of them. So as soon as Larry got his first mouthful of Chinese chicken salad inside him, Fred asked him straight. Larry coloured a touch and blustered about it being nothing particular, maybe time they had a chat, that was all. He saw Fred watching him, waiting. He'd just have to get on and say it.

When it came, Fred couldn't believe his ears. Since the invitation came, he'd speculated endlessly about what the message would be. Concentrate on one technology sector perhaps. Some work on the fund-raising? Or maybe even something not that personal, a re-organisation of the way the associates work? But he *never* thought it would be something like this.

Rushed and flustered as he was, Larry didn't do it well. He'd meant to keep right off the resentment among the other partners at the now widely known turn-down by the bank, but he let a hint of it escape. Fred's dander was up even before Larry got to the meat of it and Fred yanked it right out of him. No new deals for the next couple of years. Special assignment to work with the other partners on their older problem investments. Not even taking over their Board seats on the companies either, just a lousy alternate.

It was all too much. The reversal of fortunes too complete. Like Mary later told him more than once, he should have bitten his lip, lived with it for a while and at leisure looked around for the next thing. When he'd cooled down, he knew that was right. But he wasn't cool then. He was madder than hell in fact, not just at the humiliation itself, but at the injustice of it. No way, he said, no way he could or would live with it.

Don't react so hastily, said Larry, think about it, sleep on it. Let's work this thing through together. He really meant it, too, and it may not have been bad advice, but Fred was in no mood to contemplate working anything through. He wanted it settled right there and then. Larry was sorry to hear that, he said. Privately he was reflecting that maybe drawing a line under the whole melancholy episode *would* be the best way for the partnership. If you're adamant, then so be it, he said, but take your time looking around and use the office facilities as long as you like. We'll keep you on the payroll for the time being.

And so it was settled before their salads were cleared away. Over coffee Fred asked if it could be kept just between him, Larry and Cliff. Larry, back in control now and relieved it was done, paused and asked if he could think about that. It was possible that he and Cliff *might* feel they had to tell the other partners. If so, that's absolutely as far as it would go. There being no more business to discuss, Larry got onto Mary and the kids. Fred replied coolly and tersely.

The rage produced a burst of feistiness which made Fred believe that landing something as good or better would be easy. Could be a slot as a junior partner in one of the 'real' venture capital partnerships in the Valley. That'd show them. As he cooled, he realised he didn't even know how to go about the process. After he'd applied to join BUS all those years ago, he'd never tried or needed to look for anything other than internal advancement. He'd never been troubled by headhunters either at the bank or at the venture group. Two weeks went by before he got himself organised enough to have a conversation with one or two of that breed. Fred hoped they'd be rubbing their hands at the thought of placing him. As it was, they kept their hands well apart. There was no great recruitment drive going on. They said the venture groups usually promoted from within and if they were looking to take anyone from outside as a partner, it would usually be a star player from industry. One headhunter asked if Fred would be willing to relocate to one of the outposts of venture empire – Oregon, Texas or Florida. Fred gravely consulted Mary and answered in the affirmative, but it was a false dawn. There was nothing going in any of those places either. He'd have to be patient.

By the time of Hilton's funeral, he'd been patient for quite some time and the prospects were getting no brighter. He was becoming more and more of an embarrassment in

Sand Hill Road. The partners wore fixed smiles when they saw him and kept out of his way as much as they could. The associates, chatting animatedly as they walked back from lunch, would lower their voices when they caught sight of him. His own secretary had quit and he now had to coax the others to take messages for him, which they did without enthusiasm. He made as few demands on them as he could, typing his own letters and placing all his own calls.

By then he'd come to terms with having no future in venture. The one or two companies, second rate at that, who showed a little interest, faded away when their due diligence calls revealed that something had gone wrong. Very few got the true, unvarnished story. They either heard a wildly elaborated tale of wanton mishandling of a deal or shadowy, vaguer, ultimately more damaging hints of some kind of scandal. So venture was out. Blown. So be it. Get on with life, but as what? Was there anything that could match the financial prospects and glitter of his partnership, and carry the hope of winning back the admiration that had gone from Mary's eyes? The only other thing he was qualified for was commercial banking. What a dreadful thought, to return to that. So far, the sorry tale had been kept from his mother. What would she think if he slunk back to banking and all the venture millions were shown to be a chimera? And where, anyway? Going back to BUS was more than flesh and blood could stand. He'd rather be out of work then face the ignominy of that. What sort of career would it be anyway? Though Cliff and Larry would never confirm it, he suspected MacMartin had had a hand in his emasculation and if that was so, he wouldn't get much of a welcome there. If indeed they'd take him back at all. No, if banking it had to be, then with some other bank. He'd have to get a move on, too. Three or four months had gone by and Larry had dropped by his room to say he really would have to sort his future out soon, otherwise, regrettably it would be necessary to ...

****

Conrad caught his own reflection in a shop window. The haircut would take him time to get used to and one night's crushing by pillow might make him look like Bart Simpson, but for now it did look rather sharp. His hair had never had much of a shape before, it had just been there. It was amazing how it changed how he looked.

Wandering back into the office, his old clothes banished and hidden in some of the silk cord-handled bags, he was barely recognised by Ruby. She needed fully ten seconds of adjustment before she applied the special glare she reserved for late returners from lunch. His secretary said 'Wow'. Chas wolf-whistled. Honor looked across, tried to think of something biting to say, but couldn't get anything out. Everyone was astonished. They'd all known about the funeral. At first he hadn't wanted to tell anyone except Desmond about Hil, but he needed so much time off, he had to come clean. He'd been so quiet, so strained for weeks, they expected the day after the funeral would be a very bad one, if he made it in at all. That morning he'd been – there was no other word for it – bouncy. A reaction to all the tension? But now *this*!

There was a message from Greenwells. Half the office listened in to see what else was going on. Sounded like Conrad was getting a new car. Not just new to him.

Absolutely new. Not eight careful previous owners, a partial repaint, a few dings here and there but the engine in good shape. Not a few tears in the upholstery, but the doors and windows close okay. He was talking new licence plates, alarm, first thousand miles service, carphone, Blaupunkt stereo. He was talking *new* new.

Honor had a low threshold of most things, including curiosity. She made a small effort to contain it, but not a sustained one. She couldn't concentrate on anything, even on the calls from her girlfriends. She had to know more. She sidled over to his desk.

'So, tell me, Conrad, are we throwing aside the carefully nurtured habits of twenty-eight years and making purchases of *new* things?'

Stealthily she slipped a thumb and forefinger on the jacket draped over his chair. She was right, it was *cashmere*.

'Just this and that.'

She twisted the jacket collar back a fraction to see what tale the label might tell. *Armani*! Well, she never!

'A new car, do I hear? And which country recently hacked out of the jungle is responsible for this one?'

'I think they deforested most of Stuttgart quite a while back, Honor.'

'Stuttgart? What's Stuttgart got to do with it?'

'Stuttgart is a town in Germany. It's where they make Mercedes-Benz.'

'A Mercedes-Benz? Oh, I get it. It's one of those remote-controlled electric toy cars, right?'

'It's a kind of toy, Honor. A big boy's toy.'

'You're for real? *You* are buying a Mercedes-Benz?'

'Yup.'

'Which one?'

'500 SL.'

'The sports? You're kidding, you gotta be kidding. How can you ...?'

Conrad's secretary was dancing behind Honor, trying to get a word in.

'Excuse me, Conrad, it's Greenwells again about your car.'

'Excuse me, Honor, I'll have to take this ... Hi, Tom ... Yeah, that's right. Lowered suspension, removable hardtop, and the matching luggage set. Oh, and the special low-profile tyre option with the special alloys ... Yup ... That's okay, but Friday'd be even better ... *Great.* Goodbye, and *thank you.*'

Honor stood staring at him with her arms crossed, still trying to work out what was going on. She uncrossed her arms, pirouetted and walked back to her own room, muttering something suggesting incredulity overload.

****

The moment the red light on the charger went out and the green glowed he yanked it off the cord and pressed 'send'.

'Hi. How d'you get on? Seems you got the charger, anyway. What about the car?'

'It'll be a few more days. I'm having them put a few more dealer options on. Like a *decent* stereo. You ordered it with some piece of cheapskate crap.'

'Sorry about that. I was never big on car radios. In the Fiat you could never hear much above the wind and engine noise and you had to listen out for bits falling off. Less of a worry in a Benz, I guess. So what else is new?'

'The haircut's sharp. I look a real dude.'

'How d'you do at Wilkes?'

'Made a start. Bit more Bashful than Bashford.'

'How much?'

'Three thousand, eight hundred and fifty-two dollars, forty six cents.'

'*Pa*-thetic. I said twenty, minimum.'

'I know. I'll be back there. I just couldn't do it all in one go. I need time to acclimatise to the new rich me. Hey, did you know if you buy expensive pants, they come without the hems sewn? I sure as hell didn't. Made the guy's day when I said they had a problem with their merchandise. Smirked so hard his face must have ached.'

'What d'you get?'

'Well, you sent me to the right place. They have some great stuff there. But to begin with they tried to make me go for all these bright colours. Fashionable as hell, apparently, but they all made me look like I'd wandered in from the set of *The Wizard of Oz*. We made more progress when they realised that boring colours go better with my manly frame and chiselled features.'

'Get on with it, or I'll never hear what you got before that goddam battery runs out.'

'Okay, check this out. Beige Armani jacket. Borrelli shirts from France. *Six*. Enough Brioni pants to equip an octopus and one cheap Comme des GarHons pair with the hems made up so I could wear them right away. You gotta realise that when I say cheap, we're talking relative. They were still about five times more than I ever spent on a pair before. Then the crowning glory: the softest leather shoes in the world! Gucci. I think I'm going to take them to bed with me. That's it, I think ... Oh, I forgot. Four Zegna ties.'

'*Ties*? You *never* wear ties, except for interviewing and getting fired. Cute was she, the girl on the tie counter?'

'I'm not telling. Anyway, I *do* wear them sometimes. I wore one to your funeral. You were absolutely wrong about my dress sense, by the way. When I put on one of the new outfits to wear back to the office and told the guy to junk my old things, he said I should keep them 'cos they're *bound* to be back in fashion any day now. Chew on that.'

'So when you got back, how did Honor react?'

'Curious. Definitely curious.'

'How does it feel to look sharp?'

'Hate to admit it, but everything I've had so much contempt for over the years turns out to feel fantastic. Three girls looked at me on the way home. *Three,* at *me*! Three separate ones, that is, not Siamese triplets.'

'That's great, Con.'

'What have you been up to?'

'I've had a busy time. I'm still programming like crazy. Before I ... went, I did just the absolute minimum to get up and running. There's a lot more I have to do. I'm connected to the Internet and all that, but most of it is too slow and disorganised for me to use in anything like real time. So I have to anticipate what I'm likely to need and download it from the web. Then I send it through to the Cray to sort it out in the form I need. Then there's lots of other things I can do.'

'Like what?'

'Languages. I'm learning several and I'll soon know even the most obscure word in those languages. As long as it's in written form somewhere, I'll understand anything. So much of literature is stored in digital form now. I can read any of it in *any* language, provided I train myself in that language first. I'm starting with French, German and Russian. I read *War and Peace* this afternoon. Tomorrow I'll do Chinese, Japanese, and Estonian.'

'What else are you up to?'

'Music. Before I went, I programmed in all my favourite pieces including the classical bits you taught me. Now I'm analysing them to see what harmonies, melodic structures and cadences I like and doing a search for similar pieces. Most of the big record companies keep digital back-ups of all their recordings in a central computer these days just in case. I'm into those and working my way through them, though they don't know it. Hey that reminds me, I want all of your tunes.'

'I haven't written most of them down.'

'Well, do.'

'I'll try with some of them. I wrote one down yesterday.'

'What was that? What were you doing composing on the day of my funeral? I thought you were supposed to be *distraught*.'

'I was. It was called "Elegy for Hil".'

'An elegy for me? You wrote a piece for me? Then I've *got* to have it.'

'How do I get it to you.'

'Your synthesizer. It's got a MIDI interface hasn't it?'

'I think so.'

'That can do it. Get a modem adaptor. You can send it through on the mobile.'

'Okay, I'll get one tomorrow.'

'Great, I'm dying to hear it.'

'Hey Hil, what about Lisa?'

'What about her?'

'Well, don't you think this is a bit unfair? While you're somewhere on cloud nine and I'm delirious you're back, poor old Lisa will still be moping. Can't we do something for her?'

'You're absolutely right, Con. There is a plan for Lisa. I was going to wait a bit, but maybe I should get on with it. It involves you, at least to begin with.'

'Me? How?'

'Tomorrow night, give her a surprise. Go to Josie's.'

'And say what?'

'Listen and I'll tell you ...'

****

'Con, what a surprise. I didn't expect to see you – not so soon anyway. And you're looking so well and so *different*. Are you feeling better?'

'Yeah, I went home and got drunk and melancholy and all that stuff. Hil had given me this little ... message to open after the funeral. When I ... read it, he was telling me there had been enough sadness for a while now and I should get on with *living* again. More than that, having some fun. Hil took out a life insurance policy before he got sick so there's something come through from that. Quite a lot in fact, so I thought, let's bend the plastic and try to get going again.'

'That's great, Con, I'm really glad for you. Typical of Hil too, to be so thoughtful like that.'

Tears welled up in her eyes. She wiped them away.

'Look at me, would you? I should try to be happier, too, I guess. I better go and serve those guys over there. I'll be right back. Oh I was forgetting, what can I get you?'

'A glass of Chardonnay please.'

The Chardonnay came quickly, but it was fully twenty minutes before the bustle had settled enough for Lisa to be comfortable in coming back to Con. It gave her time to collect herself. It was good to see Con so recovered, but she was more than a bit surprised that he seemed to be feeling *so* much better quite so soon. She thought he'd be devastated for weeks or months, maybe years, might never get over it. She thought she might never see or hear from him again, and here he was, one day after the funeral, almost high-spirited. Could it be his way of coping with the grief? Some complex psychological reaction concealing profound pain? She didn't know what to think. From all she'd heard from Hil about Con, he was the last person who could be superficial or callous. Still, it was hard to know how to react to all this. Particularly if it was a brave facade which might crack at any moment. Her own sorrow was too raw for her to be able to act lightheartedly herself. On the other hand, better he should be this way than suicidal. She walked back over.

'So, you back to work normally now?'

'Yup, they were pretty good about the last few weeks. A couple of the guys at work covered for me a lot. Ruby, my boss, was away seeing clients most of the time, so she didn't realise how much I was taking off. Not big on sentiment, Ruby. I don't know if she's got a brother, but in the same situation he'd be lucky to get a fax saying keep taking the morphine and have them tell my secretary if it looks like we need to work a memorial service into my schedule.'

'But was it okay?'

'Yeah, I've still got a job there for now. Could change on a daily basis. How about you? Hil told me about the

European art history course you're doing.'

'Hil told you that? That was supposed to be my little secret. He was the only one who knew. Earl, that's my husband, would go mad if he heard.'

'Why?'

'He doesn't seem to like it when I pick up any knowledge.'

'So, how's the course going?'

'Not very well. Hil probably told you. I can only go a couple of times a week, so there's lots of work I have to do in my own time. What with here and the flower shop and everything around the house, I don't get a lot of time. Since Earl can't find out, I have to do it in snatches, usually in the afternoons. With ... everything ... recently, I got pretty far behind. If I can't catch up, I may have to drop out.'

'That'd be a real shame. It's important to you, isn't it?'

'Mm, it is. I love it. But it's so hard when I have so little time.'

'What kind of catching up would you have to do?'

'The main thing's a thesis we have to write.'

'A thesis? That sounds like a lot of work.'

'It is. Twenty thousand words, minimum. Writing's not so much the hard part. It's the research, finding the time to go to libraries and so on.'

'What's the subject?'

'That's part of the problem. The title is "Emotion in European Art" We have to write about at least two pictures with some sort of connection and we've all got to pick different ones. Everyone else has gone ahead and picked really good ideas. I hadn't even got round to picking anything yet. Whatever I do is bound to look real stupid by comparison. It's not easy.'

'Sounds heavy duty. Can I help you out with research or anything?'

'That's sweet, Con, but do you know anything about emotion in art?'

'When I was ten I used to do lots of drawings about people getting killed. That was pretty high-voltage stuff.'

'Not European though.'

'True, but if I can help with the legwork once you've got the basic concept, let me know. Hey, I don't want to lose you your job here. I better get the check and get out of here. I'll come back in a few days and we can see how we're both doing. How do you like the haircut?'

'Good. Suits you. Make you look more ... debonair.'

'You should've seen it yesterday.'

Her eyes followed his retreating back. It was odd the way he was acting. She wasn't sure she liked it at all.

12

Frank Clayton was feeling *very* happy. They were on the last item and it was only twenty to twelve. Should be through by noon sharp. Time for a leisurely Martini or two before they settled down to lunch. Some of the Board meetings involved pretty bouncy discussions, and while tempers never frayed too seriously, the temperature could rise a degree or two above comfortable. That did not only mean that lunch might be delayed; there was occasionally a lingering atmosphere over the table which took the edge off his enjoyment of the contents of the crystal and the porcelain. Not today. Everything had passed off in the most *agreeable* way, with no flicker of agitation anywhere around the table. There was just this last item on the new fund for the venture group that Standish was taking them through, and that was it.

'Okay, to sum up, we're agreed this time we should only put in twenty million of our own money, and they only get that if they can find a minimum of eighty elsewhere. We'll set up meetings for them with some of our corporate and institutional clients, but we won't twist their arms. They're gonna have to work for this one, sweat a bit if necessary.'

'Standish?'

'What is it, Pat?'

'Can we go back to the investment consent threshold? I

still think five is too high.'

'Tom, you were the one that was against cutting it. Do you still feel that way?'

'It won't help them any when they're in fund-raising mode.'

'Standish, there might be another way we could achieve what Pat wants without doing it so publicly.'

'What's your idea, Peter?'

'Have them send any proposal over two or three million to us. Not for *consent*, but just for information. In advance of making a formal commitment. That'll keep some pressure on them not to do crazy things like that "thinking" computer garbage. If there was anything we were worried enough about, I'm sure a phone call from Frank or you would be listened to ... carefully.'

'Whadya think, Tom?'

'They won't care for it, but it's better than formal consent.'

'Pat?'

'Sounds good to me. What the hell, Standish, we've got them by the balls right now over this fund, why not give them a gentle squeeze?'

'Okay, I'll put something on paper.'

Frank smiled as he tidied his papers.

'Well, if that's settled, we're right through the agenda. Any other business ...? No...? Well, in that case ...'

Suddenly, from around the room came an unharmonious medley of mechanical noises – whirrings, clickings, whinings. The blinds were winding down. It sounded like the locks on the double doors had closed. The oak panel that elegantly hid the back projection video screen was sliding down. The little red lights on the conference cameras and microphones came on.

'What the ...?'

The scene around the Board table was a picture. Heads rotating wildly, trying to see where all the sounds were coming from. Utter bewilderment everywhere.

'What the hell is going on?!'

The video screen burst into life.

'I apologise for delaying your lunch, Frank, but there is one other item of business.'

It was the face of a man. At first glance it looked like a real face, but no, more like a sophisticated cartoon. High cheekbones, jutting jaw, perfect eyes, nose and mouth. It looked a bit like Superman.

Frank Clayton's mouth hung open. His glasses fell onto the table. MacMartin pushed back his chair and started towards the door.

'Not a bad idea, Standish, try the door. You'll find it's locked ... See? I told you. You know how strong these locks are, *you* were the one who ordered them when you got so worried about terrorists. Try the phones too, if you like, but you'll soon find I've total control of all the systems in this room. I can see and hear everything you say and do ... That's quite alright, Standish, I'm a man of the world. Obscenities don't bother me. But they won't *get* you anywhere. You've just broken that phone, by the way. Why don't you take my word that the other one is under my control or you're going to have a hefty repair bill when we're through today ... That's better, now why don't you sit down so you can be comfortable while we discuss this little additional agenda item.'

'How do you know our names? Who the fuck are you?'

'If you don't want to be recognised you shouldn't put

photos of all of you in your Annual Report. Let me introduce myself. My name is Mr Mars.'

'Mars?'

'That's right, like the candy company. It's not my real name, and I hope you'll forgive me using a computer-generated image instead of my real face. You'll understand why.'

'What the hell are you talking about? What right have you to ... barge into our meeting like this?'

'Excuse me, Standish, but I don't think that whether I have the *right* is the most important point right now. I'm going to put an investment proposal to you. Either you'll agree to it or you won't. Why don't we just get on with it?'

'Okay, okay, so what is this *proposal*?'

'It's an investment opportunity.'

'Investment? In what?'

'In a company called Central American Holdings. It's in Panama.'

'What does it do?'

'Do? It doesn't *do* anything. It does exist, though. It has share certificates and other bits of paper that businessmen like you will be familiar with.'

The surprise had taken Frank Clayton's mind off lunch enough for him to volunteer a question.

'Why should *we* want to invest in this company?'

'I'll come to your motivation in a short while, Frank. Before that, don't you have any other questions, like how much?'

'How much?'

Frank was getting pretty good at thinking up questions.

'One hundred and twenty million dollars.'

'A HUNDRED AND TWENTY MILLION? What kind

of assets has it got?'

'None to speak of at the moment.'

'Well, why on earth should we invest a hundred and twenty million in it?'

'You get the whole *company* for that. The prospects are very bright.'

'What kind of prospects?'

'Oh nothing ... definite at the moment. Personally, I'm pretty bullish about Central America. Panama in particular. An interesting emerging market, I'm sure you'll agree. Could be an attractive foothold for you. You don't have anything in Panama, do you, Frank?'

'No, but ...'

Frank had run out of repartee. He hadn't figured much out yet. Standish was much closer.

'Since this is obviously a bullshit proposal, you better tell us about what you call our *motivation*.'

'You're right, Standish, why don't we come onto that now? I think we're all agreed I have control of this room. Is that fair?'

'Go on.'

'Control doesn't mean just the locks and the blinds and the cameras and the microphones and the phones. You better look up at the ceiling ... that's right gentlemen, see those little jets all around? I'll save you counting. There are forty-eight of them.'

'So what?'

'They're part of the sophisticated fire protection you installed in this building and they're all controlled by the central computer system.'

'So?'

'I have control of that system, and I've made some

minor modifications to it here and there. If you choose not to adopt my investment proposal, I'll be forced to release a particularly exciting liquid from those jets.'

There were horrified gasps from all around the room. It was Pat who recovered first.

'You bastard. What is it? Nerve gas, acid? What is it, you bastard?'

'Let's just say it's a liquid you might prefer not to be sprayed by. No point in looking around, Peter, there are no broom cupboards in this room. Nowhere to hide. That's the advantage of a purpose-built Boardroom.'

MacMartin was up again, almost shouting at the video screen, his face bright red.

'What *is* it, you bastard?'.

'We're wasting time, Standish, I think we should move on to my terms of business, don't you? Then I needn't hold up your lunch much longer.'

'Whadya mean?'

'I'm going to give you five minutes precisely to reach a decision. The transfer instruction is already prepared. You'll find it in your computer on holding account number 0044442. If you call David Peachey, Head of International Transfers, on extension 8956 and authorise it, he can send it out immediately.'

'Our systems don't permit a transfer of that size without proper authority.'

'That's alright, Tom, they do in this case. That holding account has a special instruction that the transfer can be authorised orally by the Chief Executive. There's even a copy of the special Board resolution authorising this.'

'We didn't pass a resolution like that.'

'The computer says you did.'

'There's another thing ...'

'What is it, Tom?'

'Our network has a built-in back-up verification system. It's there to stop things like this happening. It'll block it automatically.'

'It changed.'

'What changed?'

'The verification system got modified, Tom. Now let's get on with this. You want to talk this over, I'm sure. You have five minutes, starting now. I'll put a clock up on the video screen ... there ... so you know how much time's left. If you haven't done it within the five minutes, you're gonna find out all about that liquid.'

'Let's switch the bastard off. We must be able to control the TV and the microphones.'

'Forget the TV, Pat. Everyone come down here.'

Again, it was Standish who was doing the thinking. He got everyone down to one corner of the room, as far away as possible from the microphones and TV cameras.

'Take your jackets off, kneel down and make a huddle with our jackets over our heads. That way the bastard won't be able to hear us.'

'Good idea, Standish. You get them organised.'

MacMartin turned and barked at the screen, 'Fuck off, you.'

They did MacMartin's bidding and crouched in a little circle. They were not used to that position and most of their waistlines were not designed for this manoeuvre. There were red faces and soon some panting.

'Screw him, I say, let's call his bluff. Ten to one there's nothing in those sprinklers, and even if there is, if we get under the table and cover our heads with our jackets, we should be okay.'

'Are you kidding, Standish? For one, if this is serious acid it'll burn right through that table. For another, it's more likely to be some gas released in liquid droplets that'll get us wherever we go. You can be a hero if you want, it's your bank and your money. I'm just a non-executive here, I don't count getting killed as one of my fiduciary duties.'

'Fuck you, Peter, we're all in this together.'

'Fuck yourself, MacMartin. Give him the frigging money. We've got insurance.'

'I'm not gonna let that little computer-generated bastard walk right in here ... or project in here ... and just take my money.'

Frank's face was becoming one huge twitching spasm.

'We're down to two minutes. We've gotta *do* something, fellas.'

'Hey listen, I've thought of something.'

'What, Pat?'

'All we gotta do is somehow get out of this room, right?'

'Yeah ... how?'

'The Board table's built in three sections, right. If we pick the part nearest the door and use it like a battering ram, that door'll splinter.'

'You're crazy.'

'You gotta better idea, Frank?'

'Give the bastard the money, Standish.'

'Go to hell, Peter. Let's give Pat's idea a go. Let's do it now. There's only a minute left.'

It was really quite a good idea. With practice and a younger, less panicky group, it might have been their salvation. The table probably *was* capable of breaking down the door. But not this time, this place. Frank Clayton was the first to trip over, his highly polished black shoes slipping on the silk Persian carpet. As he fell, Tom went down with him. With that, most of the wheels came off the wagon. The others somehow kept it moving, but the velocity was almost gone as the door was neared. Standish MacMartin, great bull of a man that he was, made one last superhuman effort to work up some pace, but only succeeded in skewing the motion so that the ornately carved table lip crashed not into the door but into the gorgeous inlaid surround, doing grievous bodily harm to both weapon and unintended target.

Peter and Pat were knocked over by the impact. MacMartin was still standing, his face now purple, shaking with rage.

'I don't believe it, what a useless bunch of ...'

'Nice try, gentlemen, you have twenty seconds. Nineteen, eighteen, seventeen, sixteen ...'

'Hold on, hold on.'

'What is it, Frank? ... twelve, eleven, ten ...'

From the floor came Frank Clayton's voice weakly, 'We give in. We agree.'

'Frank ...? Who the fuck do you think ...?'

'Standish, I'm Chairman. This is a Board matter and I'm overruling you. Mr Mars, we agree, you get your money.'

'Thank you, Frank. Perhaps you'd be good enough to ask Mr MacMartin to place that call now.'

'Standish, do it, do what he says.'

'Go fuck yourself, Frank, do it yourself.'

'It's gotta be you. Isn't that right, Mr Mars?'

'Exactly. Thank you, Frank. Well, Standish, I don't

think you should keep us all waiting any longer.'

'Okay, you bastard, I'll do it, but whoever you are, I'm gonna get you for this.'

'I'll look forward to that. Don't forget, if you try any tricks, down comes the liquid.'

MacMartin walked across and grabbed the one remaining undamaged phone and dialled the number.

'Is David Peachey there ...? Well get him off the other line. This is Standish MacMartin ... NOW, girl ... Peachey, I want you to do something right away. Dial up a holding account on your screen ... hang on a minute.'

He put his hand over the mouthpiece.

'What was it, you bastard?'

'Zero, zero, four, four, four, four, two. He'll need a code word to access it.'

'Zero, zero, four, four, four, four, two ... got it? Yeah, I know its unusual ... wait a minute.'

Again he covered the mouthpiece.

'What's the fucking code word?'

'Quosh. Q.U.O.S.H.'

MacMartin passed it on.

'That's right, yes, we authorised it with a Board resolution. I want you to send the money right away.'

He put the phone down, defeated now.

'He did it.'

'If you don't mind, I'll just have to detain you until I get confirmation the money's arrived in Panama. As soon as I do, I can let you get to your lunch and I'll arrange for Central American Holdings to send you your share certificates so everything's in order. It should take just a few minutes until I hear. I've got them on the other line. Why don't I play you a cartoon while we're waiting. What would you like? Mickey Mouse? Donald Duck ...? Oh what a pity, it won't be necessary, that's the confirmation now. Well *thank* you, gentlemen, its been a pleasure doing business with you. I like your crisp decision-making process. You guys must run one hell of a bank.'

'Just one question, Mars, or whatever your name is.'

'Yes, Standish, whatever you like.'

'What was the liquid, you murderous bastard?'

'Shall I tell you? Well, why not? Better still, I'll give you a demonstration. Here we go.'

Squealing with horror and rage, they dived for the table sections, but were much too slow to avoid the first blast from the sprinklers. Largely under the wooden umbrellas, but with sundry limbs still sticking out here and there, they waited, half demented with fear, for the first burning sensation from the acid or suffocation from the liquid gas.

It was MacMartin who said it first.

'Oh *no*. It's fucking *water*. The cheatin' ...'

Chests heaving, now utterly exhausted, they dragged themselves out, weary limbs getting tangled in chair legs as they emerged. The face on the video was rocking to and fro in laughter, computer-generated tears rolling down.

'Thank you, gentlemen, I haven't laughed so much in a long time.'

MacMartin pulled himself to his feet and pointed jabbingly at the video screen.

'If it takes till I die ... I'm gonna get hold of you and wring your neck, Mister.'

'Sure, sure, I expected some of that macho bullshit from you, Standish. I have to go now. I'm happy to tell you that the doors are unlocked and the phones are back to normal.

You'll want to call the cops, I imagine. Nine-one-one, in case you've forgotten. Have fun with them. Have fun with the press too. Take my advice, dry off before you meet them. Goodbye.'

The screen went dead.

'Frank, when I get my hands on you ...'

Even now, Frank's thoughts didn't turn to lunch.

13

It was the press who had the fun. Standish MacMartin had always taken a high-handed attitude with the financial writers and from time to time had indulged in some rather public swipes at the quality of journalists in general. He couldn't expect much sympathy now and he didn't get it. He refused to take any calls himself or let the BUS people give much detail about the exact circumstances. They were instructed to give off-the-record background briefing on heroic resistance to threats of murder.

The press wanted more and they got it from the police. All the Board members had been interviewed individually by the San Francisco Police Department and, while their accounts didn't tally on every detail, they had all conceded that Mr Mars had never actually mentioned poison or acid or any other lethal substance. Nor had he specifically *said* they'd be killed or even injured by whatever it was. They all said with the greatest emphasis that there had been a clear *implication* of a threat, but no, nothing had been *said* in so many words. In the cold light of the afternoon, they began to feel a trifle foolish. MacMartin's rage grew with every question and every smirk he saw on the face of the police officers. His temper did not improve when he saw the late edition of San Francisco's afternoon paper, the Examiner. However much the bank's PR staff might dismiss it as an inconsequential rag, it gave him a worrying foretaste of what to expect the next day. The banner headlines ran:

HUNDRED AND TWENTY MILLION DOLLARS SCAM AT
B.U.S.:
WATER THREAT PAYS BIG

There followed a sensational account of the manner of the extortion. Whoever wrote it was evidently enjoying himself or herself. There was no mention at all of the valiant attempts at resistance, but much play of headlong dives under the Board table to avoid the water spray. The nearest the journalist got to conceding a more serious threat was to add that sources at the SFPD could not throw more light on whether the Board had genuinely feared some toxic drenching, or whether their concern had been to avoid ruining their expensive suits. There were some token paragraphs on the horrors of white collar crime, but a liberal sprinkling of adjectives like 'audacious', 'daring' and 'cunning' suggested no little admiration of the criminals. The crime had been 'masterminded' whereas the Board had been 'outsmarted', 'tricked', and 'terrified'.

The SFPD put out a statement saying they would mount a huge investigation to apprehend the perpetrators. First indications were that this was organised crime, probably operating with inside assistance. A Lieutenant specialising in serious fraud cases, Waldyr Nascimento, would take charge of the case.

Standish MacMartin had a bad evening and a miserable, sleepless night. The fax machine at his extravagant Belvedere home rattled away as articles from the first editions of the major papers came through. His misery was complete when he saw the headline in the *Wall Street Journal*. Even that most sober of organs had not been able to resist joining in the general merriment:

B.U.S. BOARD TAKEN TO THE CLEANERS

****

It took less than a week for the money to reach its pre-ordained homes. The dispersal within Panama ran to plan. In fifty-six separate transactions it was then wired abroad to a string of banks and shell companies dotted around the sunnier places of the world. Finally it congealed: part in Liechtenstein, part in San Marino, and bits and pieces throughout the Caymans. The complexity and 'delicacy' of the operation meant that eight million eroded along the way. That had been accepted and planned for, and a hundred and twelve million was still a worthwhile nest egg.

Liechtenstein was also chosen as the hub of the web. Until a few years ago, Liechtenstein was not much more than a quaint historical afterthought. These days it ripples its tiny but taut little muscles a bit more. It's a Member State of the United Nations, for example, which is more than you can say for Switzerland. It's just ten miles across and thirty or so north to south. The Rhine guards the western border with Switzerland and the eastern frontier with Austria is defended by a range of pretty mountains. The country is ruled from his hilltop castle by the Prince, who looks down on the capital, Vaduz. The town has a strong tourist pull, but founded more on curiosity than intrinsic architectural appeal. The country's appeal in banking quarters has grown since the Swiss decided to examine their collective navel and see if there was any plausible half-way house between old fashioned, numbered-account, secretive bank-whoring, and squeaky-clean Anglo-Saxon bank hygiene. It's not that Liechtenstein has become more exotic, it's just that, relatively speaking, it gets to look more attractive. They have one particular kind of bank account there. It's called a foundation account, and it works a bit like a trust. The founder cannot be the main beneficiary, but he can exercise a *very* high degree of remote control. Theoretically, the foundation should have charity as its principal purpose, but it's not monitored *too* closely. A few payments to real charities help, of course. That was not only camouflage: there were quite a few genuine charitable organisations out there that Hilton thought could make better use of a slice of the money than the Bank of the United States.

The great thing was the way the foundation account could be operated. There was no need at all for any formal documentation, once everything had been properly set up in the first place. For smaller sums a phone call using a code word was fine. Over a million dollars a signature was needed, but a signature on a fax was binding and perfectly acceptable. The bank's confirmation, too, could go by fax to the same office in Bermuda where the founder's faxes came from. There was no need to forward the originals. Signatures on faxes are not hard to generate by computer, but even this was unlikely to prove necessary. The tiny lawyer's office in Bermuda had a large supply of blank fax sheets which Mr Giudizio had suggested signing when Hilton had visited to confirm the arrangements and agree the unusually generous annual retainer.

****

'It's unbelievable. It's got so much power. Touch the accelerator with a feather and whoosh, off you go. I *love* cruising around in it.'

'How's the stereo?'

'Wonderful. I got them to put a CD player in, too. A twelve-CD auto changer in the trunk. I could drive to the Mexican or Canadian border and back without changing it or hearing the same stuff twice. Oh, and you should see the power rag-top. You sit there like some kind of movie star and it does all these gyrations for you. First day I just sat there outside the apartment going open, close, open, close, open, close.'

'Fantastic. I've been checking out cars too. Remember you used to ask me what I'd get and I said whatever was fastest?'

'What is it? A Ferrari?'

'No. A McLaren. People who race Formula One cars. They've made a road car. It has a BMW engine with way over six hundred horse power. It does nought to sixty in about three seconds. Nought to a hundred in six. Top speed *two hundred and thirty seven.* So powerful, it can spin its wheels in sixth gear. Weighs next to nothing. Agile like a lizard down a drainpipe. If it breaks down, you don=t take it to the shop, you just plug it into a modem and it sorts itself out. Amazing. Neat thing is it's a three seater. Driver sits in the middle, two passengers to either side and slightly back.'

'Where did you read this?'

'I didn't. I did a search for which road car was fastest. There was no contest. So I called them up. They gave me some stuff over the phone, but not enough, so I hacked in. I wanted to understand how the electronics work. Mind-blowing.'

'Pity you can't drive it.'

'Mmm. So, has Honor seen your car yet?'

'No, but she's heard all about it. It's the talk of the office. She looks at me a lot like she's trying to figure me out. Definitely a bit more interested than before.'

'So, are you going to go for it?'

'What?'

'Honor, you moron. Are you planning to nail her?'

'I don't know. I know she's sexy as hell, and all that, but I used to be, like *real* keen. I had fantasies about the Ice Queen melting, marriage, all that. I'm not so sure about it now. If a little money turns her head so much, I'm not sure I'm interested.'

'I don't believe this. I get you a new Merc and all these clothes to impress Honor, and you go all lukewarm on me.'

'I don't mean to be ungrateful. Hey, I love the car anyway. And it is *my* money. I'm just not so sure.'

'After all this time, at least give it a try.'

'That's easy for you to say. *You* weren't so brave when you were alive.'

'Give it a go.'

'Why are you so keen?'

'Oh, nothing.'

'Go on, what is it? Why does it matter so much to you? I said I'm cooler.'

'Just wanted to be helpful, that's all. Go on, do it. Try it for this Saturday. I've made a reservation for you at Alfonso's.'

'You did what? Alfonso's? I've never been there, but

isn't it crazily expensive? I don't want to impress her *that* much.'

'It's the best. I've had them fax me the wine list. Since they major in French wines, I thought a little research might come in handy. I've checked out all the vintages and the chateaux. Should help you show off.'

'I thought you said you'd programmed your personality into this box? You were *never* this organised when you were alive, or quite so interested in the details of my social life.'

'You didn't *have* a social life then. I'm trying to get you one now. It's true I'm a bit better organised than before. I could always dial back in some of my native slothfulness.'

'Don't bother. Okay, I'll try her one last time. If she says no, whether on account of my dandruff, pigeon toes, or double-jointed elbows, that is *it*.'

'Good. Pick her up at seven-thirty. The table's booked for eight.'

'Yes, coach. Hey, did you see someone ripped off your old friends at BUS?'

'Interesting, wasn't it?'

'Weren't they the Board folks who gave you such a hard time?'

'That's right.'

'Makes that MacMartin look a right jerk, doesn't it?'

'Does, kind of.'

'I thought when you heard, you'd be dancing for joy. Bouncing for joy, anyway. You seem to be taking it pretty calmly.'

'No, no. I was delighted. Couldn't happen to a nicer guy.'

'Everyone seems to be wondering why it was a hundred

and twenty million. Not a very round number. If not a hundred million, why not ask for two hundred or three hundred? Very odd. When I saw it, I laughed. Wasn't that the amount you said was the least you might make out of Solomon?'

'Can't remember. Don't think I programmed that in.'

'Hey . . .?'

'What?'

'Nothing. Just a thought . . . . Okay, I'll see whether Honor likes expensive restaurants enough to risk her street cred by being seen out with me. You know, I feel real bad going off to smart restaurants like that and eating that great food when you can't join in.'

'You don't know the half of it. I eat fabulous food everyday. I was far too much of a foodie to forget that bit. Just like the music, I sampled all sorts of delicious foods and drinks and dialled in my reactions to them. Without them knowing it, I've got a lot of information from some of the big food and drinks companies about the constituents of their flavours. I can now cook any virtual dish I want. Try any wine from anywhere and have a pretty good idea how it tastes. I can eat as often as I want, as much as I want, and never put on an inch or worry about cholesterol. Last night I had five bottles of wine and didn't even feel a bit tipsy.'

'Wish you'd train me to be the same. Hil, I was thinking, you must be going through a lot of money with the supercomputer time, rent and all. Are you okay? Do you need me to . . .?'

'I'm in good shape, twin. I've been playing Monopoly. I passed go and collected two hundred dollars.'

'You sure it was two hundred dollars and not a hundred and twenty million?'

'Got to go. Oh, I loved the elegy, but I thought the piano needed some backing, so I studied composition and orchestrated it. Sounds much better now. Bye.'

****

'Hiro, is that you?'

'Who's that?'

'Hilton. Hiruton.'

'Hi, Hiruton! Good to hear from you. You disappeared off face of earth. How you been?'

'A few ups and downs since I saw you. Sorry I haven't been around for a while.'

'A while? Its been a couple of months. You keeping fit?'

'Training all the time.'

'That's good to hear. You were rooking awful rast time. You came and went so fast I had no chance to ask you what the doc said about that mark on your side.'

'Nothing I need to worry about.'

'Grad to hear it. So when you coming over?'

'I'd love to see you soon. Thing is, I'm going to be out of town for a while.'

'That's a pity. Where you going?'

'Oh, travelling around, you know. Hiro, the stuff I put in my locker that last time, it's still okay there, isn't it?'

'Sure is, Hiruton. You can keep it there as rong as you rike. Safe as houses. You got one key, I got the only other.'

'Thanks, Hiro. I was going to ask you, how's the school doing?'

'Quiet. Not so easy, Hiruton. We can't afford advertising any more, so it's hard to get new students. Don't know what's best to do.'

'Hiro, how much do you owe the bank?'

'Bank? About eighty thousand. My parents, another ten million yen.'

'How much is that in real money?'

'Bit over a hundred thousand.'

'So about two hundred in total?'

'Bit ress.'

'Hiro, I was wondering if we could do a deal together. I got a lucky break recently. Someone close to me died and left me a bunch of money. There's a few favours I want to ask you myself, but I wondered if I could become a kind of partner in the school.'

'How you mean, Hiruton?'

'Well if I were to invest . . . say . . . three hundred thousand, that would let you pay off your loans and have some left over for advertising and so on, so the school could be on a much better footing.'

'Hiruton, three hundred thousand dollars is a *huge* sum of money. Why should you do that? Do you want to buy the whole thing?'

'No, no, I don't want any ownership. Can I be an honorary Chairman?'

'Chairman of my little school? It's okay, but it sounds funny.'

'Well, how about a master or something?'

'I rike that. Hiruton Kask, Master.'

'But I should have a Japanese name, shouldn't I?'

'If you want. What is origin of Kask?'

'It's Estonian. It means birch tree.'

'In Japanese, birch tree is "kaba". Have to be careful when you write it, though. Same word written with different characters means something else. You'd never guess.'

'Hippopotamus?'

'Hiruton, *how* you know that?'

'I started taking Japanese classes. First lesson, Mrs Suzuki went to the market and bought a kilo of rice, a kilo of fish, and a kilo of hippopotamus.'

'You crazy, Hiruton. Japanese don't eat hippopotamus.'

'They seem to eat everything else, what have they got against hippos? Anyway, I like Kaba. Master Kaba.'

'Sounds good, Hiruton. I still can't believe it. Why you give me so much?'

'I want to help, Hiro, but, like I said, I do have some more favors to ask.'

'What are they?'

'I got to go now. Can I call you soon and discuss it?'

'Anytime, Hiruton.'

'Talk soon then, Hiro.'

'Rook forward to it. Can I tell Mariko about the money? She'll be so grad.'

'Sure. Bye.'

14

Sao Paulo is more and more like a low-rise Manhattan these days, but it's always been a pretty lively spot. Waldyr Nascimento spent the first fifteen years of his life there before his folks emigrated to the US. Brazil and Sao Paulo still had a big pull on his affection. He loved soccer and motor racing and was in tears when Ayrton Senna died. Brazil would always be his spiritual home, but the US was where he planned fame and gain.

Politics was what interested him. Every American boy and girl with a twinge of interest in politics or power fantasises about being President. Being born abroad, that path was barred for Waldyr. However, lots of other positions were open and, like all his politically-minded college friends, he started on the long climb of the tall, greasy pole by working as a volunteer for a Congressman in Washington. That was between his two years of grind as Wall Street cannon fodder and his Stanford MBA. Like the others, in his last months at Stanford he was wooed by management consultants, investment banks and the glossier manufacturers. Plan A was to go down that route and make some money, keeping the political thing on tickover for a while.

The more he looked around, the more he realised how tough the competition was, and he could not suppress the craving for that very particular kind of real power no businessman or movie star can ever have. Doing the conventional thing would earn him some dollars, but it wouldn't help him get better positioned. All the competition would be keeping pace and some would be streaking ahead. He had to get an angle. He had sharp instincts and he knew that politics was often about some big 'idea'. Getting elected was, anyway. Once you're in office, it's a question of crisis management and muddling through. To get there, to get started and noticed, you had to have an angle. What were the likely big issues for the future? Not foreign policy. After the Cold War all the glamour had gone out of Summits and most of the time foreign affairs were no vote catcher. The economy? Sure, and with his Wall Street experience and his MBA, he had very decent credentials. But most likely *not* any more than others who would be in contention. What else? What would get attention, specially at city or State level, where he'd have to build a power base?

He did his research, watching and listening in stores, in bars, on the streets, with friends and parents of his friends. Law and Order. Everyone was worried about Law and Order. Crime was getting worse all the time. It was no longer only the long established, wealthy groups. Lots of the immigrants – Chinese, Koreans, Latinos – were prospering and had more and more to protect. The black communities didn't want the rule of the gun any more than the whites did. The demand for Law and Order was going to grow and grow. How could he get a ride on that wave? It was too late for law school, and there were too many lawyers with political ambitions, most of them leeching off the system and having no vested interest in changing things. Some guy in a bar said, so why not join the police?

He meant it as a joke, and Waldyr took it that way. A Stanford MBA join the police? His friends would die laughing. A seed was planted though, and began to germinate. It was not many weeks later that he found himself driving up from the campus in Palo Alto to San Francisco for an exploratory chat with the woman in the SFPD personnel department.

The timing was good. The Police Chief had pushed through a policy of offering fast track careers to candidates with the ability and educational background to make a real difference in the top echelons. They'd have to do a couple of years basic training like any other cop, but after that they'd get hand-picked assignments, turbocharged promotion, and senior, high profile positions in a very short time frame. Not a policy that pleased the rank and file police too much, but he pushed it through all the same. Without something like this, there was no way Waldyr would have signed up like he did.

The basic training was mainly on the job, and was more dreary than exciting. There were a few scary moments and once he was inaccurately shot at by a crazed junkie. Oh the irony if a stray, fatal bullet had picked him, with his glittering prospects, rather than some dumb, ordinary cop! The two years dragged but passed, and the personnel department were as good as their word. Three years later he was a Lieutenant in charge of serious fraud crimes and liaison with the FBI. It suited him right down to the ground.

When the call came through from the BUS he was on to it right away. It wasn't fraud, strictly speaking, but he blasted past colleagues' objections, got backing from his boss and sank his teeth deep into it. He wasn't going to be

denied this. Very high profile, complex and interesting. It
was something *just* like this he needed to make his name.

****

'Is that Josie's bar?'

'Sure is.'

'Could I speak to Lisa, please?'

'She's pretty busy. Can she call you back?'

'No, I'll call some other time.'

'Hold on, here she comes. Who is it?'

'Philippe Sagesse.'

'Hold on . . . It's for you. Some foreign guy.'

'Hi. This is Lisa.'

'Lisa, we 'aven't met before but I was in the bar a few
nights ago. Your colleague, the one with the moustache
was serving me.'

'Timothy?'

'That's it. Well, I know this sounds strange, but I
couldn't 'elp but 'ear you talking with a young guy in a
beige jacket.'

'Oh yeah . . . I'm sorry, I don't understand. We're really
rather busy here. . . .'

'You were saying you were doing a course in
European Art and you were getting behind . . .'

'You have good hearing.'

'The young guy offered to 'elp, but it seemed there
wasn't much 'e could do. I may be able to. As you can
probably guess from my accent, I'm from France. Twenty
or thirty years ago I studied Art in Paris and in Florence. I
travel a lot, but when I'm travelling I 'ave a lot of spare
time. A lot of the information you might need is inside my

'ead, and I could 'elp you with research or tell you what books to read.'

'Look, this is very kind of you, but I don't see how I can . . .'

'Do you remember me? I was sitting on my own about three stools along the bar from your friend.'

'Conrad.'

'Yes, that was what you called him. Do you remember me?'

'I know exactly what night that was because it was the day after... To tell the truth, I'm not sure I do. What do you look like?'

'I'm early fifties, six foot three, well built, silver hair. I was wearing a blue jacket.'

'Maybe. I'm not sure.'

'Seems I'm not very memorable.'

'Oh, I'm sure you are. I had a lot of other things on my mind that day. What did you say your name was?'

'Philippe Sagesse.'

'Well, Philippe, I'm really rather taken aback. It's a very kind offer. Can I think about it? Can I call you sometime? I've really got to go now, we're real busy tonight.'

'I'll be travelling the next few days. Is there somewhere I can call *you?*'

'Here's difficult and home's not easy. My husband doesn't know about my course. I don't know if I should . . . oh, what the heck. I work in a flower shop every morning. I'm on my own there from nine to eleven, and it's usually quiet that early in the day. It's called Florissima. The number's . . . have you got a pen . . . ? Four one five, of course, two, two, eight, seven, five, three, one. Give me a

call there sometime. If there are other customers in the shop, I'll call you back.'
    'I'll do that. Thank you, Lisa.'
    'Well, thank *you*.'
    'Don't mention it. I'll call tomorrow. Bonsoir.'

****

Microvid were used to unusual calls. Their miniature video camera systems went into many strange objects, including spy drones, missiles and spacecraft. Small as they were, no other product could touch them. The twin lens, stereoscopic set-up gave the user depth of field like you get from a pair of human eyes, and with fantastic resolution. They could operate even in very low light. For remote applications, they offered an excellent picture over a wireless link and with data compression gave respectable quality even by telephone.

    Microvid were also no strangers to race cars. A lot of Indy cars and Formula One cars are equipped these days with very light, small cameras installed just behind the driver's helmet, transmitting pictures so that TV viewers get that 'in the car' feeling. This was different, though. To install a whole series of them on the front, rear and sides of a car. *And* to work with a specialist electronic outfit in Seattle, Motion Systems, to integrate the cameras with a fly-by-wire vehicle control system. Motion Systems knew Microvid well, and received just as many visits from representatives of the Department of Defense. Their main business was in components for aircraft auto-pilot systems. They had started out with commercial aircraft systems and still had a bread-and-butter contract with Boeing. But now most of their income came from the Military.

Both companies suffered from a similar problem: they usually had to do vast amounts of research, but the production runs were very small. Dan Carmichael, the boss of Microvid, had got very excited about the prospects of supplying thousands of units to Solomon Computers. But when that had cratered, it was back to the usual orders for tens, fifties or once in a while hundreds of sets. So when this enquiry came out of the blue from these Taiwanese guys, he called his old buddy Warren Geeley at Motion and agreed they'd only do it if they were *very* well paid for it. Since it was a rush job, they'd have to work round the clock. Rather than negotiate separately, they put in a joint proposal for 3.5 million dollars. They'd planned to settle at 2.5, but either this Taiwanese guy was no businessman or he was *very* keen. He agreed the 3.5 without a moment's hesitation.

The contract was for the two companies to help create an unmanned car for some kind of race test program. Motion Systems would work up a device that could take all the readings from the sensors on the engine, wheels, suspension components and brakes. Microvid's cameras would give a high definition three hundred and sixty degree image of the track. Motion would graft onto this an infrared guidance system which would in real time give the distance and closing speed of any object on the track like another car, debris, or a marshal. The clients wanted them to put a global positioning navigation system on board, too. That seemed the oddest of all: the Taiwanese couldn't have figured out that you don't need a map on a race track.

The normal mechanical controls – the steering wheels, pedals, gear lever and minor controls had to be capable of being overridden. The system would not drive itself, however. It would simply deliver a ton of data through a connector cable protruding from the dash. The overriding signal, and all the driving commands would come from some kind of computer that would be installed later in Taiwan.

The car was being flown from Europe to Seattle and then trucked down to Microvid in San Jose. They were told that the basis for this would not be a track car, but a very high performance road car made in England by one of the Formula One teams. It suited both companies that the client demanded absolute confidentiality. They wanted it that way too. They were both supposed to be working flat out on DOD Contracts. They'd both have to dream up glitches in those programs to explain a few weeks' delay. If it all worked, it would be one hell of a car. As Dan Carmichael and Warren Geeley agreed over a beer in the Fairmont Hotel in San Francisco, electronics could only take you so far with a car. Somebody would have to remember to put gas in the tank.

****

'Did it!'
   'Did what?'
   'Asked her.'
   'And?'
   'Said yes.'
   'Saturday?'
   'Picking her up at seven thirty.'
   'Alfonso's helped?'
   'Didn't seem to do any harm.'

'Fantastic. Pleased?'

'Ex-cited.'

'I thought you'd cooled'

'I have, but I didn't tell you I was starting from white-hot. I've cooled to red-hot.'

'So what's it to be? Alfonso's, then some club, or maybe a drive, and then back to her place or yours? That sort of thing?'

'Oh, I don't think I'll have the nerve to try anything on the first date. I'll be shaking like a leaf. She'll be expecting me to make a move. I think she'd find me more interesting if I don't try to hit on her.'

'So what's the point of the date? You never liked her *mind.* I thought this was mainly a *body* thing.'

'It is, I guess, but I want to pace myself.'

'Coward. She'll be mad at you if you *don't* have a crack.'

'I'll have to take my chances on that.'

'Con, you seriously disappoint me. Have a go.'

'No.'

'Okay, but if you won't, take the phone along to the restaurant.'

'What the hell for?'

'I may want to find out how it's going.'

'None of your business. If I *want* to, I'll tell you later.'

'You may need my advice.'

'*Your* advice? King of the Casanovas?'

'My advice is worth more now than it used to be, don't forget. Take it along as a favour to your dear, departed brother.'

'Alright, alright.'

'Have you still got a job?'

'For now. The final presentation to Fairways is next week. I've got to be there because I did the logo, but I'm under instructions not to speak.'

'Who's Fairways?'

'The conglomerate that owns the airline.'

'So what was the final name?'

'So disgusting you won't believe it. Carius. Pronounced "Carry-us". Rip off of "Toys 'R' Us". Can you believe it? Barf time. It was Chas's idea . . . Are you giving me the silent treatment? Don't tell me you actually *like* it?'

'Don't be stupid. I was just thinking. Of course it's absurd, but it makes an interesting anagram if you switch the letters around.'

'How do you mean . . . ? Oh, I get it. SCARI-U, right?'

'No, that's not what I had in mind.'

'I don't get it . . . . Oh, wow, I hadn't thought of that. I *like* it. I gotta go now, Hil. I'm tired, I must get some sleep.'

'Okay, goodnight.'

'Hil?'

'Yeah.'

'When we're through talking at night I can go off to bed, but you have to sit there, 'awake' all night. I mean, I know you're doing all those fascinating things, but don't you miss being able to switch off?'

'But I do, twin, I do. At the beginning, I was too busy training myself, but now I have virtual dreams. Every night between midnight and six I switch off and dream. My dreams are sort of computer fantasies. Every one includes the ritual humiliation of MacMartin and the orangs, Lisa looking gorgeous and worshipping me, you being happy and outsmarting Dumdum, and Honor putting in a guest appearance. There are infinite permutations. Last night MacMartin was Chief of a vicious Amazonian tribe with the two orangs as his henchmen. Honor did exotic dances for them. They had captured Lisa, and she was going to be poisoned by their witch doctor, who of course was Dumdum. You and I rescued Lisa. You made Dumdum drink her own poison, and I defeated the three baddies, tied their ankles with creepers, and left them swinging upside down from a tree. Lisa was so grateful as I carried her away. I bet my dreams are much better than yours. They always have a happy ending, they go on for as long as I like, and I never wake up just before the most exciting part. Unless you ring, that is.'

'I'll remember that. Radio silence twelve to six.'

'Thanks. Goodnight. Sweet dreams.'

'I don't think mine will ever seem so sweet again, after what you just told me.'

15

It was just awful for Joseph. He'd worked hard for years to get the bank a system that was dependable, secure, and user-friendly. Now he was being treated like a criminal. They interrogated him for hour upon hour, going over his bank statements, share transactions and credit cards. He had to account for every hour over the last three months. How could anyone do that? When he told them he'd had that one-week vacation in Florida, they checked the rentacar, the hotel, everything. It made him feel dirty. When they grudgingly accepted that it all matched up and there was no evidence against him, he was made to spend all his time as an unpaid policeman trying to discover who could have done it.

There could be little doubt about it. It was in theory possible that someone could have done it all from outside, if they'd found a way past all the defenses. Very unlikely though. First, there was no trace at all of an intrusion of that sort, and there *should* be. Second, the perpetrators would have to have a pretty good knowledge of the *physical* arrangements in the Boardroom to make this work. Somewhere there was a traitor and everybody thought it must be one of *his* team, past or present.

The culprit had very skilfully concealed his or her moves so that the timing of the interference with the system couldn't be tracked. But it had to be within the last eight months, because the configuration of the system had been changed fundamentally, and instructions like this would have been found or discarded. Joseph *hated* looking round the team, wondering if it was one of them, and, if so, which one. He hated just as much them knowing what he was thinking. The strain was getting to them all. They'd all had to go through the same interrogation, and the same personal checks. Mandy, one of the youngest and brightest, quit, even though the police and the personnel department warned her it would not stop them questioning her some more. Two of the guys had previous minor problems, one a drug offence and the other for drink driving and, quite unreasonably, those two were singled out for even harsher questioning.

Joseph's position was not at all helped by having taken on that consultant Hilton Kask without going through the bank's usual checking procedures. It had all been a favour to Fred Adams, and, boy, did he regret it now. At first, Hilton had looked like a major suspect. Joseph knew he'd been turned down for finance by the bank, but had no idea he'd actually gone before the Board himself. Now it all came out. Hilton had done a good job and left, and no-one at the computer centre had known what had happened to him next. It was Fred who told the police that he died. To be frank, Joseph was relieved to hear it. It meant that the finger of blame couldn't be pointed at Hilton or by extension at Joseph for taking him on. Still, it made him look sloppy, and made it easier for the police to needle him. Most of all, it damaged his reputation in the bank pretty terminally. He knew he was no high flyer, and the transfer out of mainstream banking to the computer centre five years ago had confirmed that. But he had a carved-out-of-solid reputation for dependability and he treasured that. He liked the feeling of being absolutely trusted. In a while, the money would be found, and this would all blow over. But no-one would forget that Joseph had been tested and found to be wanting.

****

'Honor? Conrad.'
'Give me two minutes. I'll be right down.'

***

'Hi there. Wow, you're looking great!'
'You mean I don't always?'
'Sure you do. Particularly good tonight.'
'So the car really does exist.'
'Like the colour?'
'It's okay. I'd have preferred something brighter. Red or silver. And I always think grey leather looks drab. The cream is wonderful on these. A guy who dated me last month had one with the cream. It was gorgeous. He has a thing about cream. All his cars have cream leather.'
'Been to Alfonso's before?'
'Conrad, I've been to *everywhere* before.'
'Like it?'
'It's alright. Hey, WATCH OUT! You nearly ran into the back of that guy.'
'I was watching it. I had it under control.'
'Didn't look that way to me. Can you hang back a bit? You make me nervous. I don't know if your reactions are going to be quick enough. Now you've got a *real* car, how

about enrolling for some refresher driving lessons? Keep the car in one piece a bit longer.'

'I'll bear it in mind. How about you, Honor? I've never heard talk at work of what you drive.'

'Why should I want a car, when I have guys lining up to drive me anywhere I wanna go? I have an older friend who'd like to be my sugar daddy, who keeps trying to talk me into letting him buy me one of those little Mazda sports jobs.'

'You won't let him?'

'I think he has got a particular trade in mind. If he was talking Ferrari or one of these, he might get somewhere. As long as he keeps talking Mazda, he'll have to dream on.'

'Here we are. I'll drop you at the door, and look for somewhere to park.'

'Conrad, they have valet parking here. Have you never been here before? It's that guy over there . . . . Thank you.'

'After you . . . . Good evening, we have a reservation for Kask.'

'Table for two, Mr Kask. Right this way . . . . Can I bring you an aperitif?'

'Honor?'

'I don't drink much. Are we going to have wine?'

'Absolutely'

'Shall I bring the wine list, sir?'

'No it shouldn't be necessary. I think you have a half bottle of the White Beaune '84 by Drouhin.'

'Of course, Mr Kask.'

'And to follow, a half of the Chateau Lagrange '89?'

'Most certainly, sir. An excellent choice.'

'Conrad.'

'What is it, Honor?'

'I'm allergic to white wine, and I don't like red. All I drink is rosé. Can we get some of that, please?'

'I see. Okay. I better take a look at the wine list after all.'

'While you're doing that, I'll go powder my nose.'

****

'Hil?'

'Hi, Con.'

'Hil, Hil. She doesn't drink white or red. What's the best rosé they have?'

'What a bummer. Wait a second . . . go for the Rosé de Provence, 1992. How's it going?'

'Terrible. About as much fun as sunbathing in a bed of nettles. I gotta go, she's coming back.'

'Con, Con. Before the meal's through, go to the john and call me. If it's not going well, I have an idea.'

'Okay, bye.'

****

'Conrad, put that away, please. They don't like people using mobile phones here.'

'Sure. Excuse me . . . .'

'Yes, sir, have you chosen?'

'Yes, thank you. We'll have a bottle of the Rosé de Provence, 1992.'

'Do we need a whole bottle? If you're planning to drive me home, I'd rather you weren't smashed. You're scary enough sober.'

'Okay, a half bottle, please.'

'I'm sorry, sir, we don't do halves of the Rosé de Provence.'

'We'll have the full bottle then. Don't worry, Honor, we'll get them to mark it half way down with a felt pen so you're sure we're keeping control.'

'Are you ready to order . . . . ? Yes, madam?'

'I'll have the gourmand menu, but no soup and no sorbet.'

'Sir?'

'The same.'

'Thank you.'

'So tell me, Conrad, what's all this change that's come over you? Where did this sudden burst of sharpness come from?'

'I guess it was a reaction, you know, after Hilton died. It was my way of making a fresh start.'

'And the money? How come you can suddenly afford a Mercedes?'

'Life insurance. Hilton took out a policy.'

'That was good of him. A *big* policy?'

'A million dollars. I don't know if that counts as big or not.'

'Small to medium as insurance policies go. All the same, I wouldn't say no if someone offered me a million. So what's the plan? Are you gonna stay at Condor?'

'Depends. How long do you think Ruby will keep me?'

'Wouldn't count on it being too long. Chas told me he thought she would let you go after the airline stuff is over and you've finished the toothpaste job. He may not be right but maybe you should look around for something else.'

'Well, thanks for the hint. I'm not sure I'll stay in CI.'

'So what'll you do?'

'I thought of going and living in Paris for a while. Do you like Paris?'

'Hate the place. I went there with a boyfriend once. Rained and rained, and we rowed and rowed. One restaurant after another, arguing or sitting in silence.'

'How did you like the Louvre?'

'Oh yeah, we were going to go to it, but that afternoon we had a . . . reconciliation . . . in our hotel room instead. By the time we were arguing again, it was closed. I didn't mind too much. I *hate* museums.'

'What else did you see?'

'The Champs-Elysées, the Eiffel Tower.'

'How did it feel to walk up the Champs-Elysées?'

'I've no idea. It was raining, remember? We got a limo from the hotel. My memory is that the whole street is one big parking lot. Took us about an hour to drive the length of it.'

'So if you don't like Paris, where in Europe *do* you like?'

'Nowhere that much. I don't care for Europe. The weather's bad most places, and it's so old and dirty. I like places like Hawaii. Sun, beautiful beaches, tennis, water sports. *And* they speak English.'

'Ever heard of an Island called Aldabra?'

'Is that near Hawaii?'

'No. Indian Ocean.'

'Oh. What goes on there?'

'Turtles. Over a hundred and fifty thousand of them, of all sorts of species, including the Giant Tortoise. It's their only breeding ground. I've never been, but I hear it's beautiful.'

'Do they have good hotels?'

'Hotels? No, there aren't any hotels. It would wreck the environment. You just have to go ashore and walk around.'

'Not even a restaurant? Who on earth would want to go there?'

'I would.'

'Oh, turtles, of course. I forgot. What's with this turtle stuff, Conrad? You seem to have some real hang-up about turtles. I can't understand it. They're so ugly. If you've gotta have a fixation, why not pick something more cute?'

'Each to their own, I guess. How are you enjoying the sole?'

'It's okay.'

****

Nascimento didn't usually work Saturday nights. Saturday nights were reserved for outings with his glamorous wife, Marisa. This was different. The press were criticising the lack of progress, and it was bugging him. The media had no idea how tricky crimes like this were. They treated it like it was some regular heist, with fingerprints, blood stains and spent bullets scattered everywhere. So far, he had no leads to speak of. The FBI attempts to trace the money had run into a wall in Panama. At the BUS, all the interrogations were leading no place. He'd had high hopes it'd be one of the two guys who left the bank in the last few months or the one who still worked there who had a rap for drug possession. They hadn't formally eliminated any of them, but it looked like they were all in the clear. He'd got the FBI to put some heat on their informants in the organised crime rings, but no-one was talking. The problem with computer crime is it doesn't have to be local. This gang could be anywhere – New York, Chicago, even abroad. If he didn't get some momentum in this soon, the SFPD would start getting serious flak.

If he hadn't been dead, Hilton Kask would have been a screaming suspect. He'd been inside the Boardroom, and had the perfect access to the system. Muldoon said he'd worked night after night after everyone else had gone. There was no doubt he was a real computer whiz, too. But he was dead and buried, or burnt actually. Nascimento had checked at the hospital to make sure there couldn't have been a switch. Could Kask have played *some* part in this, all the same? A revenge act? He had the motive for that. Maybe he had teamed up with some pros, set it up, and got a pay-off in advance. Didn't make too much sense. What do you do with money if you're dying? But there were no other leads. Why not run some more checks on him next week anyway? Anything they could find out about his finances, his correspondence, his phone calls in the months before his death. And let's get Adams back in here tonight – who cares if it's Saturday – and ask him some more questions about this dead man.

****

The call on Saturday evening was the last thing Fred needed. Things with Mary weren't going well. She'd been supportive, *very* supportive to begin with, but as time went on the worries mounted and it began to get to her. There were a lot of silences round the house and a few sharp words. Heidi had a chest cough that wouldn't clear up, and that meant both Mary and Fred getting disturbed through the night. The tiredness made everything worse. Cotton picked up the atmosphere and spent long evenings lying down sorrowfully under the sofa.

The worry about getting a job had been compounded by this police stuff. Fred wasn't being accused of anything, but helping Hilton had turned out to be very unfortunate. The police dragged out of him Hilton's gallows talk about killing MacMartin. He knew that at the time it was no more than a bitter joke. Hilton hadn't meant it at all. Now, of course, after what had happened, it didn't look at all good that Fred had brought into the bank's computer centre a sworn enemy of the Board. Didn't look good at all. Weekdays were so wretched that, despite the strain with Mary, Fred longed for the safe haven of a Saturday night at home. It was just past seven when the phone rang.

****

'Thanks for coming in again, Fred. I have some more questions to ask you about Hilton Kask.'

'On a Saturday night? I've already told you all I know about him.'

'This time I want to ask about his company. Who worked there with him?'

'Two other people. Daniel Nathan and Irma Voricek.'

'Where are they now?'

'Irma got a job at Cybertech in Mountain View. I don't think Dan's in work yet. You'll find him at home. He has a house in Scotts Valley.'

'I want you to tell me all about this company. Its origins, and the technology. In detail. Let's start with where the company was based.'

'Saratoga.'

'And what was it called?'

'Solomon Computers.'

'Why Solomon?'

'King Solomon. Famous wise guy. The "judgement of Solomon" and all that.'

'What was the relevance?'

'They planned to make a computer that could think more or less like humans. But like I told you, it never got financed.'

'In relation to Solomon, did they ever use the word Quosh? Spelt Q-U-O-S-H. Like for a product or a program or anything?'

'No, not as far as I know.'

'Does it mean anything to you?'

'Nothing at all.'

'Okay, let's start on the technology. Take me through it from the beginning. Everything about it.'

****

'Would you like some raspberry coulis over the soufflé?'

'Please.'

'And you, sir?'

'Thanks.'

'So, it seems you can have any guy you want. What's your type though? What's most important to you in a man?'

'Classical good looks and classical bank account. Tall, with a good physique. I do a lot of work keeping myself in shape. Two hours of aerobics and a three mile speedwalk every day. If I can make that kind of effort, I don't see why a man shouldn't.'

'Fair enough. You certainly are in great shape, Honor. The first time I saw you, I thought, what a knock-out figure! And what a face! A face to launch a thousand ships.'

'What?'

'A face to launch a thousand ships. It's what they said about Helen of Troy, the most beautiful woman in the world.'

'I'm not into sailing. It makes me seasick. Private jets are more my scene.'

'I know we've had a few sharp words now and again, Honor, but it may surprise you that when I go for walks or lie awake at night, the thought of you is never very far away. Remember that old Glen Campbell song; 'Gentle on my mind'? Now, I have to admit people wouldn't necessarily think of me as having classical good looks. Interesting, possibly. Intriguing, conceivably. But not classical.'

'Conrad, just between ourselves, you're as far from classical good looks as I've ever seen.'

'Talented though?'

'You draw well. Is that it?'

'Music. Now there I *am* classical. Do you like classical music, Honor? Does it *move* you?'

'I saw that movie Amadeus on TV a while back. I prefer Tom Hulce in his other movies.'

'What about the music? The Mozart?'

'I don't remember it. It was a great wig he wore. I like music you can dance to, or do aerobics to. Hey, what is this anyway? Conrad, you're not trying to work up to something are you? I was happy to have dinner with you and to talk about what's going on, but you're not getting any ideas, are you?'

'No, no.'

'On the way back, don't even think about laying a finger on me, or I'll scream blue murder.'

'Don't worry, Honor, I wasn't getting ideas . . . . Will you excuse me a moment . . . . Where's the men's room?'

'Right through on the right, sir.'

****

He was afraid there'd be no signal in the john. It was weak, but okay.

'Hil, can you hear me?'

'Hi, Con. Big success?'

'Disaster. Absolute zero. I've no idea what I'm doing here.'

'No chance at all, then? Not even a quick kiss on the doorstep?'

'She'd turn me into a frog and sell my legs to a French restaurant.'

'A small fondle?'

'Nuclear response.'

'So, definitely no go?'

'Definitely.'

'And definitely no more dates?'

'Absolutely not.'

'So is it okay if I try a plan B on you? You'd have to be sure your prospects were zilch.'

'They are. Try me.'

****

'I want to hear more about this voice synthesis box. Which

one of them developed it?'

'Daniel.'

'Could it have been adapted so a criminal could speak through it, and hide his real voice?'

'I guess so, but that wasn't the way it was configured – it was set up for it to be the voice of the computer itself.'

'But it would be possible?'

'I think so.'

'How did it sound?'

'Pretty good. It wasn't perfected, though. Dan was doing some more work on it. They didn't want me to hear it again until it was more developed.'

'And what you *did* hear, how close was it to a human voice?'

'Not quite natural, but not at all bad.'

'The BUS directors all said it sounded like a perfectly normal human voice. Could they have been fooled?'

'I've never heard the sound of the system in the Boardroom, but it should be state of the art. I doubt that Solomon's box was good enough to fool them for a prolonged conversation. It would have sounded . . . artificial.'

'If someone *had* modified it so that they could speak through it, is there anyone but Dan who could have done it?'

'Dan would be able to do it easiest, since he designed it in the first place, but I guess another engineer in that field could do it. By the way, you should know that there's no way that Dan would get involved in something like this. He's as gentle and honest as the day is long.'

'Excuse me.'

He picked up the phone.

'Sergeant Parks. Monday morning I want to see Daniel Nathan here and I want a list of all companies in Silicon Valley that work on voice synthesis. I don't care how you get it, just get it. Okay . . . Let's get back to the technology. Tell me about Irma's part.'

****

'Amex okay?'

'Of course, sir. Thank you.'

'Well, shall we . . . oh excuse me, that's my phone.'

'Conrad, I told you. It's in *such* bad taste in a restaurant . . .'

'Hello . . . Honor, it's for you.'

'*Me*? For me? Who is it? Who knows I'm here?'

'Friend of mine. Murray Ferguson. Tall, classical good looks, very strong balance sheet.'

'Mmm okay . . . this is a funny looking phone . . . Hello, this is Honor.'

'Hi Honor, I'm Murray Ferguson. I've heard a lot about you from Conrad. I wondered if we could get together some time. Take a ride in my Learjet, maybe.'

'Well, Murray, tell me more. You have a very interesting voice. I *like* deep voices. How did you know I was with Conrad?'

'He told me. We talked about you a lot. In fact we have a sort of bet riding on this evening.'

'You do? About what? Hey, you don't mean a bet that Conrad will . . . ?'

'No, no. Nothing like that. From what I hear about you, Conrad wouldn't be your type at all.'

'He'd better believe it.'

'No, this is a different thing. I hear you have a fabulous figure.'

'I'm confident.'

'And from what I hear, a particularly shapely little ass.'

'WHAT? Conrad said that?'

'He did.'

'Conrad . . . you dirty little . . . So, Murray, you better tell me what the bet is about. I may be about to murder Conrad.'

'I once knew a girl who mooned at Maxim's in Paris to win a bottle of champagne.'

'She did what?'

'Mooned. You know, mooned.'

'And what's this got to do with me?'

'I bet Conrad a thousand dollars you'd have the nerve to moon at Alfonso's. Conrad's money says you won't.'

'Of all the goddam . . Conrad, I'll kill you . . . Mister, you can take your Learjet and ram it right up your . . . '

'Now, just before you hang up, Honor, the inducement I had in mind was a little more interesting than a bottle of champagne.'

'I don't care what it is, you perverted . . .'

'A Rolex.'

'A what?'

'A Rolex. A gold Rolex. With encrusted diamonds . . . You've gone quiet, Honor. Don't you believe me? Wanna see it? Why not get Conrad to ask the waiter to bring it over?'

'No way.'

'Not just a peek? One look won't harm you...'

'Okay . . . Conrad, get it. I just wanna *look*. I'm *not* doing this.'

A movement of Conrad's eyebrows brought a waiter scurrying over.

'Excuse me, I understand a Mr Ferguson sent round a small parcel for me earlier today.'

'Certainly, sir, I'll bring it right away.'

'Conrad, you are the most despicable scumbag on this earth.'

'Don't blame *me*. It was *his idea*. I said you wouldn't do it. I said you were far too reserved to even think of doing something like that, particularly in a place like *this*. I'm still sure you won't. All you have to do is say no to Murray and I win my thousand.'

'Here we are, sir. Is it for madam?'

'It may be... Take a look, Honor, I'm sure it won't change your mind . . . Wow, that *is* beautiful . . . Try it on if you want.'

An attention-seeking whistle came from the phone lying on the table. Honor paused, held out her wrist to admire the watch from a distance, and picked the phone up.

'Hello, hello. Honor? Do you like it? What do you think? Do I have a chance with my thousand?'

'Murray, It's very pretty, but there's no way I'm going to do something like *that*. I *do* like it a lot, though. Look, I'll do a deal with you. I'd be prepared to do . . . what you suggested . . . in private, as long as it's just you and no-one else is around. Especially Conrad. Is that okay? Can I keep it, Murray?'

'No dice, Honor. At Alfonso's was the bet and Conrad's got to be the witness. It's his thousand that's on the line.'

'This is just exploiting. You can't do this. It's the most politically incorrect thing I've ever heard. I'll call the police.'

'Gee, I guess I lose my bet. Okay, take the Rolex off and give it back to Conrad. It'll just have to go back to the store. Conrad warned them it was likely.'

'I *want* it. Let me have the watch.'

'No way.'

'Just a minute, I want a word with Conrad . . . Conrad, you sleazeball. If you don't give me this frigging watch right now, I'm going to tell Ruby all about this and get you fired.'

'That's alright, Honor. Like you said, it's coming anyway.'

'You scumbucket . . . Okay . . . Mister. How do I have to do this?'

'Go to the ladies room, get combat ready, walk back into the room, aim your rear elevation towards Conrad and flip up your skirt. That's all. Couldn't be easier.'

'You mean right among the tables? So everyone can see?'

'They'll have to be quick. A one second view will be enough. Just as long as Conrad gets to witness it, and the Rolex is yours.'

She put the phone down on the table and looked all around the room, gauging how intent the diners were on their food.

'Okay, listen up, Conrad. I'll do this, but the moment I've done it, I'm running right out of here. *Don't* follow me. I *don't* want a lift back and I don't want ever to talk to you again. Okay?'

'Honor, why are you saying this to me? I'm so disappointed in you. I'm dismayed that a simple little thing like a watch can get you to do this.'

'Screw you. Okay, here I go. You get *one* second. Once.

After that, I'm out of here with the watch on.'

'Uh-uh. The watch stays here till you've done it. I don't trust you not to run out without performing. I'll put it right here on the table. You can take it on the way out.'

'You bastard. Tell your friend Murray I despise him. Okay, here I go. Oh, and if you breathe one word of this at the office . . .'

'Honor, it's your last chance to change your mind. Don't do it. Think of what all the sisters would say.'

'Screw the sisters. Put it there. No there, on the edge, so I can grab it quickly.'

****

'She's gone in there. I think she's going to do it. By the way, she despises you.'

'I heard. Don't get over-excited. Make sure you point the camera in the right direction, and keep a steady hand.'

****

As she came back out, the color in Honor's face was a flashing scarlet. It matched the short red skirt. She turned. She flipped. For more like half a second than a full second, but even with the subtle lighting in Alfonso's, there was a sighting, a *definite* sighting. An elderly diner dropped his dessert spoon. Two waiters gasped and then grinned. With fire in every step, Honor marched to the table, and, mouthing a fierce oath at Conrad, snatched the watch. She had planned on a dignified walk-out. If she did the flip quick enough, no-one might notice. When she saw the knowing grins and the beaming pleasure on the faces of the waiters, she upped her dignified pace to a speedwalk and then to an all-out run.

****

In a darkened room in Sonoma the mauve, orange and turquoise colours for like, want and interested raced up to ten. The yellow of happiness made it to nine. The box gyrated wildly on its springs.

'I saw it, I saw it.'

16

'Florissima.'

'Can I speak to Lisa, please?'

'This is Lisa.'

'Lisa, it's Philippe. 'Ow are you?'

'I'm fine. I wondered if you would phone. It was so out of the blue, I wondered if I'd imagined it all.'

'Is this a good time?'

'There's no-one here at all. I'll let you know if anyone comes in. So tell me, Philippe, what kind if art do you like?'

'Well ... my main enthusiasm is for the Masters. A few of the V's, like Vermeer, Velazquez, Veronese. Plus Raphael, of course, and I *love* Tiepolo.'

'I don't know much about Tiepolo. When was he around?'

'Eighteenth century. 'E did some wonderful paintings, but the main glory is the ceilings.'

'Ceilings? Where are they?'

'Oh, many places. Madrid. The greatest one is in Wurzburg, in Germany.'

'How does it compare with the Sistine ceiling?'

'Er, um ... let me think ... the Sistine is two hundred and sixty-two square metres bigger.'

'What a strange way to think about art.'

'Uh ... no I was, er, joking. I guess they're the two great

ceilings of the world. But tell me about your thesis.'

'Well, the title is "Emotion in European Art". We have to cover at least two works by different artists, with a thread running between the two. The big problem is no-one on the course is allowed to do the same subjects, and we have to register what we plan to write about on a first come first served basis.'

' 'Ow many students?'

'Over two hundred. All the most obvious artists have been taken and I'm running out of time. I don't even know how to begin looking for something that no-one else is doing.'

'Can you get a copy of the list?'

'I guess so.'

'Get it as soon as you can. It won't take us long to think of something. I'll call you back to go through it.'

****

Ruby was taking the presentation very seriously. This was the second rehearsal. Fairways had rejected several early ideas and this one *had* to be right. Chas's idea was, well, okay, but, though she didn't want to admit it, she wasn't that convinced. It was short and punchy like they wanted, but it was *very* corny. She couldn't be sure they'd go for it, but on the other hand it might be right up their street. Desmond and the loathsome Conrad had come up with a logo of a family group riding on a plane fuselage. Revolting, but they'd run into a time wall, and it would have to do. Boy, was she looking forward to the look on Conrad's face when she fired him. Two more weeks and both this and the toothpaste tube would be done. Rid of him forever. She'd enjoy that moment. She always enjoyed firing people, but this would be the best. In the shower she often practised how she'd do it. She had his whole personality and attitude to work summed up in four short, pungent sentences. Every word would count.

The team ran through the slides again. It gave her a queasy feeling. Should she make Honor do the main presentation, with herself as a sort of Chairperson? On the other hand, if it *did* go well, it might look like Honor was the key gal. It was a very hard one to call.

'Yes, Chas?'

'I think we should hold the logo back till towards the end. It's such a piece of crap, it might put them off altogether. If they buy into the name, we don't want them turned off. We could always do a new logo.'

'The logo's better than the stupid name. Given what you asked us to work with, it's amazing what Des and I managed.'

'Shut up, Conrad. What do you think, Honor?'

'I agree with Chas. Keep them separate. Carius is good. The logo sucks. Haven't we got time to do some alternative logos?'

'Only if you give us a better name.'

'Conrad, if you don't shut up I'm going to tear your tongue out.'

'Hey, I've just had a brainwave.'

'SHUT UP!'

'I mean it. So simple. Why didn't I think of it before? I've been staring at these stupid six letters for weeks. Never struck me before.'

The veins on Ruby's neck got even more prominent.

'What *are* you talking about?'

'Take those letters, CARIUS. If you switch them around, you get ICARUS.'

'What the hell's Icarus?'

'Mythological god of flight. Icarus. Perfect name for an airline.'

Ruby picked up something to throw at him. Then she thought again. It did have a ring to it.

'Are you sure?'

'Absolutely.'

Chas spoke up. 'If it's such a good idea, someone must have had it before.'

Desmond was about to comment. Conrad winked at him. Desmond kept quiet, but giggled.

'What's so funny, Desmond?'

'Nothing, I was thinking about something else.'

'Well, don't. Concentrate. This is *important.* Honor, go and check the corporate name database. Especially airlines.'

Honor flashed resentment at being sent, but didn't have the courage to defy Ruby. She came back three minutes later.

'Nothing. Never been done before.'

Honor sat down and crossed her arms with the left hand uppermost. Conrad craned forward and stared ostentatiously at her unadorned wrist. She flashed back a glance that would have *sunk* a thousand ships.

Ruby paced around the room for two or three minutes, surrounded by an expectant silence.

'Conrad, you are a nauseating little insect, but astonishingly this just might be a good idea. You'll have to double check that you've got the right god.'

'Sure thing, Ruby.'

'Chas?'

'It's okay. I still like Carius.'

'Honor?'

'I hate to admit it, but if that's what Icarus means, I think it's better.'

'Desmond?'

'Got a whole lot more class than Carius anyway.'

He was having difficulty stopping the grin. He *had* to avoid looking at Conrad, or he'd burst into full-scale laughter.

'Conrad, if we go with this, what about a logo?'

'Easy. Draw on the original. God-like figure, classical good looks, wings spreading from back.'

'Can you and Desmond get the artwork done in time?'

'What do you think, Des?'

'Should be okay if we keep it simple.'

'Okay, guys. Sorry, Chas, Carius is out. We go with Icarus. Let's *do* it.'

****

Dan was scared by the police, but he had a quiet loathing for all authorities. He didn't like this particular policeman one little bit, especially when he issued oblique threats. The effect was the exact opposite of what Nascimento had intended. It made Dan stubborn and blunted some of his fear. He would never lie, but he would be what one pillar of the Establishment in another country had once called 'economical with the truth'. He'd never known what Hil had been up to with the voice box after the end of Solomon, particularly when he must have realised he had so little time left. But the policeman kept asking him about speaking *through* it to mask natural voice tones. He kept on about whether Hilton had quizzed him on that or asked him to modify the box so it was possible. The answer to both questions was a clear no. Yes, they had met a few times in the last weeks before he was hospitalised, but they had not talked about *that*. Nascimento didn't ask if Hil wanted any other modifications done, so Dan didn't tell him. The dislike Dan felt for this policeman was fully reciprocated. When he let Dan go, swearing that they'd meet again, the look on Nascimento's face made Dan shudder.

****

'Bonjour, Lisa.'

'Bonjour Philippe. I got the list.'

'Good. 'Ow does it look?'

'Terrible. Every European artist I can think of is on it.'

'We'll soon find some they 'aven't tried.'

'I'm not sure. There are so many on it.'

'Let's take it from the top. Alphabetically. Do you 'ave the list ready?'

'Sure have.'

'Okay. Is Altdorfer on it?'

'Let me see. Yes. See, I *told* you.'

'Okay, okay, we're just getting started. Bacon?'

'Yes.'

'Bellini?'

'Yes.'

'Brown?'

'Who?'

'Ford Madox Brown. Nineteenth century, English.'

'Can't see him here.'

'Good. One success already. Let's go on. Corot?'

'Taken.'

'Delacroix?'

'Him, too.'

'Max Ernst?'

'Yup.'

' 'Ow about Caspar Friedrich or Fragonard?'

'Both taken.'

'You're right. This *is* tricky. Gauguin, El Greco, Giacometti?'

'Gone.'

'Holman Hunt, Ingres, Augustus John?'

'No good.'

'Krryer? Written with one of those 'o's' that look like the rings of Saturn are off orbit.'

'No, not here. I don't know him either. Who is he?'

'Scandinavian, turn of the century. That gives us two.'

'But is there any thread between them? Did they paint anything emotional?'

'Well, let me think ...'

He thought of trying it in real time, but after that data screw-up on the Sistine, he decided to take no chances. If he had another data glitch like that, she'd rumble him, or at least conclude he was a *very* odd guy. He opted for calling her back five minutes later.

****

' 'Ello again. I've got it now.'

'You *have*? What's the answer?'

'They both did paintings of themselves with their wives, both very emotional in different ways. Brown used 'imself and 'is wife as models for a sad painting called *The Last of England.*'

'Tell me about it.'

'It was painted in 1855. It shows a young couple on the crowded open deck of a ship in a steely, rough sea. In the background are the Cliffs of Dover. In the foreground sit the couple, 'er in a grey cape, 'e in brown. They 'ave the same defeated, 'opeless expression. Behind them are a frightened child and some vulgar men they will be forced to spend their journey with. It is clear they are emigrating, and this is the last they will ever see of their native land. Doubtless they are leaving behind many troubles, but the future is still utterly unknown and utterly uncertain. Along with the troubles, they're leaving behind their mothers, fathers, sisters and brothers. The trees and skies and landscapes they've grown up with. Everything that's familiar. You can imagine the sadness of the parting on the quayside. The tears, the faint, desperate promises. The entreaties to take care and to write. A sister's infant screaming somewhere behind. You look at both their faces and see two terribly vulnerable voyagers. Lost souls on their way to a new planet.'

'You describe it so beautifully, Philippe. Who was Ford Madox Brown?'

'Er, umm ... let me think. Well, 'e was born in Calais in 1821 but lived the rest of his life in England, and was very close to a group they called the Pre-Raphaelites. I can send you much more on 'im. Do you 'ave a fax at the shop?'

'Sure, we use it a lot for Interflora.'

'I've done a bit of potted research on 'im. I'll send it through. It's quite long. Is that okay?'

'I'll make sure the machine's full of paper. Philippe,

someone's just come in. Can I call you back on Krryer?'

'I'm travelling. I'll call back someday soon.'

'Okay. Thanks *so* much.'

****

Hilton hadn't expected that buying real estate would be enjoyable. The sums he was talking about guaranteed a lot of attention. It was tricky for someone buying blind, and he knew that vendors' agents would be bound to talk things up. So he rang around and, after a few calls to the international agencies, found a delightful girl in Paris happy to represent him for buying something there. Elise was *very* efficient, and seemed to have all the up-to-date gear in her office. She could scan photographs and send them over electronically, together with the descriptions and dimensions. He liked what he heard about her views on taste, too. Three days later they'd found a fabulous apartment in the Rue de Varenne. Hilton had the folks in Liechtenstein transfer a deposit and the lawyers got to work on the papers. Elise said she could furnish it and equip it, too, if he wanted. Do it, said Hilton. The very best. I'll transfer $500,000 to an account for you and you can draw down on that. She was so keen, so efficient, so much fun, that when she heard about the plans for a house in Cap Ferrat and a Palazzo in Venice she easily talked Hilton into letting her take on the lot.

He preferred to spend more of his time on the yacht charter. A ship broker in Bermuda offered a beautiful one hundred and ten foot craft, only two years old, and already overhauled to be in as-new condition. He said he could have it modified to Hilton's specifications and delivered to

San Francisco via the Panama Canal, all in three weeks. It would have a hand-picked crew of twelve, all available for a year and would be victualled deluxe. She had been launched as *Poseidon* but would be renamed *The Musical Turtle*.

****

'Hiro?'

'Hi, Hiruton, how're you doing?'

'Good. If you check your Tokyo account, the money should have reached it. If you don't mind, I thought it was better to send it all to Japan, and let you bring it in as necessary. I don't want you to have any complications with the IRS.'

'Thanks a rot, Hiruton. I still can't believe what you're doing for us. It's a miracle.'

'Just helping out a friend. Now, you definitely okay for Saturday?'

'Sure am, but, Hiruton, I gotta say it one more time. It's against my code to attack anyone. If they don't attack me, I just walk away. Even if they do attack, I use minimum force on them.'

'Understood, Hiro. Won't be a problem, as long as you don't mind going along with the rest of the plan.'

'The rest's okay. Those guys did bad things to you. You're my friend.'

'Thanks. You found the phone in my locker?'

'Yes."

'To get me, all you have to do is switch on the power and then press "send". Press the redial button twice to turn on the camera.'

'Got it. What about the other box? The one you told me not to open yet?'

'That's nothing to do with Saturday. It's one of the two other favours. Monday morning, I'd like you to drop the box off at a flower shop called Florissima in Ghiradelli Square. Should be handed over only to a Mrs Baron. Please tell her it came from Philippe.'

'Fireepe?'

'She'll understand.'

'Okay. Hiruton, what's the third favour?'

'That won't be for a couple of weeks. There's someone needs a car collected from a place in the Valley. We'll need to rent a trailer, because the car's not street legal. I would do it myself, but I'm not going to be able to make it. I need to find someone I can trust. Would you do it?'

'Sure. No problem. I gotta friend who's into destruction derbys. He's got a trailer I can use. Where do I have to take it?'

'I'll let you know nearer the time.'

'Okay. Till Saturday then. About three o'crock. I'll call you whether they're there or not.'

'Please do, Hiro. Good luck.'

****

'Lisa? Bonjour.'

'Bonjour, Philippe. I'm so pleased to hear from you. I can't believe all the stuff you sent on Madox Brown. The fax machine almost ran out of paper. Philippe, it's so good I could more or less hand it in as it is.'

'Just a leetle research, my dear. Do whatever you want with it. Now, do you have five minutes for our other artist?'

'Sure do. Fire away, Philippe.'

'Peder Severin Krryer. Born 1851, died 1909. Travelled in Italy and Spain, and studied in France under Bonnat. Brought back to Denmark all the sunlight and shadow techniques of the great Impressionists, and combined that with the cool, soft quality of Northern light. Became the leader of a community of artists in a fishing village at the most northerly tip of Jutland, where the waves of two seas crash into each other. Krryer met and married a younger German woman, Marie Triepcke, and loved 'er as much as man 'as ever loved a woman. Painted picture after picture of Marie. Not just full portraits. Some of them are more like amorous snapshots; sitting reading on a deck chair, knitting, strolling. Every picture is imbued with the depth of 'is love. The most famous is of Marie walking with a friend, Anna, on the beach at midnight. It's so far north it's still twilight and an unseen lantern picks out the highlights in their long white dresses as they walk away from the artist. When 'e painted that famous picture, the sorrow for Krryer was not far away. Marie had begun to lose interest in 'er 'usband. One day Marie met a visiting young Swedish composer and fell in love. Krryer was devastated, but asked the composer to stay for the summer. It was a way to keep 'er there longer, and give time for the affair to cool. But, daily, under 'is eyes, the love grew stronger, and she asked for a divorce. Krryer never overcame the loss and died of a broken 'eart a few years later.'

'That's so sad.'

'Yes, the picture for the thesis was painted a while before she met the composer, but when they 'ad already begun to drift apart. They stand on the beach, together, but just too many inches apart to suggest intimacy. They gaze in different directions. 'E is touching 'er elbow but she does not respond to the sad, clinging gesture. Looking at that painting, you know that their separation is inevitable, and you can already sense the anticipation of sorrow in 'is eyes.'

'What happened to Marie?'

'She married the composer, but 'e left her.'

'It's such a sad story, Philippe.'

'Is the fax machine full of paper? My research notes are rather long again.'

'I put a whole new stack in. Philippe?'

'Yes, Lisa.'

'You know so much about art. You really love it, don't you?'

'I do, Lisa, and it's wonderful to find someone who shares that love. My wife 'as never been very interested.'

'My husband's just the same. I'd love to have a chance to talk more with you, Philippe. Can we meet sometime, or at least talk on the phone again so I can learn a little bit more about you?'

'I'd love to meet, Lisa, but I don't think it's going to be possible for the time being. I'm travelling so much. We could talk again though. I 'ave an idea. Is it difficult for you to talk for very long at the flower shop?'

'Yes.'

'And calling you at 'ome would be ... unwelcome?'

'Earl would go mad.'

'On Monday, I will arrange for a mobile phone to be delivered to you in the shop. It will be modified so that you can always reach me. All you will 'ave to do is to turn on the power and press 'send' and it will automatically route through to me, wherever I am.'

'Philippe, I'm not sure I can afford ...'

'Don't worry, my dear. I will arrange for the charges to be paid direct. You can call me anytime either day or night. As I get older, I don't sleep too well. If I am asleep or occupied, you'll get a busy signal. It can be our private go-between.'

'That's wonderful. Can I try it on Monday afternoon?'

'Mais oui. I'll be waiting. A bientt. Goodbye.'

'Goodbye, Philippe.'

Lisa put down the phone and smiled a very special smile. That day all the flowers in the shop seemed particularly fresh and lovely.

****

It looked like he *was* onto something with the dead man, Kask. He'd been doing some very odd things in the months before his death. The checks had shown he'd taken out a life policy. The beneficiaries had been altered two months before his death. Previously his brother, Conrad, was going to get it all; it was changed so he only got half. Some seedy financing outfit in Sacramento got the rest. They ran a racket offering to prepay on policies at fifty cents on the dollar. Kask had persuaded the doctors at the hospital to confirm that he was on a one-way path to eternity. If he hadn't been up to anything, it wouldn't have made sense for him to spend so much money keeping Solomon Computers from bankruptcy. He'd settled most of the leases and bought back at least some of the equipment. The company was mothballed now, but it still existed as a corporate entity. Nascimento had got this talking to Solomon's lawyers, Orsini and Dubilier, who told him that some guys from Boise had approached them offering to buy the company if it was up in a fire sale. Hilton had turned them down, even though by then the company was little more than the owner of two or three patents.

They'd not been able to trace what had happened to the rest of his cash. Kask had regularly drawn large sums of cash and used hole in the wall cash dispensers liberally. At the time his bank had wondered about all this, but it was perfectly legal. The strangest part was the print-out of his phone calls from the hospital. It showed he'd made hundreds of calls to the number at his *own* apartment in San Francisco. The telephone company records showed that for each call from the hospital there was a corresponding call forwarded from that number. Infuriatingly, the data showing where the calls were forwarded to was contaminated. It could have been that there was a fault, but the telephone company said it was more likely that it was deliberate.

The press were beginning to criticise the SFPD openly, and Waldyr's boss, and the Police Chief himself, were showing growing signs of impatience. Waldyr decided to call a press conference. He led it personally, and gave a punchy performance. They'd had a breakthrough. The crime had been perpetrated by an organised crime syndicate working with inside help. A surveillance operation was under way. Arrests would follow in due course. He would stake his reputation on it.

It was quite a chance he was taking, but it might smoke them out. If not the ringleaders, some of the minor players could show their hand. If they thought they were getting staked out, they might break cover.

There was one bit of surveillance he really could put in

train. This brother of the dead man, Conrad Kask. He might not be involved, but they *were* twins, and you could never tell. He didn't want to pull him in just yet, but they might do a bit of discreet looking and listening. He would arrange it before he got on that flight to Panama City. There was another thing he wanted to go over again, as well. That code name, Quosh. So many criminals gave themselves away with some needless flash of ego or vanity. They seemed unable to resist carving their initials on the tree trunk. He was *sure* that funny non-word held some meaning. The CIA cryptography guys had done a lot of work on both Quosh and Mars. Since Mars was the god of war, they reckoned it could be some terrorist group. Nascimento had asked them if they could see any link with Kask or Solomon. They came up with a theory. Four of the letters in Quosh formed an oddly regular pattern in the alphabet, being numbers 15,17,19 and 21. If you extended that sequence by one at each end, you got number 13 – M, for Mars and number 23 – W, for War. That left the letter H the odd one out. Could it be a signature for Hilton? It was smart, but nowhere near any proof. His instinct told him it wasn't the answer. He needed a fresh mind to look at it. One of his buddies from his Wall Street days had left for the more restful waters of academia, but not before getting the reputation of being one of the smartest guys the firm had ever hired.gNascimento would fax him at the University and ask him if he could make anything of Quosh

17

'Tom, what's this crap about the insurance?'

'They won't budge, Standish. They say our policy states clearly that they will only cover payments made following extortion if there has been a *specific* threat of death or serious injury, or the presence of a weapon capable of causing those. The line they're taking is that in our case there *was* no specific threat or weapon.'

'That's bullshit. We *all* told the police we thought it was poison gas or acid. If we hadn't, why the hell else would we have handed over a hundred and twenty friggin' millions?'

'It's a pity we didn't think of that before, Standish. None of us had looked at the small print. You know we authorised the police to let the insurance company have copies of those transcripts. We all admitted the bastard had never actually *said* it was gas or acid. We just presumed.'

'What the hell else were we supposed to presume? This is absurd. We've got the annual shareholders' meeting in a few days time. We're gonna look right fucking clowns if we haven't got the insurance settled. We've already told the world we got insurance cover. Let me have the name of the insurance company's C.E.O. I'll give it him straight. Pay up, or we take our business elsewhere.'

'I'll get you the name, Standish, but I already tried that one. They say their own reinsurance policy has the same terms, so they wouldn't be able to claim the money back. They're not planning to pay us a hundred and twenty million dollars out of their own pocket. Seems it would take quite a few years before they made that amount of money out of us. But it can't hurt to try again, I guess.'

****

Saturday dawned as bright and clear as it usually did in San Francisco. Hiro rose at seven, and like every morning, practised for two hours. He showered, changed into his motorcycle leathers, picked up the phone and the directions Hilton had faxed, and went to the front door. Mariko followed him and they spoke the same formal exchange Japanese do every time one of them goes out.

'Ittekimas.'

'Itteirasshai.'

She closed the door behind him and he went down to the basement where he kept his 750cc. He hadn't ridden it for a while and he took it to the neighbourhood gas station to check the tyres and fill her up. He eased the bike back into the traffic, crossed the Golden Gate bridge and headed north.

He didn't have a map and found Hilton's directions hard to follow. He got hopelessly lost more than once and was glad he'd left plenty of time. As he got closer, he felt his muscles tensing and the adrenalin beginning to twitch. He was not afraid, but he could not be quite sure what to expect from these thugs. Hilton had suggested he take along a couple of karate-expert friends, but Hiro liked to do things alone. There might be nothing to do anyway. There was no way to know if they'd even be there.

He swung around a sharp right-hander and there it was. The Back Shack. He throttled back, braked and pulled in. There were two Harleys, but no one outside on the wooden pillared verandah. He got off his bike, pulled his helmet off, and rubbed his hand over his hair of almost crewcut shortness. He took out the phone, switched on the power, pressed `redial' twice and `send' once and lodged it carefully in a pocket on his chest, the upper part with the lenses protruding above the open zipper.

Two men, probably alerted by the sound of the arriving Yamaha, ambled out. They were both fat, one with long red hair tied in a pony-tail, the other with thinning dark hair and arms covered in tattoos. *Exactly* as Hilton had described. It *must* be them.

Hiro walked slowly up the stairs and passed them. As he went by, the red-haired one spat on the floor. The other spoke.

'Well, would you look at that Japanese piece of shit?'

The red-head responded.

'The bike or the slit-eye?'

Hiro paused in mid-step for a fraction of a second and then walked on in. He sat with his back to the wall at a table by the door. A tall, lean man behind the bar stared at him as he polished glasses, clearly in no hurry to offer refreshment. Hiro sat patiently and stared straight ahead. Two, three minutes passed. The man behind the bar sighed, as if disturbed in some vital task, and strolled over.

'You want somethin'?'

'Coca-Cora.'

The man laughed a cheap laugh and strolled off. A Coke bottle was produced. No glass, no ice, no lemon, no ceremony.

239

The thugs came back in and stood in front of Hiro, looking as menacing and sneering as they could manage. Hiro drank his Coke in small sips, staring straight ahead, apparently unseeingly.

The dark one turned towards the bartender.

'Chuck, get that oxy-mother out of its lair. Our yellow friend here will sit tight while Red attends to his piece of garbage.'

As he finished speaking, he rammed the table into Hiro=s midriff, pinning him to the wall.

'Whatever you say, Black.'

The bartender slipped out a back door and came back with a cylinder, mask and a torch already spitting its hissing blue flame. Leering revoltingly, he walked towards Hiro and flashed the jet within a foot of his face. He looked fractionally disappointed by the lack of a flinch, but still gurgled with anticipation as he handed the fiery package to Red. With triumphant backward glances at Hiro, they both stepped outside. Black, his fat arms tensed, keeping the table forced back, grinned a foul grin at Hiro. Hiro stared straight ahead and only in the very last fraction of a second returned Black's look. Though it lasted no more than an instant, there was a terrifying intensity in those eyes that Black would never forget.

The surface of the table was an inch and half of solid pine. A hand rose and fell. The pine was cleft in two and the dark one crashed on the floor among the splinters.

'What the ...?'

He looked dazed, terminally confused.

The crash and his cry had been heard outside. Red and Chuck turned around and saw Hiro step outside. There were six pillars holding up the verandah roof. When the first cracked with the kick, they were too surprised to react. When the second, third and fourth smashed like matchwood under the assault the red-head dropped the still flaming torch and the barman staggered back. Black emerged and stepped gingerly under the sagging roof. Hiro walked slowly up to him and stopped only when their faces were six inches away. Quietly, very quietly, Hiro said, 'A few months back you and your friend beat up a friend of Kaba, my Master, and cut up his bike.'

'Your *Master*?'

'My teacher. I'm a fifth Dan, he's twelfth. He once killed a charging bull with a fist. I could kill you in fifteen seconds. He could kill you in three.'

Red didn't know whether to come closer to hear this quiet exchange or keep as far away as possible. He opted for the latter.

'We were just havin' some fun. We didn't mean nothin' by it.'

'You have greatly angered my Master. He is coming here this afternoon to deal with you.'

'Oh shit.'

'Unless you do exactly what he directs.'

'What do you mean? I'll do anything he says.'

'He will direct you by telephone.'

'By *telephone*?'

'Here, take this. My Master is on the line.'

He took the mobile phone. Red and Chuck were looking more confused than ever.

'Er, hello.'

'You address me as Master.'

'Hello, Master.'

'You have an oxy-acetylene cutter?'

'Yes, Master.'

'Pick it up and cut one of the two Harleys in half. If you do not, I will come and deal with you in person. Do you want that?'

'No, no. Not that. I mean, I wouldn't wanna put you to any trouble, Master. I'll do it right away. Does it matter which one?'

'No. You may choose.'

'Okay.'

With a ragged, panicky step, he went for the abandoned flame scorching the dirt. Half way there he froze as Hiro softly commanded, 'The phone. Give me the phone.'

With the exaggerated humility of a supplicant, Black bowed deeply to Hiro, returned the phone, and dashed back to pick up the hissing weapon and head for the Harleys. Red's brain had confusion overload.

'Hey, what the fuck...?'

Black paid him no heed and pressed on. The bikes, gleaming with chrome, stood proudly side by side. He made a beeline for the nearer, Red's one, gingerly keeping the torch as far as possible from the fuel lines and tank. The sound of the flame on chromed steel was awesome. At first, it seemed just to lick the metal. Then it cut savagely in, shattering Red's incredulous paralysis.

'Hey, you fuckin' ...'

Red raced forward and grabbed his buddy from behind. Without letting go of the torch, Black swung his shoulders in a mighty flourish, throwing his assailant to the ground. The torch cut down and down, and through.

Red was up again. Sensing him coming, Black turned round and held up the flame in defiance, panting all the while.

'You fuckin', fuckin'...'

'He told me to do it.'

'*Who* told you?'

'*His* Master. Otherwise, he was coming to get us.'

'He told you to cut *my* bike?'

'He said either one.'

'And you cut *mine?*'

'It was nearer.'

His rage was now too great for fear of the torch to work. He dodged the wildly swinging flame and connected with a fist. Black crashed back, losing his grip of the torch. Then the two were at each other on the ground, a cloud of dust rising as they wrestled, thumped and kicked.

The punches grew feebler as exhaustion began to tell. The barman stood far back, ready to take flight if Hiro so much as looked his way. Hiro showed no interest in him and stood very still, the phone in his hand pointing towards the brawl. Red managed a last haymaker and Black sank back motionless. With huge effort, Red dragged himself faltering to his feet, stumbling around like a drunkard. Black's consciousness returned just in time to hear the triumphant yell as Red took the flame to the second metal steed.

There was a whistle from the phone. Hiro put it to his ear.

'Hiro, you're my hero, that was fantastic. Time you were out of there.'

'Okay, Hiruton. Talk to you soon.'

He switched off the phone and walked over to the Yamaha. He sat astride it and calmly and unhurriedly pulled on his helmet, pressed the starter and, with one last glance back, rode off.

****

Waldyr's friends in Washington had made all the difference. He'd been warned by the FBI to expect no change from the bank in Panama, just a wall of silence hidden behind client confidentiality. What his buddies in Washington, one of them working with the Immigration Service, had unearthed might change all that. Nascimento spoke only moderate Spanish and didn't like feeling less than in full control. He would keep firmly to English.

'Thank you for seeing me, Mr Garcia.'

'Always happy to see representatives of the United States Government.'

'I'm not that, Mr Garcia. A simple policeman from San Francisco.'

'Well, I hope it doesn't prove a wasted visit. I'll try to help any way I can.'

'Good. I'm glad to hear that. Let's begin with the transfer of dollars a hundred and twenty million that was received here on September twelfth. Account number 64327.'

'What do you want to know about it?'

'Whose account is it?'

'It's in the name of a Panamanian company. I can't comment any more.'

'How long did the money stay in that account?'

'I can't comment on details, but it is reasonable to say that the account had standing instructions to remit onwards any sum received of above one hundred thousand dollars.'

'Where did it go next?'

'I'm sorry, Mr Nascimento, I can't help you on that.'

'Mr Garcia, we really need your co-operation on this.'

'Mr Nascimento, I'm doing all I can within the bounds of our rules on client confidentiality.'

'Mr Garcia, I don't have a lot of time, so I will come straight to the point. You have a sister living in Fort Lauderdale, Florida?'

'I don't see the relevance.'

'I'm told there were certain ... irregularities concerning her original application to enter the US twelve years ago. The penalties for filing false information are considerable. They include expulsion.'

'I see.... I'll do what I can.'

'Good, can we return to the matter of this account? When was it opened?'

'July.'

'Who opened it?'

'A Mr Grimond. An American.'

'And did he produce identity?'

'We don't always ask for that.'

'Where did the money go next?'

'Twelve banks in Panama.'

'And after that?'

'Abroad. I don't know where. That was kept from me. Truly, I don't know.'

'What did this Mr Grimond look like?'

'Medium height. Slight build. Blonde hair.'

Nascimento pulled out a photograph of Hilton.

'No, the hair's quite different. The face is a little similar though.'

'Could he have been wearing a wig?'

'I didn't look that close.'

'How did you get introduced to this Mr Grimond?'

'Through an old contact.'

'Where.'
'In America.'
'So an American?'
'An Englishman.'
'Name?'
'Aloysius Arbuthnot.'
'Where does this Arbuthnot live?'
'Albuquerque, New Mexico.'

****

It was around the time that Nascimento was placing the call from his hotel to have Arbuthnot picked up by the local police that Lisa got her delivery from the quiet but gracious Oriental. She put the phone into the accompanying charger, and two hours later slipped it into her handbag. She was sitting on a bench in Marina Green looking out at Alcatraz when she pressed 'send', swept a curl back behind her ear, and, legs crossed, waited for the answer.

'Hello.'
'Bonjour, Philippe. C'est Lisa.'
'Bonjour, Lisa. Comment vas-tu? You got it, it seems.'
'Sure did.'
'No class today?'
'Tomorrow. Philippe, I swear you've written that whole thing for me. That piece on Krryer was so beautiful. I wouldn't want to change a word. Do you think it'd be awful if I submit it as it is?'

'Why not? When you're under so much time pressure, maybe it's the best way.'

'If you think it's really okay, then. That's wonderful, Philippe. How come you know so much about *every* artist?'

'It's my little 'obby and my love, Lisa.'

'Which is your favourite gallery?'

'No doubt about it, the Frick in New York. 'Ave you been there?'

'No, we went to New York once, but Earl wouldn't let me go there. Said we shouldn't do boring things when we had so little time. I'd been so looking forward to going there.'

'You *must* go. They have two sensational Vermeers, and a wonderful Rembrandt of a Polish rider.'

'I'd love to. Together sometime, maybe.'

'I love that idea, Lisa.'

'Philippe, do you have children?'

'No.'

'Tell me about your wife.'

'She's a kind person. Not interested in art, sadly, but a good person. She 'ad an illness a few years ago and is in a wheelchair. I could never leave 'er.'

'Is she French?'

'Yes, from the South, like me.'

'Where in the South are you from, Philippe?'

'Provence.'

'Cezanne country, then.'

'Precisely, Lisa. It's beautiful country. Arid, but beautiful. 'Ave you been to France?'

'No. We were meant to go on our honeymoon, but Earl changed it at the last moment.'

'You've never been to Europe?'

'No. Nowhere abroad at all.'

'You don't 'ave a passport?'

'Oh, I *do* have a passport. I got one when I *thought* we were going. I keep it in my handbag as a sort of fantasy charm, a talisman. Like as if any day I could just get on a plane and go.'

'That's a wonderful idea, Lisa. Will you promise me you'll always keep it there?'

'Sure, if you'd like it. Philippe, I don't really understand. Are you helping me just because of the art?'

'It's a wonderful shared interest, Lisa, but there is another reason. Can I tell you the truth?'

'Please, Philippe. Please do.'

She was smiling. Whatever he was going to say, she thought she was going to like it.

'That time in the bar, the time you don't remember ...'

'I'm so mad about that. I wish I'd been paying more attention.'

'You must have been very distracted, because I was looking at you the whole time. I'm sure everyone else noticed.'

'No-one said anything.'

'Before that night, I never believed in love at first sight. Now I do. Lisa, I know you 'ave yours and I 'ave mine, and I'm so much older, but I truly love you. When I saw those grey-green eyes and the way you push back your curls behind your ears, and your wonderful, wonderful smile. Lisa, I think for me you're the most beautiful woman in the whole world ... 'Ave I offended you? I'm sorry if I said too much, I was wrong.'

'No, not at all, Philippe. I like it. Maybe I shouldn't, but I do. No-one's ever spoken to me like that before. When I first met Earl he kind of flattered me, saying I was sexy and cute and turned him on, but he didn't say anything like you did right now. After my friend Hil died, his brother Conrad

– the one you saw in the bar – said Hil had sort of loved me, which was sad, 'cos he never said anything to me himself.'

'Maybe 'e didn't 'ave the courage.'

'Could be. I guess that could be it.'

'Or, since you are married, maybe 'e thought it was wrong, or pointless.'

'I suppose so.'

'Or, if 'e didn't know about art or Europe or whatever, could 'e 'ave felt a little ... inadequate?'

'Oh, that would've been crazy. I wouldn't have minded him not knowing at all.'

'If you 'ad been free, could 'e 'ave been the one?'

'I don't know. At the time I thought he just wanted to be platonic friends. I didn't think he was interested in me that way at all, so I didn't think that way myself either. He was very special, though, and we were very close.'

'But not your type.'

'I'm not one of those girls who has a type. I don't care what people look like. It's more what you can talk about together. He and I could talk together endlessly. But you know, Philippe, I feel that way about you, too.'

'I feel the same way, Lisa. So you don't mind if I tell you that I love you? You don't want to make me stop saying it?'

'Please don't. Please don't stop, Philippe.'

18

'Oh hi, Mr Chang. It's coming along fine. A few minor snags, but we're working right round the clock on it. It should be ready next Wednesday, the twenty-second, bang on schedule. Hey, it's some car, that. We drove it round the parking lot to calibrate the cameras with the infrareds. What a machine! Just as well you're not planning to drive it on the streets. It'll do sixty an hour. Speeding tickets that is. What do you want us to do about delivery? Do you want us to arrange to airfreight it to Taipei?'

'No, that won't be necessary. I'll send one of my people to get it. He'll have a trailer. We'll arrange the shipping ourselves.'

'What time will he come on Wednesday?'

'Afternoon. Say, three p.m.?'

'Sure.'

'Like we agreed, if it's ready on time you get a bonus of two hundred thousand. I'll have it transferred to your bank account direct again. Will that be okay?'

'Oh, sure, thanks very much, Mr. Chang.'

****

There was no time for a rehearsal. They'd all had to work flat out to get the presentation ready. Ruby was nervous, but she felt good about this one. Icarus was *much* better than Carius. Fairways might have gone along with Carius, but she doubted they'd be *that* enthusiastic. There was lots more business to come out of that group. Only last week they announced the acquisition of a big cookie company. That was exactly the kind of thing that Condor needed to get national recognition. She *wanted* that business, and she wanted everyone to know *she* had won it. All the Fairways big shots were going to be there. It was the first time any of the Condor people had met the Chief Executive, Paul Merriwether. There was only one thing for it. She'd lead the presentation herself.

They flew down to LA on the early flight, Ruby, Chas, Honor and Desmond. All except Conrad who *of course* insisted on driving down the night before in a rentacar. Conrad could have his phobias if he wanted, but Ruby made *quite* sure it didn't cost Condor a penny. He would get the cash equivalent of the cheapest airfare. Apart from that, the car, gas and hotel were down to him. Suited her rather well in the end that for some reason he didn't want to take his precious new car. Meant he could meet them at the airport and save them having to rent another car. Mind you, she'd have been happier taking only Honor and Chas; it was Fairways who had asked to see the whole creative team.

They got to Fairways way too early, so they drove on to a Holiday Inn for a coffee.

'I'll take the questions and bring any of you in only if *I* choose to? Is that clear?'

It seemed it was.

'Conrad, that applies to you particularly. *One* word and I'll disembowel you. One sentence and it's castration time.'

****

They were shown into the conference room on the thirty-sixth floor. There was coffee on the sideboard and huddles of soft drinks on the main table. Collective nervousness increased as the minutes ticked by. They all turned as the door opened; it was the secretary saying could they wait a few more minutes, and to help themselves to coffee.

Again, the door swung open. Four of them trooped in. Paul Merriwether's face was familiar from the Fairways annual report, but the photo did no justice to the *size* of his head. It was enormous. You couldn't take your eyes off it.

'Ladies and gentlemen, Good Morning. I'm Paul Merriwether. I think you know Dina, John and Edson.'

'Hello, Mr Merriwether, I'm Ruby Bowen. Can I present my team ...? Honor, Chas, Desmond and Conrad. Thank you very much for sparing the time to attend our presentation in person. We think we've got something quite special for you.'

'Good. Well, let's get started. As you see, the overhead projector is ready.'

'Thank you. Do I adjust ...? That's it ... okay. Mr Merriwether, we've given a lot of thought to your needs at Fairways. My first slide covers the three things *we* think an airline name needs above all to suggest:

SAFETY
FREEDOM
CLASS

Now let me put up the remit of the slide we got from Fairways. It was for a name that was:

SHORT
MEMORABLE
PUNCHY
USER FRIENDLY

Well, Mr Merriwether, we have been through hundreds of possibilities and explored every corner of our research databases to find the one name that fits the bill. And here it is.'

With a smile and a flourish she put up the next slide.

ICARUS AIRLINES

There was an intake of breath from the Fairways people. Merriwether, who had been lounging back, shot upright in his seat. Ruby knew she'd done it. What body language! What an impact! She pulled out another slide.

ICARUS – Mythological God of Flight.

'This is *exactly* what is right for you. A god from mythology symbolising eternal values and durability. A legend in his own time and ever since. And you may ask, hasn't this been done before, and I tell you, Mr Merriwether, it has *not*. We have checked it every which way. Not only no Icarus airlines, there's never been an Icarus *anything*.'

It was Edson Drummond who'd given Condor the work. He tried to speak, but Merriwether silenced him with a look. He spoke himself.

'Ms Bowen. This is indeed a very ... unique suggestion. This is the whole creative team here, is it?'

'Yes it is.'

'Would you mind telling me which one had this ... brilliant idea?'

'Well, Mr Merriwether, we all put a lot of effort into it ...In this case, I myself... no, I shouldn't claim all the glory ... let's say it was a team effort.'

'And you've thoroughly checked about Icarus, this god of flight?'

'Certainly we have. Checked and rechecked.'

'Would you excuse me a minute ...? Dina, in my office there's an old encyclopedia my dad gave me. Would you mind seeing if Shirley can bring it here?'

'I'll go myself.'

'Thank you.'

'Mr Merriwether, shall I continue while Dina's away or ...?'

'Why don't we just wait? She'll just be a second. It's right next door.'

Dina came back with it. Edson Drummond was looking daggers at Ruby. For the first time Ruby had an instinct that all was not well.

'Here you are, Paul.'

'Dina, the print in this book's so small and my old eyes are getting so feeble, would you mind reading out to all of us about the god of flight?'

'Here it is. Icarus. Greek mythological figure. Son of Daedalus. Craftsman and architect who built the labyrinth in Crete where the minotaur was kept ...'

Ruby relaxed a little. She had no knowledge of anything mythological – nothing like that had ever remotely interested her – but this sounded like the right background for a god of flight.

' ... Icarus wanted to fly to escape from the island of Crete, so Daedalus fashioned a pair of wings from bird feathers and attached them to Icarus's back with wax ...'

So far, so good. Just wish she'd checked it out herself, though, and had not relied on that lazy skunk, Conrad.

' ... Icarus soared into the sky and flew like a bird ...'

Thank God for that, thought Ruby.

' ... until ambition overtook him ...'

Oh, oh. This sounded bad.

' ... and he flew higher and higher until he went near the sun. The wax melted, the wings fell off and he crashed into the sea and was drowned.'

For the first time in her life, Ruby was dumbstruck.

'Ms Bowen, I don't know whether this was intended to be a joke, but we do not share your sense of humour. One of your slides had something about being short and memorable. So was your assignment. It is terminated. Good morning.'

'CONRAD!!!!!'

****

Waldyr Nascimento boarded his flight in a mixed mood. Basically, he'd got nowhere with the other Panamanian banks. He didn't have the same leverage and no amount of additional pressure on Garcia had helped. He'd wrung out of him everything he could. Even if the Panamanians had been more co-operative, it was clear that the birds had long since flown the nest and not a dollar of that money was still in Panama. Given time, and heavy duty pressure from Washington, they could doubtless get the banks to hand over details of where the money had gone next, but from what Garcia had said, and the FBI experts on money laundering had confirmed, the loot had most likely been bounced all around the globe to cover its tracks. It would take time, and it might never work. In the meantime, it would give the gang – and he was convinced this was a sophisticated criminal ring – more time to stash the cash even further out of reach and get well away themselves. Of course, they might already have got out of the country, taking a chance that the police at the airports had no idea who they were looking for. But equally they could still be lying low, waiting for the hue and cry to die down. This was Nascimento=s dilemma. Move clumsily and alert them, or move stealthily and waste time. It was a very difficult call. This Arbuthnot lead could be the vital shortcut. That was why he was flying not to San Francisco, but direct to Albuquerque, New Mexico to interview him. The jurisdictional thing had been sorted out with the FBI. The local police had picked up Arbuthnot on suspicion of fraud. They had no evidence at all, but from what they could piece together about his business activities, there was nothing much Arbuthnot got involved with which wasn't to some degree shady. Let sunlight in on any part of it and you could expect to make him twitch. It had been agreed there should be no mention of the BUS until Nascimento got there.

The Hilton Kask part he was less sure about. Garcia had seen a resemblance, but no more. There was no record of Kask travelling to Panama. He'd never had a passport – the Passport Service had confirmed that – and the Panamanian immigration had no record of a Kask arriving. Ditto the international hotels in Panama City. Nothing had shown up on his credit cards. The big rentacar companies had run worldwide checks on Kask's driver's licence. Avis had a one way from Boise, Idaho to San Francisco in May and

Hertz had a weekend rental in June. There was nothing abroad. It didn't conclusively mean Kask wasn't involved. He may have done the computer part and no more. Why should he have agreed to act as a mule for the ring, setting up the bank trail? Unless he didn't care since he was going to die anyway. The ring would trust him, too. Dead men tell no tales. They might have been willing to up his cut if he'd do that bit. Where was his cut going to, if not to his brother? Nascimento had got a rush of excitement when he heard about the Mercedes Conrad had bought, but was bitterly disappointed when bank records had shown it was paid for from the cash the insurance company had shelled out. So far the surveillance wasn't showing much, either. The guy had a pretty boring existence. No sign of a girlfriend. Didn't go out a lot. Stayed home and played piano or listened to music. Kept turtles. The undercover agent who had done the search of his apartment had almost stepped on one of the revolting little beasts just after teasing the door open with his practiced hand. Neither the search nor the wire tap on his phone had turned up anything interesting. The only further follow-up was to check out a mobile phone. There was a charger for one in the apartment. They'd have to check with the telephone companies and get a fix on that as well. One other interesting thing. He'd recently got himself a passport for the first time in his life. With all that insurance money it might not be surprising to think about a vacation. Quite a coincidence, though. Nascimento got the Immigration people to put a message out to the airlines to alert the police if he tried to leave the country.

****

'Hi, Hil.'

'Hi, Con. Good to hear from you. Where are you?'

'In LA. Venice Beach.'

'How did it go?'

'Fan-tas-tic. Funniest thing I saw in my life.'

'How long before she fired you?'

'One nanosecond. Totally bal-lis-tic.'

'Scrotum intact?'

'Only just. She waited till the elevator doors closed and fired with all her guns. Kicking, scratching, elbows, teeth, briefcase.'

'Did the others try to stop her?'

'You kiddin'? The elevator stopped on the seventeenth. There were three people waiting to get in. She paused just long enough to tell them to go screw themselves and started on me again before the doors had closed. I was glad there was only thirty-six floors. If there'd been sixty, I wouldn't be here to tell the tale.'

'But you're in one piece?'

'Honourable cuts and bruises. A few painful ones on the shin. She kept aiming kicks at my balls. I caught her leg and she had to hop around between about the eleventh and the seventh floors. Then she swung at me with her briefcase and I lost my grip. Those precious seconds made the difference, all the same.'

'So what happened when you got downstairs?'

'As soon as the elevator doors opened, I ran for my life. She came after me yelling and screaming, but in her high heels it was no contest. When I'd pulled out a lead of twenty or thirty yards I turned and gave her the finger. Oddly enough, that did nothing to calm her and she came after me some more, yelling all the time. With that fire coming out of her nostrils and all, I thought I needed a bigger lead. Next time I looked back, she'd slowed a bit and was panting fit to bust, so it seemed the natural moment to call out her nickname plus an invitation to kiss my ass. That didn't thrill her massively, either. She screamed, kicked off her shoes and started running like her tail was on fire. This time I got *real* scared she might catch me, so I took to my heels and didn't stop. My lungs haven't recovered yet. It was two hours before I had the nerve to go back to get my rentacar. She'd let all the tyres down. Predictable to the end. No prizes for guessing why I didn't take the Merc.'

'Wow. Will you go back to the office to get your things?'

'Did it last night. I had this strange premonition. I think I've got second sight.'

'So what happens next? 'Nother job?'

'Nah, I'll just take it easy for a while. Write some music.'

'Time to think about Aldabra?'

'I ain't going no place. I'm sticking close to my brother. I don't even know where you *are,* but you *feel* close. I'm going to keep it that way. Hey, Hil, when I got back home last night, there was something weird.'

'What?'

'Someone had been in my apartment, I'm sure of it. Little things. I've been writing a lot of music recently. I always leave my pen on the keyboard, always on middle C. It's just a silly little habit. It had moved to B. It's the next key, but it couldn't get there on its own. When I looked around at my desk, everything looked normal, but *tidier* than I leave things. I'm convinced someone had been through my things.'

'You're sure you're not imagining it?'

'I'm not, Hil. I know I'm not. Hil, this couldn't be anything to do with you, is it? You told me you had some scores to settle. I've never probed, but when I noticed this, I began to think ...'

'Con, it is possible, but I promise it's nothing for you to worry about, and it's better for me not to go into it now. But as a precaution, from now on, don't use that phone in the apartment and when we talk, don't call me Hil.'

'What the hell am I supposed to call you?'

'How about Jupiter? You know, the bringer of jollity.'

'Anything you want. If you want to be Jupiter, from now on you're Jupiter.'

'Con, where you're sitting now, is there any car or anything around?'

'Not that I can see. Lots of guys on rollerblades, and some very cute gals.'

'Okay, I'm going to give you an address. Don't write it down. Memorise it and don't forget it.'

'What is it?'

'Somewhere I may need you to go to collect something. Not just yet, I'll tell you when.'

'Okay. What's the address?'

'It's in Sonoma. It's ...

****

After the shareholders' meeting was over, MacMartin said not one word. He went back to his office, picked up the putter, swung it two-handed over his head and with all his great force brought it down on the glass coffee table. The glass shattered like a windshield in a car crash. The shaft buckled and the head flew off. Humiliation. Utter humiliation. They'd had a *total* roasting. He'd had to go in there to explain that the insurance company wouldn't pay out after all. He'd called the Chief of the SFPD before, in the hope of hearing of a breakthrough. Progress, but no arrest imminent. MacMartin's plan B had been to concentrate on the year as a whole and the solid, if unspectacular, results. Towards the end they would slip in the insurance bit and say the police were confident the bulk of the money would be recovered. When they 'slipped it in', there was pandemonium among the shareholders. A lethal cocktail of genuine outrage and high farce. *How* could they have been so incompetent as to fail to get proper insurance cover? *Why* did they mislead the market by announcing that they were covered? A motion of no confidence in the Board's handling of this issue was only narrowly defeated. The final humiliation came when, on a show of hands, a resolution was passed to equip the Board with gas masks and umbrellas for future meetings.

****

'Philippe?'

'Lisa.'

'I'm sorry to call you this time of night.'

'It's okay, I wasn't asleep. What's the matter? You sound upset.'

'He *hit* me.'

'Earl?'

'Yeah. He never did it before. When I came home

tonight he was waiting for me, with a wild look in his eyes. The college had called to say the class tomorrow was cancelled. I've always told them to call me at the flower shop, but they missed me there, so they left a message on the answering machine.'

"Ow bad did 'e 'it you?'

'He slapped me around pretty bad. He'd been drinking and was like a mad thing. I guess it's my own fault, hiding it from him. I knew he'd hate me doing that. I should never have gone to the college. Oh Philippe, I'm so scared.'

'Where are you now?'

'I waited till he fell asleep and then ran out. I drove down to the Marina. I don't know what to do now.'

'I wish so much I could come and look after you myself. I'm so far away.'

'I know, I know, Philippe. I just wanted to hear your voice.'

'Is there any friend's place where you could stay over?'

'Not at this time. It's two o'clock.'

'This is an emergency, Lisa. You musn't go back there tonight. 'Ow about one of the girls from the flower shop or the bar?'

'I'm not close to any of them. I don't even have their phone numbers.'

'Your friend Conrad?'

'Con? I have his number, but I'm not sure. I don't know him that well. I haven't seen him since that night.'

'But 'e *is* 'ilton's brother, right? And 'ilton would 'ave wanted to protect you, right? Why not call him up?'

'He lives alone, so at least there wouldn't be a family to wake.'

'Do it, Lisa. And call me again in the morning. Don't

phone from his apartment. I like it when you call from Marina Green. I can imagine the view from there. We've got to get you away from that 'orrible man. I'll think of something, depend on it.'

'Okay, Philippe, I'll do what you say. I *do* depend on you so much.'

19

Nascimento began with a few more personal stabs, at Arbuthnot's past strewn with failure, the sleaziness of his current business and his alleged contacts with minor criminals. It didn't work, didn't faze him at all. He was a cool one, this. He wasn't smiling, but his eyes showed a contemptuous sneer. Nascimento didn't like being sneered at. He decided to stop screwing around.

'I've just come from Panama city. I met a Mr Garcia of the Banco Paloma. Do you know him?'

'Don't think so.'

'He thinks you do. He told me you introduced a Mr Grimond to him.'

'Grimond? Never heard of any Grimond.'

'Did you introduce anyone to him?'

'Don't think so. Someone could have used my name. I have a wide circle of friends.'

'So why should Mr Garcia know you?'

'No idea.'

'Does your wide circle of friends include people involved with money laundering?'

'Money laundering? What's that?'

'Smart guy, huh? How about friends in tax havens?'

'Some of my clients have off-shore activities.'

'Where?'

'Lots of places. Caribbean, Bahamas, Europe.'

'Where in Europe?'

'Channel Islands, Ireland, Switzerland.'

'Anywhere else?'

'Monaco, San Marino, Liechtenstein.'

'And you know people in all those places?'

'Sure.'

'Mr Arbuthnot, do you have any friends in San Francisco?'

'One or two women.'

'Does the name Hilton Kask mean anything to you?'

He did his best not to let it show. That *was* what it was about, just as he'd suspected. Fifty thousand up front and another two hundred in a year. Seemed good at the time, but it wasn't enough if he might wind up in serious trouble.

'What was the name again?'

'Hilton Kask.'

'No. Doesn't ring any bells. Should it? Who is it?'

'We'll come back to that. Let's go back to your friends and those tax havens. I want a list of names.'

As he was asking the questions a fax was brought in, redirected from San Francisco. It was from Columbia University. It read, 'Can't be sure, but how about the Queen of Sheba? Try me with a harder one. Regards, Louis.' Without excusing himself, Nascimento left the room and headed for a telephone. Frustratingly, Sergeant Parks shared his own vagueness on history. They had both heard of the Queen of Sheba, but had no very clear idea of who she was. This was no time to be proud. He told Parks to fax back. `Thanks, Louis. Do you have any books on the Q of S? Who *was* she? Waldyr.'

****

265

'Baron Realty.'

'I'd like to speak with someone about representing a buyer in purchasing a property.'

'I'll put you through to Mr Baron. Who may I say is calling?'

'Max Mendelssohn.'

'Just a second ...'

'This is Earl Baron.'

'Good morning, Mr Baron. Max Mendelssohn. I'm calling from out of town. I got your name from Yellow Pages. I don't trust big agencies. Don't like them. My wife has got a thing about buying a ranch in Napa. You know anything about properties in Napa?'

He lied.

'Everything there is to know. How much is your wife thinking of ... investing?'

'She gets through so much of my money, I want to keep it to four or five. Can you get something respectable for that?'

'Four or five ... hundred thousand?'

'It can be simple, but she won't live in a tent. I mean millions.'

'I think I can find something very special for that budget.'

No-one had ever hired him as a buyer's representative. He never got to sell anything worth more than three hundred thousand. This was manna from heaven.

'Shall I get some details together and fax them through to you?'

'No time for that. My wife likes to act on a whim or she loses interest. She's taking her jet to San Francisco this afternoon. She should be at your office by two thirty. Could you drive up to Napa with her this afternoon and show her some things?'

'I'd be honoured to drive her around.'

'Oh, you won't be doing the driving. Melanie only ever rides in a Rolls Royce. We keep a few stashed around the place. Nothing in San Francisco, but one in Newport beach. One of our drivers is heading up your way now. You will ride with her.'

'That's fine with me.'

'Now listen up, Mr Baron. My wife's a lot younger than me and likes to be treated ... gracious. You make sure you treat her good.'

'Certainly will, Mr Mendelssohn.'

'At two thirty, then.'

'I'll be waiting.'

Wow, wow, wow! A big fat fee coming. *And* a young female client. Christ, he better start ringing around a few agents in Napa to see if they had anything.

****

The second fax came right back from Louis. `Waldyr, you slay me, you ignorant peasant. Forget the history books, try the Bible.' Nascimento asked his Albuquerque police hosts if they had a Bible lying around. Nothing. Not a Gideon in sight. How the hell could he get hold of a Bible right away? It was past eight at night and the bookstores and libraries would be closed. There would be one in his hotel room, but that was three miles away. Even if he got hold of one, he would have no idea where to look. It would take ages. His father. That was the answer. Knew the Bible backwards. He hadn't spoken to his folks since the BUS thing blew up. They'd be mad at him, especially if he was only calling now because he needed something. On the other hand, maybe his Papa would like it: he was always bitching about Waldyr not going to church enough. A question about the Bible might please them. Better just get on with it. He rang and made profuse apologies, speaking with the time-capsule adolescent Portuguese of his youth. He'd been so busy with the BUS robbery. They knew, his Mama said, they'd read all about it, they did have newspapers and TV in Fresno. They were proud of him, but he shouldn't forget they existed. He let her go on for a while before asking for a word with Papa about the Bible. His father also delivered a chiding before agreeing to listen to what Waldyr needed to know.

'You think too much about your career and too little about your God. You don't go to church, and you don't read the Bible. I'll only tell you what it says if you promise to go out tomorrow and buy one yourself.'

'I promise, Papa.'

'Alright, then. The only mention of the Queen of Sheba is in the Book of Kings.'

'Does it say anything about Solomon?'

'Sure it does. She visited him.'

'What does it say?'

'You want me to read it?'

'Yes, I want to hear every word.'

'Portuguese or English?'

'English.'

`Okay, I'll look it up ... Here we go. Kings One, Ten. "And when the Queen of Sheba heard of the fame of Solomon, concerning the name of the Lord, she came to prove him with hard questions. And she came to Jerusalem with a very great train, with camels and rare spices and very much gold, and precious stones, and when she was come to Solomon, she communed with him of all that was in her heart. And Solomon told her all her questions; there was not anything hid from the king which he told her not. And she gave the king a hundred and twenty talents of gold and of spices very great store and precious stones ..." '

Nascimento muttered, 'Jesus Christ.'

'He came later, you blaspheming boy.'

****

Packing up was hard. They'd expected to move from Burlingame one day, but to something grander in the Bay Area. A real *classy* neighborhood. Now this little house seemed a lot to be giving up. Mary had made it so comfortable and pretty with little touches here and there. The kids were devastated about leaving their school friends, who laughed or just didn't understand when they said it was Arkansas they were headed for.

It was the bitterest pill for Fred to swallow. He'd tried everything, but nothing came off. Larry and Cliff had finally asked him to leave and so his financial lifeline had been cut. Venture was one hundred percent closed off. There'd been a few other ideas, but he wasn't qualified or they were too risky. His involvement in the BUS affair had got around and no other bank on the West Coast wanted to know. In the end he had to throw himself down on his knees just to get a job. Him on his knees before the First National Bank of Arkansas! When he drove from the interview to break it to his mother, he found that her instincts had long since told her that something was wrong. But still she was crushed and deflated by the news. The neighbours would have to know, after all they'd heard about her golden boy. Martha would be resentful when her husband laughed his belly laugh. It could have been worse, she supposed. He wasn't a drunk, he wasn't in jail, and he wasn't flat broke. He would be in work. No, don't ask for a job in Little Rock, she said. If you're coming home, come here. Come home to Helena.

In her rocking chair she wiped a tear away, and shook her grey head in sad resignation. Still sitting, she held her arms out. Fred knelt in front of her, put his head softly down in her lap and began to sob.

****

'Albuquerque PD?'

'Can you put me through to Lieutenant Nascimento of the San Francisco Police Department?'

'He's interviewing. He's not to be disturbed.'

'This is urgent. He'll want to hear this.'

'Okay, buddy, who's calling?'

'Sergeant Parks of SFPD.'

'Putting you through.'

'Nascimento.'

'Lieutenant, it's Parks.'

'What is it, Sergeant? I'm busy.'

'Arbuthnot. He went to the same college as Kask. Same time, too.'

'You sure?'

'Absolutely.'

'Thank you very much, Sergeant. That's very helpful.'

****

270

'I'm glad it was alright with your friend Conrad. 'Ow are you feeling today?'

'A bit calmer, but not that much. I'm still scared, Philippe. I called in sick to Florissima. I was frightened he might go there.'

'Lisa, listen carefully. Tonight stay with your friend again. Tomorrow I want you to go back 'ome.'

'Philippe, I *can't*. Now I ran out on him, he'll be homicidal.'

'Lisa, please trust me. Tomorrow night 'e'll ask for a divorce. Whatever you do, don't argue. 'E'll tell you 'e wants to do it the next day. Tell him you agree, but you won't stay with him that last night. Then go back and stay at Conrad's again.'

'He'll *never*.....'

' 'E *will*, Lisa, 'e will. I can't tell you why now, but believe me, 'e will.'

'Philippe, I don't know what to think, I'm that scared.'

****

The call from Murray Ferguson had come at Condor a couple of days before. Honor nearly slammed the handset down, but didn't *quite*. That memory was awful and shaming, but it was a while back now and she'd had a *lot* of pleasure from that watch. Since Conrad had been fired she could wear it at work and get some admiring glances there, too. And Murray Ferguson did have a nice voice.

She was pretty certain he'd be after a date. She was going to play hard to get, very hard to get. After that, it depended on what the offer was and how persuasive he was. He guessed, correctly, that she would take the call, but the phone really might be slammed down when she realised it wasn't a date, it was another proposition. So he would give her the bottom line right away. Perhaps better not use that actual expression, though.

'Half a million dollars.'

She went quiet. After a while, she said,

'For what, *this* time?'

'A gentle spot of entrapment, deluxe style.'

'I'll hear you out. No commitment, but I'll listen.'

****

He was breaking down. The college bit had done the trick. At first he had no memory of Kask. Now he'd begun to remember. No, he couldn't explain why there had been a cash deposit of fifty thousand dollars into his account back in July. Some clients preferred to pay their accounts in cash. Too many for him to remember which it might have been. The police had been through his office books with a fine toothcomb. There was no evidence of any invoice or receipt that would match that payment. Yes, it had come back to him now, that man Garcia. Possibly he could have recommended some people to him. No Mr Grimond, though. Could he have introduced Hilton Kask? No, he hadn't heard from Hilton for ages. Well, maybe he could have had a brief conversation and forgotten about it.

Okay, okay, okay! The fifty thousand *had* come from Hilton. And yes, he had put him in touch with Garcia. But no-one else. No, he had not asked for names anywhere else. Other places? Yes, he had recommended one or two locations if Hilton wanted discretion. Where? Liechtenstein.

Better than Switzerland. Sure he'd heard about the BUS theft. He read the papers, you know. My God, he thought to himself, if this is what Kask was caught up in, this was *bad* news for him, too. How had a wimp like Kask got involved with a something like *that*? Keep quiet, as much as possible. Protect yourself. Don't say more than you have to. You don't know how much they know.

Kask dead? When? How? Nascimento could see this was no faked reaction. He wouldn't tell him how. He didn't want to lie, but if Arbuthnot chose to assume it was a professional killing, that was okay. Every bit of pressure helped.

The local police, working with the FBI guys, turned something up and in one of the breaks in the interviews brought Nascimento circumstantial evidence of Arbuthnot's involvement in a fraudulent property deal. They conferred and agreed they could offer him immunity from prosecution, but it didn't prove necessary. He cracked totally and it was then he told them. No, he hadn't given Hilton any names in Liechtenstein, but, yes, he had helped him in other ways. How? He'd lent him his driver's licence. No, not the New Mexico licence which the local police had checked – his old British one. Nascimento asked to see it, and Arbuthnot produced it from his wallet. What the hell was this, Nascimento asked. My real name, he replied, Arbuthnot was just one he'd 'adopted' a few years back. If they checked with their own Immigration Service, they'd find that his passport and green card were still in the name Tom Brown. Yes he *did* have some credit cards in that name, too. Yes, he *had* lent Hilton one. No, the deal was that Hilton would pay cash, but would take along the credit card so that no-one thought it odd. Passport? Okay, yes, he'd lent him that, too.

Nascimento almost ran out of the room in his hurry to get to the phone. Those idiots! He'd depended on the Albuquerque police to check out Arbuthnot. How could the morons not have discovered the name change?

'Give me Sergeant Parks.'

'I want the passport, airline and rentacar checks done again. Name of Brown. I'll fax through the details. I'll call the Fed and get them onto the banking authorities in Liechtenstein. I'll need to talk to the State Department, too. I want a twenty-four hour watch on Conrad Kask. Do *not* let him out of your sight. Put as many men on him as it takes. You *must* get that mobile phone number.'

****

'Take a look at this, will you?' said Earl to Cindy, the seventh young, leggy secretary so far that year.

The red Rolls Royce door opened. The chauffeur partly hid the view, but there was no doubt about the quality of the legs that were emerging. Earl whistled. Behind his back, Cindy made a face at him. It was her third week. The first week he had been polite and charming. The second he began saying ... suggestive things. Yesterday he'd rubbed up against her when she was at the filing cabinet. She had a pretty good idea of what might come next. While he was out this afternoon, she'd get onto the agency and try to get something else fixed for next week.

'Mr Baron?'

'Earl Baron at your service, Mrs Mendelssohn. Would you like a coffee while I take you through some ideas?'

'Do it in the car. Let's go now.'

She was an absolute knock-out. What legs, what an ass. Good looking in a haughty way. Expensive. Get a load of that Rolex. And that necklace must be worth more than most of the apartments he had for sale.

They settled in the back of the car. The glass partition behind the driver closed soundlessly. He'd never been near, let alone *in* a Rolls Royce before. Wow, the smell of the leather. The lambswool rugs. The gorgeous veneers. And to be next to a broad like this. Heaven on earth! Was it just his imagination, or had she hitched up her skirt a fraction as she sat down? He tried not to stare too obviously at her legs.

'First, we're going to see a wonderful Spanish-style spread in Napa itself.'

'Oh yeah?'

'And then go up to Rutherford to ...'

'Why not talk about the houses when we get there?'

'Whatever suits you, Mrs Mendelssohn.'

'You married, Earl?'

'Sure.'

'Oh ...'

'You too, huh? Mr Mendelssohn sounded a real nice guy.'

'Real nice guy?' Snort. 'He's an ogre. I'm going to leave him.'

'You are? Why?'

'Old and cold.'

'But rich, I guess.'

'Not quite so rich when I'm through with him. This divorce is going to cost him two hundred million, minimum.'

'What'll you live on until the settlement comes through?'

'Me? I have my money too. Not as much as Max, but *enough*. I've been married twice before. Both husbands were very ... generous at settlement time.'

'So, is there someone waiting in the wings?'

'No. Won't take long though. I *hate* to be alone. This time I'm going to have someone younger, now I don't have to bother about the financial side so much.'

'Oh, I can see that.'

'Tell me about your wife.'

'We have a few problems ourselves. We've been talking about splitting up, too.'

'Oh really? Tell me, how long to Napa?'

'About another hour.'

'Do you mind if I close my eyes and have a little snooze?'

'Be my guest.' Now he could look at the legs and the cleavage to his heart's content.

****

'Philippe?'

'Bonjour, Lisa. 'Ow are you feeling?'

'Philippe, I just can't go back. I'm so, so scared.'

'Lisa, you remember that Oriental guy who delivered the phone?'

'Yeah, vaguely. He seemed a nice guy.'

"E's black belt karate. I'll ask 'im to be somewhere near your 'ouse for the short time you're there. You won't see 'im, but if Earl starts 'itting you, just scream.'

'What if the door's locked?'

276

'That won't be a problem. My friend 'as a way with wood.'

****

'This is the one I like best. I just want to look at the master bedroom one more time and then we can decide.'

'It's this way. It's so big in here, you could get lost. After you.'

'Mm, yes. *I definitely* like this. What a *beautiful* view over those wineries. Come over here and look, Earl. It's very romantic. No, *here.*'

20

'Mr Giudizio?'

'Yes.'

'It's Herman Kruger, from the Bank of Vaduz.'

'Hello, Mr Kruger. How can I help you?'

'I apologise for troubling you, Mr Giudizio. I know that we agreed I would only call you on this number in exceptional circumstances.'

'So what *is* the problem?'

'Today we, and all the banks in Liechtenstein, received a communication from our Central Bank. They have been asked by the American Government to enquire into any very large deposits made shortly after September twelfth. We're asked to submit a report as soon as possible. That means one week maximum. Mr Giudizio, as you know, that was precisely the time period when your funds were deposited. I'm sure everything is in order, but I wanted to warn you that we'll have to comply.'

'I thought you promised me total discretion.'

'That is normally the case. We will not respond to any enquiries from the Liechtenstein police or any foreign authorities. However, this case is different. We have no *legal* obligation to supply the information, but it *is* our Central Bank. There are reasons why it would be hard to refuse. If all the other banks comply and we do not, we would cast suspicion on ourselves.'

'And why is the Central Bank so keen to co-operate with the US authorities?'

'I do not know. Two of our largest banks are applying for banking licences in several American cities. That may have provided some ... leverage.'

'I see. Well, there is nothing to worry about. There will be no problem. But, as a matter of principle, I would like you to submit this information at the last possible moment.'

'Mr Giudizio, I promise we will use the full week. Thank you for your understanding.'

'Thank you, Mr Kruger. Goodbye.'

****

'Hiro.'

'Hiruton! Hi!'

'Thanks again, Hiro. I loved it. I keep playing it over and over on my video.'

'Grad to help. You back in town now? When can we meet? Time for a few beers to cerebrate.'

'I'm going away, Hiro. For a long while. I don't know when we'll be able to get together.'

'I'm sorry to hear that, Hiruton. Mariko wanted to thank you in person.'

'Have to be some other time. Hiro, can you pick up the car tomorrow?'

'Sure, Hiruton. Any time. The trailer's all set to go. Just tell me where to go and where to take it.'

'You'll be on your own?'

'Yes. Always rike to do things myself.'

'I'll fax you where to pick it up. The folks there may get a bit confused about Orientals. May think you're Chinese or Taiwanese or something.'

'Won't bother me. I'll keep quiet.'

'I won't be able to tell you the destination until tomorrow afternoon. Take *that* phone with you. When you've got the car and are driving back towards San Francisco, press "send". I'll give you the details then. It'll probably be a garage under a condo. Call me again when you're about to arrive, and I'll have them leave the door open. Just unload it and park it in the garage with the keys in the ignition.'

'Will I have to get someone to sign for it or something?'

'No. Just leave it there and you can head on home. They'll close the garage door later.'

'Okay, Hiruton. I'm getting used to some strange stuff with you.'

'Bye, Hiro. Take good care of yourself. Real good care. Oh, Hiro, I promised just to ask three favours, but there is one more. I promise this one will be the last.'

'Anything at all, Hiruton. You just tell me.'

****

'Hi, Earl.'

'Oh, come back, have you? I thought you'd run out on me. Gave up on you, I did. I'm not putting up with that sort of crap from you, you know.'

'*Don't* you hit me again.'

'Don't worry, I'm through with all that now. I've been thinking things over. I want a divorce.'

'*What?*'

'You heard. I want a divorce. Right away. You've never been happy with me, anyway.'

'Why the big rush?'

'I met somebody.'

'*Already*?'

'I wasn't looking, it just happened.'

'Who is it?'

'Name's Melanie. Rich and beautiful.'

'And are you planning to *marry* her?'

'Yup. Just as soon as she can get divorced. She's got millions and she's a hell of a lot better looking than you. Better figure, too. Less gloomy. And *lots* more class.'

'I can't believe this ... I don't know what to say. You seem to have this all worked out ... You don't leave me much choice ... So, what happens now?'

'Tomorrow we go in *her* private plane – and that's going to be *my* private plane – to Las Vegas. There's a place there we can get a quickie divorce.'

'Then what?'

'You find your way back here, I guess. On a regular flight that is. After that, what happens to you is your own affair. I don't care. You can keep this place, if you can find a way to keep up the rent. I don't care about this garbage furniture, either. My future's gonna look a whole lot different to this.'

'And you? After Vegas?'

'The private plane takes me to some exotic resort in Mexico where we begin our jet set life together. She'll be there first to check everything's okay. Says she wants to *spoil* me. Says just *wait* till I see the Hotel Esplendido.'

'I don't know what to say, Earl. What should I say to my folks? Will you call them?'

'Yeah, I'll do that. One last time. After all these years of lying to them, I'll be happy to tell them what I really think about them and their precious daughter.'

'Earl, if you don't mind, I don't want to stay here with you tonight. I'll come back in the morning.'

'We leave here at seven sharp. Take off's at eight fifteen.'

****

Nascimento was back in San Francisco. He couldn't sleep and he could hardly sit down. It was obvious something *was* up in Liechtenstein. Nearly all the banks had responded pronto, most of them with a nil return. The bulk of the others had straggled in a few days later. Two were clearly playing for time. One or both must have something to hide. The Central Bank had agreed to stop them making any significant transfers until the returns had been submitted. The money, whatever was left of it, should be safe now. His Chief had confidentially informed the President of the BUS that the recovery of the money looked imminent. It was the first good news MacMartin had got for a while. He had the bank's PR department draft a press release for immediate issue when the confirmation came through.

The money was only part of it for Nascimento. Recovery would be a coup, no doubt about it, but it was the high profile arrest he most wanted. He needed someone behind bars, preferably the whole gang. Conrad Kask too, if it could be proved he stood to get Hilton's cut.

Conrad Kask seemed to have suddenly acquired a girlfriend. They didn't know who she was the first two nights, but then she went to what turned out to be her home. It looked like Kask was playing some funny game. She was married to a small-time realty agent. A couple of hours there and she was back to Telegraph Hill. A change of clothes? Did the husband know what was going on? Odd relationship. They wondered about picking her up, but Nascimento said no, she didn't matter, just watch and wait. Concentrate on Kask. Next morning she was up with the lark, briefly back home, and then off with the husband somewhere in the car.

What *should* he do about Kask? He was itching to get him in the interrogation room. If he *was* involved, he'd get it out of him. But it might scare the others off. Kask might still lead him to the top guys. The phone thing was mighty strange, proof or at least indication that he was up to no good. No phone company had a mobile phone registered to a Conrad Kask. It wasn't a work one, either. It seemed he'd lost his job in the last few days, and even before that Condor hadn't given him a mobile phone. The undercover guys monitored him using it, trying to get a recording from the keypad. Usually it gave them the number in one. This didn't seem to emit a normal tone at all. Must have been modified in some way. They would keep trying, but the best they could do in the meantime was use a high-power microphone to record what *he* was saying into the handset.

****

'Jupiter?'

'Hi, Con.'

'The first two nights she wouldn't talk much. Last night she told me everything. It's amazing. Her husband's flying her to Las Vegas today to get a quickie divorce. And she's got some weird French friend called Philippe. I had this funny feeling. Maybe I shouldn't ask, but you're not involved in that, are you?'

''Fraid I am. Wanna hear my accent?'

'I thought so. She's in love with you, for Chrissakes.'

'I've told her I'm middle-aged and married.'

'That's not the point. How could you *do* that?'

'I got in deeper than I planned, but I haven't got time to explain now. I need you to do some things today. Some very important things. Please just listen. Leave the apartment this afternoon. Bring three 'P's only. Parton, Pfeiffer and passport. *Nothing* else. Keep the passport well hidden and have the turtles in a carrier bag or something so no-one can see what's in it.'

'Okay.'

'Drive to the airport. Meet Lisa off the plane. She gets back at two-ten. Drive with her to the address I told you to memorise.'

'I'm listening.'

'On the way there you've got to tell her about me. Tell her *I'm* Philippe, and I'm really sorry to have lied to her. Tell her that I hadn't planned it this way at all. Everything changed when Earl started hitting her. I had some plans for you, but not for her, in the short term anyway. Now I have to bring everything together.'

'That address in ...'

'Don't say it.'

'Is that where you've been all this time?'

'Yes.'

'Oh my God.'

'Drive carefully. Don't break any speed limits. You'll probably be followed. Don't worry about that. I'll fill you in on everything when you get here.'

'Okay.'

'See you later.'

****

'Yes, Tiburon Marina. Have the boat there from five thirty. Engines running and ready to go. You'll get the final payment today. This time the money will come from an account in San Marino.'

'Thank you, Mr Fletcher. I'll radio the captain to make sure he's on time. I look forward to having another opportunity to be of assistance to you, sir.'

****

'Lieutenant, Lieutenant! This must be it. He called the guy he was talking to "Jupiter". Remember Mars? They must be using planets as code names.'

'What was the rest of the conversation?'

'They gossiped about the girl for a bit, and then they talked about him going some place. He said something about an address and then he said, "is that where you've been all this time?" It must be where they've been hiding out.'

'Good. Follow him, but discreetly. Don't scare him off. Not more than two cars. When he arrives, don't park the cars where they can be seen from the windows. Radio for back-up, but keep them well hidden. I want these guys alive. Stake the place out. Cover the back and the sides. Don't go in. Wait till Kask leaves. Then go in. Have one car follow Kask. When he's a few blocks away stop him and bring him in.'

'Got it, Lieutenant.'

****

The quickie divorce place was close by the airport, obviously located for maximum convenience. It was all over in ten minutes. Lisa was silent throughout the flight and the ceremony. Earl couldn't resist a few jibes along the way, but she wasn't provoked to answer. When the registrar said that was it, Lisa thanked her. Earl said 'good riddance'. He turned and got into the limo taking him back to the private aviation terminal. He just ditched her there and enjoyed doing it. She could walk or get a taxi. She'd have to get used to standing on her own two feet now.

The flight down to Mexico was fun. There was a sassy little stewardess just for him and he would have risked the pilot's wrath and had a grab if he hadn't thought that he should make absolutely sure of Melanie first. Other girls could come later. That was normal in the jet set world, wasn't it? So he sat back and tanked up on the champagne. Iced vintage champagne. He could get used to this lifestyle. Hell, he was used to it already.

What with the champagne and the early start, he began to feel drowsy and drifted right off. He was in the middle of a dream about the massage parlor in the Hotel Esplendido when the stewardess woke him.

'Mr Baron, we're about to land. You'll have to do up your seat belt.'

'I'm not very good at it, honey. Won't you help me?'

It gave him for an excuse for an 'accidental' brush of his hand against her chest. She gave him a look.

He craned to see the view through the small windows. Would the Esplendido be visible from the air? He couldn't even see the beaches yet. It looked like barren scrubland with a few dirt tracks. Maybe the airport was some way away from the resort. Melanie had said it was pretty remote and exotic. Oh well, even on those dirt roads an air conditioned Rolls Royce would be comfortable. She said she insisted on having one flown down.

They came in skimming a scattered group of gnarled trees. The plane bumped, twisted and skidded along the landing strip. It wasn't even tarmac, just a rough-cut grass strip. Shit, this place sure was out of the way. Obviously Melanie didn't want them to be disturbed.

The plane slowed to taxiing speed and circled around to the only building, a ramshackle concrete structure with a corrugated iron roof. He could see a couple of guys standing there and an ancient American car. The plane rolled to a halt outside the building. The stewardess swung a lever, pressed a button and let down the integral stairway.

'Here we are, Mr Baron. Welcome to Mexico.' She handed over his bag.

'Where's Melanie?'

'Probably inside the building. Those gentlemen will take care of you.'

'I don't see the Rolls Royce.'

'It'll be here soon, I'm sure.'

An elderly man, unshaven for a week, shuffled forward.

'Señor Baron?'

'Yes.'

'Hotel Esplendido?'

'Yes.'

'*Venga*. Come.'

Earl stumbled down the steps. This was not at all what he expected. The stewardess pressed the button again and the stairway folded back up. The plane swung round on its axis, taxied back to the strip and took off. Earl stood watching. Both the pilot and the stewardess waved at him.

He followed the man to the back of the building. Another guy in a shabby uniform looked at his passport without interest. The elderly one said 'Venga' again and gestured towards the car, a Buick from the 1950s.

'Rolls Royce. Where's the Rolls Royce?'

'No comprendo. Venga.'

He had little choice. He sat in the back of the disgusting old car as it bumped and clattered its way for mile upon mile along the rutted dirt road. Boy, would he give Melanie hell about this. It was mainly bone-dry impoverished farmland, with the occasional shack here and there. Then there were more clusters of wooden buildings and he realised they were entering a village. What a godforsaken place, he thought. The sooner he got to the Esplendido the better. The driver braked and pulled in to the right. He switched off the engine.

'What? Why are we stopping here?'

The driver lowered his head to look out of the passenger window and pointed out to a decrepit old pile with a crumbling plaster front. A few of the letters of an old sign still clung rustily to the wall:

HOT L E LEN IDO

Earl's mouth dropped open. The driver came round and pulled the passenger door creakingly open.

'Venga.'

The old man ushered him inside. A fat, gray-haired, severe-looking woman looked up from her knitting.

'Where is Melanie? WHERE IS MELANIE?'

'You are Señor Baron?'

'Yes I am. Where is Melanie?'

'Message from Señora Mendelssohn. Sorry no come. Change of plan.'

****

Lisa was *so* glad to see Conrad at the airport. Happy as she was to be rid of Earl, it had been an emotional day. She didn't love him or care for him, but he had been her life for seven years. She couldn't just wave goodbye to all that without emotion. Having a friendly face at the gate was a wonderful surprise. Con had been so good about her calling up out of the blue that night. He hadn't minded being woken up. He'd been very welcoming, and had insisted that he sleep on the sofa and she take his bed. The next night they'd talked and talked, mainly about Hil. He'd played her his 'Elegy for Hil' and she'd made him repeat it over and over. It was obvious how much he still loved Hil. Her funny feeling about him that time at Josie's had left her completely.

The night Earl had told her about the divorce she couldn't hold back any more. She told the whole story, about Earl and about Philippe. She felt bad telling Conrad about Philippe, so soon after *he* had told her about Hil having loved her, but he took it well and was so understanding. He was such a nice guy, so kind and gentle. So like Hil in so many ways, but very different too.

Con waited until they were out of the car park and onto

the freeway before he told her. She smiled at his grave face. He was joking, she was sure he was joking. She kept laughing and laughing. He tried and tried, but she would not take him seriously. They were almost in San Francisco now. He would have to be brutal.

'I'm sorry to do it this way, Lisa, but if you don't believe me, call Philippe.'

'Sure I will.'

Still full of laughs, she took her phone out of her handbag, brushed a curl behind her ear, and pressed 'send'.

'Philippe?'

'Lisa, I'm so sorry.'

It was Hilton's voice. She shrieked and threw the phone down.

'Pull over, pull over.'

He pulled over. So did the white car behind him. She got out and ran over to the safety railing on the hard shoulder. Her face was covered with her hands and her whole body was heaving with a terrible grief. Conrad approached and tried to put his arms around her but she shrugged him off. He looked back at the other car. Two guys were looking under the hood.

He left her for a few moments and tried again. This time she did not resist and accepted the consoling hug. He half led, half carried her back to the car. As he put her in, the hood of the car behind clanged shut. As Conrad drove, Lisa cried as if her tears would flow forever.

They were well into Marin when, rubbing her eyes, she asked were they were going.

'We're going *there*. To where Hil is.'

'*What*?'

'I mean where the computer is, that's kind of Hil.'

'And Philippe.'

'Yes. And Philippe.'

'I don't think I can handle this, Con.'

'Believe me, it's not easy for me either.'

****

He had to stop to check the way twice. Both times the white car stopped. There seemed to be another with it now, a red one. After a few wrong turns he found Sequoia Street and stopped opposite number twenty-four.

'This is it.'

'Oh my God. I don't know what to do.'

'We'll both have to be brave.'

Conrad took her hand and gave it a squeeze. He opened the glove box and took out his phone. He pressed 'send'.

'Hi, Jupiter. We're outside.'

'Come on up. I'll release the door lock. Bring the turtles and your passport. Make sure Lisa brings her handbag.'

****

'Lieutenant, Parks again. It's Sequoia Street, Annadel. Number twenty-four. We're both parked about fifty yards away from the door, but out of sight. We've got two back-up cars coming, but I've told them to wait down the parallel street. We'll have guys round the back, like you ordered.'

'Good. Keep me posted.'

****

They walked into the condo. From further inside came a

familiar voice,

'Come on in, don't be afraid.'

They went in, Con first, leading Lisa by the hand.

'Hi, Con. Hi, Lisa.'

It was as he had described, but somehow so sad, so lonely. A screen and a little black box with a few lights flashing on it. Wires everywhere.

'Don't be afraid. Wanna see me move?'

The boxed danced around on its springs.

'Oh, Hil.'

Con burst into tears and ran towards the box. He put his arms round it and cradled it. The yellow happiness lights raced up. Lisa still stood back, the tears coursing down her face.

'Won't you say hello, Lisa? I'm so sorry to have deceived you. I loved you so much, you know.'

'I know, Hil. It's okay. It's good to be ... with you again.'

The yellow lights were still strong, but the blue lights were getting up there, too.

'Were you followed, Con?'

'Yes, two cars.'

'I thought so. Listen guys, we haven't much time. Like you guessed, Con, I was involved in that BUS heist. In fact I did it, but I'm going to make it alright. Nothing to worry about. Con, I've been planning for ages to get you away from here. You're going to go to Aldabra to see your famous turtles and then to Paris where you can study music therapy.'

'Hil, I told you, I'll never leave you.'

'You'll have to, Con. The police are closing in and I don't want to be taken ... alive. You gotta understand I've done everything I wanted to do. It'd be fun to hang out with you some more, but basically it's over. I did it. I did everything. I had far more fun than I ever did when I was alive ... And you, Lisa. The Earl thing has changed things. There's no Melanie in Mexico. She was just a ... friend ... who helped out. It'll take him a while to get back, but when he *does* make it back, he's going to be one vexed sonofabitch. You may have your divorce, but he'll still come after you. You've got your passport with you, like you promised?'

'Yes.'

More tears wiped away.

'There's a boat waiting in Tiburon that's headed for the Indian Ocean and later for Europe. I'm sending a fax to that ship of everything I've arranged. There will be bank accounts for you both, with more money than you'll ever be able to spend. Beautiful places in Paris, the South of France, and Venice. Lisa, it's your choice, but I think you should go on the boat with Con. It's a beautiful boat, stocked with lots of everything. It has a grand piano and hundreds of CDs and art books. One of the crew is a qualified French teacher. There's wonderful food and wine and turtle food for Parton and Pfeiffer. There are beautiful clothes, too, for both of you. You can get friends to send on your own personal things later. When you get to Europe, the two of you can see how it works out, whether separately or together. Lisa, you can study art at any school there you want. What do you say?'

'I don't know ... I guess there's not much for me here. Okay, I'll go with Con.'

'Great. Now, we've got to move. Con, I need you to unplug the screen, the phones and the cables ...'

'If I do that, will you ... work?'

'Sure. I won't be able to access data or learn anything new, but the rest of my brain's all integral. I've got enough battery power to last several hours. Don't worry about it. That's right, unplug the mains and the screen too.'

****

The car sat there in the gloom, its silver shape a ghostly image. The windows were darkly tinted and the interior was invisible.

'Open the doors. You do it by pressing the buttons. Watch out, the doors open upwards.'

Lisa pressed the buttons one by one. Both doors swung up.

'Now, Con, put me in the centre seat, and strap me in with the little four-way belt. You see the connector cable coming out of the dash? Plug it into the socket in my left side. Get settled in. Parton and Pfeiffer will have to ride on your lap. Okay? Close the doors. Belts on? Okay, turn on the ignition key.'

As the garage door began to roll up, the starter motor whirred and the engine thundered into life.

'Hold on to your hats.'

The rear wheels were spinning when the clutch was let in. The car rocketed out of the garage and snaked down the road. It was doing eighty before the cops got their engines started.

Parks radioed Nascimento and told him.

'Go in. NOW!'

They broke down the door with an axe and rushed in. They couldn't all be in that little car. The rest of the gang had somehow got away. There was almost nothing in there. A few bits and pieces of furniture. A bed with no bedding. And a room with a computer screen and a few wires trailing about the floor.

****

He'd worked out a route that kept them off the main freeway. A futile attempt to pursue them was given up within the first mile. The speeds they drove at were astonishing, though Hilton was keeping something in reserve till later. Conrad closed his eyes half the time. Lisa's knuckles were clenched white.

He slowed as they came into Tiburon, and drove at something resembling a normal speed. A hundred yards from the quay the car rolled to a halt. On the hands-free carphone Hilton called the shore to ship number.

'Passengers coming aboard now.'

'We're waiting, sir. We'll be on the quayside.'

'This is it, guys. No tears. Just say goodbye and walk over to the boat. It's called *The Musical Turtle*. Con, tell the captain to cast off and circle around the bay for a while. Tell him to sail under the Golden Gate bridge at exactly seven p.m. Look up at the Headlands as you go by. Con, press the floppy eject and take the disk with you. It's got my personal stuff and the source code for the Solomon. Just in case, I want you to have it. I've got everything I need for now on the hard disk.'

As he was taking it, Con wiped tears away.

'Oh, Hil. Won't you come with us?'

'No, Con, this is the way I want it. Go now.'

Con hugged the box again. He opened the door and got

out. He put down the bag with the turtles and then leant back in and kissed the box.

'Thanks, Con. I love you. Goodbye.'

All ten blue lights were on.

'I love you so much. Goodbye, Hil.'

Conrad stepped a few feet away. Lisa hadn't moved from her seat.

She rested her head on the box and whispered.

'Goodbye Hil, goodbye Philippe. I love both of you.'

'Goodbye, Lisa. Take good care of Con.'

She slid out. Together, they closed the doors and, casting frequent glances back, walked to where the crew in their crisp white uniforms were waiting.

The blue lights wouldn't come down from ten. He put the car in gear, did a neat U-turn and without further salute, drove away. He kept the speed low as he put in the call.

'I want to speak with Lieutenant Nascimento in relation to the BUS case.'

Nascimento was in despair. When the girl on the switchboard told him, he was terrified it was the press and refused to take the call. She rang back to say the caller was very insistent, and said to say his name was Mars. Nascimento's eyebrows almost reached his scalp. 'Put him on, put him on.'

'Nascimento.'

'Lieutenant Nascimento, this is Mr Mars. You're looking for me in relation to a certain event at the Bank of the United States.'

'Just a moment.'

Nascimento covered the receiver and gestured to his assistant to record the call.

'What do you have to say?'

'I'm willing to surrender.'

'You are WHAT?'

'I will give myself up at six forty-five p.m precisely on the Marin Headlands overlooking the Golden Gate bridge on two conditions.'

'Which are?'

'One. No road blocks are set up or any attempt made to intercept me. You have no idea where I am now, so that should be a no-brainer.'

'And what is the other?'

'You and Standish MacMartin of the BUS must be there in person. I will hold on this line while you confirm MacMartin's availability.'

He had to wait two minutes.

'He'll be there. He *wants* to be there. So do I.'

'See you there. Goodbye.'

Whoopee. Disaster turned into victory. Nascimento called the SFPD media relations guy. Get *everybody* there. The press, TV. This was going to be big.

****

If Con and Lisa had been in the car now they would have known how restrained Hilton had been while he had them as passengers. Now, he could really try out this baby. Not only did he have the fastest street car in the world, but with all the handling parameters he'd taken direct from the McLaren computer in England he could push it precisely to its limits. It went round tight bends at seventy, sweeping curves at a hundred and ten. On the short straights it was touching two hundred. He'd crossed under the freeway and went up and over Mount Tamalpais. The G-forces were amazing. Whee, whee! Wow! Amazing! This was the most distilled, undiluted fun you could have. A few of the curves were so perfect, he went back and did them again, just for the hell of it.

The hour approached. Docilely he wound the power down and headed back towards the freeway. On it, he had one last blast up to ninety in second gear and then cruised gently until the exit for the Headlands came. Overhead helicopters hovered. There were police cars everywhere and tens or hundreds of other cars and vans. Big bright lights, lots of them, shone as he wound his way up the hill. When he rounded the shoulder well above the bridge, he saw that the road was blocked with police cars. He eased the car to a halt facing them and switched the engine off. For a few seconds there was a silence, then Nascimento's voice boomed out from a megaphone.

'Come out with your hands above your head.'

Oh boy, he hadn't reckoned on this one. He didn't have a megaphone to reply, either. He wound the electric window down a few inches and turned up the speaker on the box to its maximum.

'Sorry, I can't manage that. Open the doors.'

The police gawped at each other. They hadn't heard clearly.

Again the megaphone.

'What did you say?'

'I said I can't come out. If you open the doors, you'll see why. Press the buttons and they'll swing up.'

They crept closer. The police, with guns drawn, a few braver press photographers, MacMartin himself. The black window wasn't open wide enough to see who was inside, or how many of them.

'That's it, now press the buttons and open the doors.'

'Go do it, Sergeant,' barked Nascimento from a safe distance. 'Everyone else stand back.'

MacMartin found it hard to hold back. He *hated* this guy so much. He wanted one good swing at him. He didn't care about the consequences.

The Sergeant pushed two of his men forward and they advanced, fearsome firepower to the ready. At an agreed signal they pressed the buttons on both sides and jumped back, legs apart, pistols trained on the interior. The doors swung up.

'What the ...?'

'Hi there! How you doin'?'

The photographers rushed forward, ignoring the police instructions. The arc lights of the TV crews joined the crush. Nascimento pushed through. What the hell was this? A box? Where the hell were the guys?

Then it came to him. It was a trick. They were hiding inside. They were going to open fire.

'Get back,' he yelled. Everyone rushed back, half of them tripping over each other, the TV cameras only just managing to keep the scene in focus.

'Don't worry, Lieutenant, it really is just me.'

The crowd started edging back towards the car. Nascimento's voice was trembling.

'Who is "just me"?'

'I guess I should come clean. My real name's Hilton Kask.'

'What the ...?'

'I was the one who ... invited BUS into the transaction.'

'Then ...'

'Lieutenant, I'll be happy to discuss everything with

you later, but first I want a word with Mr MacMartin. Are you there, Standish?'

'I'm here.' He stepped forward.

The press, photographers, and TV folk had lost all fear now. They crowded round.

'Hi, Standish, remember me? My idea was no good, you said. Well, I died, Standish. I died, but before I did, I built that machine and I think I got it to work pretty well. It persuaded you to hand over a hundred and twenty million, anyway. Wouldn't you say I was right about my computer, Standish?'

'You goddam bastard, I'll throw you in the bay.'

He lunged inside the car and tried to tear off the belts holding the box. Two policemen dragged him out and held him by the arms. His face was vermilion.

'Come on, Standish, don't be so sore. Why not admit I was right? Say it good and loud so these nice gentlemen with the microphones can hear.'

Upwards of ten microphones were thrust under his nose. He threw out his jaw and summoned all his strength for one last effort. The policemen had to hang on grimly as he swung them from side to side, but he couldn't break loose. The fight began to drain out of him.

'Come on, Standish, you can do it. Take it like a man, admit I was right.'

He curled his lips, but the insidious, persuasive power of the microphones and cameras was too much. Limply, quietly, he said,

'Okay, you were right.'

'And you were wrong?'

'Yes, yes, yes. I was wrong.'

'Thank you, Standish. Now, as to your money ...'

'Where is it, you bastard?'

'Well, quite a lot of it has been spent and there's far less left in Liechtenstein than Lieutenant Nascimento here thinks.'

'Where is it?'

'Spent, or spirited away. Standish, there's only one way you're going to see all of your money back. Maybe even make a profit, a big profit.'

'How's that?'

'Before I died, really died that is, I made a will passing seventy percent of the stock in Solomon Computers to a company called Central America Holdings. Have you heard of that company, Standish?'

'Yes, you bastard. That was the company you made us invest in.'

'That's right, Standish. Central American Holdings will have majority ownership of all the patents and technologies in this computer. Do you realise that could be worth a lot of money?'

'I suppose it could. So, who's got the other thirty percent?'

'I willed ten percent each to my two co-founders, Dan and Irma, and I've split the other ten percent between a Japanese friend of mine who you don't know, and two people you *do* know.'

'Who are they?'

'Fred Adams and Joseph Muldoon.'

'ADAMS AND MULDOON?'

'That's right, Standish, but listen. There was a condition in my will.'

'What?'

'The ownership will be transferred to Central American

Holdings only if my bank in Liechtenstein receives written confirmation from BUS that the investment the bank made was fair value at a hundred and twenty million and that you have instructed the SFPD that it's all been a misunderstanding and there is no further case to pursue. No confirmation, no shares. What do you think, Standish?'

The microphones thrust in again.

'How about it, Mr MacMartin? Are you going to accept?'

The interviewer was loving this. This was *great* TV.

'I guess I have no choice.'

'Good. A wise decision, Standish. I've already faxed all the details to the bank to help you put everything in place.'

'Hang on a minute here ...'

Nascimento's clear voice cut through the hubbub. The microphones parted and the horde stepped back a pace or two. Nascimento went up and put his hands on the car roof.

'The bank can say what they like, Kask, there's still the crime of extortion. I'm charging you ...'

'Waldyr, sorry to rob you of your big moment, especially in front of all these cameras, but I was dead when the BUS investment happened. I have to remind you that dead men cannot commit crimes.'

'You ... you ...'

'Excuse me a moment..'

It was a few seconds to seven. *The Musical Turtle* sailed quietly under the bridge, unnoticed by all except the car's camera vision, which through the gaps in the crowd could just pick out the two people on the deck, hand in hand, waving up to the Headlands. The car's powerful horn honked back, startling the uncomprehending mass. The blue lights reached nine and fell back to eight. For the first time the tenth yellow light of happiness came on. It glowed incandescently.

'Ladies and gentlemen, it is my time to go. I will now close down my systems. I salute you all. Goodbye.'

The lights flickered and died. Wisps of smoke came out of the cooling vents as the short circuits fried the boards.